10-05-09

Devil *at the* Crossroads

Also by Olive Etchells

No Corners for the Devil
Footprints of the Devil

Devil *at the* Crossroads

Olive Etchells

Constable • London

Constable & Robinson Ltd
3 The Lanchesters
162 Fulham Palace Road
London W6 9ER
www.constablerobinson.com

First published in the UK by Constable,
an imprint of Constable & Robinson, 2009

First US edition published by SohoConstable,
an imprint of Soho Press, 2009

Soho Press, Inc.
853 Broadway
New York, NY 10003
www.sohopress.com

A copy of the British Library Cataloguing in Publication
Data is available from the British Library

UK ISBN: 978-1-84529-414-4

US ISBN: 978-1-56947-592-8
US Library of Congress number: 2009007943

Printed and bound in the EU

1 3 5 7 9 10 8 6 4 2

Mixed Sources
Product group from well-managed
forests and other controlled sources
www.fsc.org Cert no. SA-COC-1565
© 1996 Forest Stewardship Council
FSC

For my delightful grandchildren:
Jennifer, Tom, Alex, Katie, Matthew,
Sally and Thomas

Acknowledgements

Once again, for their expert advice and comment, I offer
sincere thanks to:

David Price, Police Superintendent (retired)
David Etchells, my dear 'Ancient Mariner'

Chapter One

Carrick Roads lay blue-grey and sunkissed beneath a cloudless November sky, a faint breeze touching waters that for days had been whipped into frenzy by high winds and rain. It was not yet nine in the morning but the yachting fraternity were out in force, tacking back and forth and relishing the change in the weather.

Creeks and small rivers dissected land on either side of the estuary, and on a certain stretch of the western bank stood a house, set on rising land and backed by trees. It was an old house, stone-built and serene, with a deep porch and big, many–paned windows that glinted in the sun. Through its gardens a path ran down to a tiny beach where there was a wooden jetty with stout mooring posts.

Inside the house Helen Pascoe was up in a bedroom with her hands pressed flat on the window ledge, deep in thought as she stared at the tranquil plump fields of the Roseland peninsula across the water. Her life had changed, her children had been uprooted from their schools and their friends, but at last they were all settled here, ready to face the winter. Things would get better. Things always got better at Trenoon.

Trenoon, Trenoon . . . the very name of the house was magic, it caught at her heart. As a child, knowing she was to be brought here on a visit, she would whisper the name into her pillow before going to sleep. The word itself meant 'farm on the downs', though it wasn't a farm and it wasn't set on downs. Nobody knew who had named the house, but records showed that it had been built long ago for a sea captain.

Helen liked to think of him as being in command of one of the early Falmouth Packets – fast sailing ships that had carried mail across the oceans of the world. She pictured him needing a comfortable home in which to raise a family, but wanting it to be linked to his seafaring life. If that had been his aim he had achieved it with Trenoon: though seemingly remote, it had been within easy reach of a developing Falmouth, not to mention having one of the world's largest natural harbours outside its front door.

That long-dead sea captain had created a beautiful, beautiful house, and the amazing thing was that it was hers, all hers! For the last six years it had belonged to her – great-uncle Benjamin had seen to that ... But she was daydreaming, and if they didn't set off soon they would miss the next ferry. Unless she was doing a big food shop it was easier to sail to Falmouth rather than make the roundabout journey by car and have trouble parking. 'Katie!' she called as she went down the stairs. 'Are you ready?'

With a squeal, a clatter and a thud, her youngest child erupted into the hall. Katie never merely entered a room, she burst, leapt, catapulted into it. That was the way she was. Still very small, she was dark, thin and wildly energetic – a twelve-year-old embodiment of her father.

True to her Cornish parentage the sea was in her blood. Today, wearing a red fleece with the words *I Love Ellen* across her chest, she was making yet another pilgrimage to the National Maritime Museum, followed by her usual Saturday visits to the docks and the sailing school with her friends.

She ran out to the car, while Helen let out a resigned breath and followed her. Whenever she went out with Katie she felt as if she were being sucked into a whirlwind, her careful, orderly nature battered and unsettled. She knew that people must find them very different from each other, not just in personality but in looks: the dark, dynamic daughter with her mop of wild black curls and the gentle, fair-skinned mother with her smooth, honey-coloured hair, green eyes and a figure always verging on plumpness.

Once in the car Katie fixed her alert, glittering gaze on her mother. 'So how long can I stay?' she asked, continuing a conversation begun over breakfast.

'I want you home in daylight,' said Helen. 'I'll be in all afternoon so if you ring me from the pier before you take the ferry I'll pick you up at this end.'

'Right, and what about the sleepover? Have you decided?'

'No, I haven't. I don't know Holly's parents all that well, do I? I'll ring her mum when I get back from shopping.'

Katie rolled her eyes. 'It's a sleepover, Mum – one night! Holly's mum and dad are OK and so are her brothers. There'll just be the six of us sleeping over – all from school. Her mum's going to put mattresses on the floor of their games room. It'll be really good. *Please*, Mum.'

Helen set off up the narrow lane behind Trenoon. Sometimes she wondered if she was the only mother in the entire United Kingdom who didn't like sleepovers. Steve hadn't been all that keen, either, but the days of him backing her up were over. She drove through Pengorra village and headed for the road leading to Flushing. Laying a gentle hand on Katie's thigh, she asked, 'Would you like it if I didn't care where you were or what you were doing?'

There was no reply; no reassuring, 'No, of course I wouldn't!' Her daughter was grinding her teeth, a habit she had when considering something. At last she conceded, 'I wouldn't actually *like* it, but it would make things a bit simpler. Holly's mum lets them all go where they like. She says she wants them out of her hair. She's really cool!'

'Is she indeed? Well, I'm not Holly's mum, and I don't suppose I'm cool, but there's no way *you're* going to go wherever you like. And I don't particularly want you out of my hair, either. Your dad and I love you and we want to keep you safe.'

Eyes that were all at once old and cynical swivelled towards her. 'I don't see how Dad can keep me safe when he's in London.'

'He knows what we do down here and how we live. He knows where I let you go,' answered Helen calmly. 'We talk about you all the time.'

Katie rolled her eyes again. 'OK, so can I go?'

'I'll decide after I've talked to Holly's mum.' Silence fell between them and a minute later they turned on to a grassy drive next to a white cottage overlooking the water. Some outlying residents with parking space had standing arrangements with motorists who drove to Flushing to take the ferry, but this was Chrissie Boon's house, where the Pascoe family were always welcome, with or without their car.

At that moment Chrissie herself, still in an ancient dressing gown, was putting a bag of rubbish in her dustbin. 'Hi,' she beamed. 'Just the two of you today? There's a good five minutes to go so you'll make it with time to spare. Before you dash off, Helen, is everything all right round at Pengorra? My neighbour's just been over there and he had to pull to one side to let four police cars go past, heading for the village. Lots of men, he said, both uniforms and plain clothes.'

Katie was poised to go down the hill to the quay, so Helen answered while walking backwards to join her. 'We did see one police car parked by the green – I noticed it because it was so unusual – but I've never seen four policemen in Pengorra, let alone four cars. I'll be back on the 11.15, so I'll call in and we'll compare notes.' With a wave she hurried after Katie, wondering what could have happened to need the presence of the police.

The day was mild for mid-November, but all at once the back of her neck felt cold, as if she were in a draught. She almost shivered, and then laughed at herself. The sun was shining, the village was as lovely as ever and, down below but still out of sight, the ferry boat would be bobbing at its mooring. Everything was all right, of course it was. Katie was safe with her, and the other two were still in bed, she'd looked in on them before leaving the house. Police or no

4

police, all was right in *her* little world. Right, echoed a mocking voice in her head – except for a marriage in ruins.

Leading the way, Katie found she was quite pleased about the police cars. Police meant trouble, and trouble was interesting – it was exciting. Cornwall was bliss, Trenoon was heaven, but that was because of the sea. Life ashore was different; it was good, of course it was – but exciting? Please! Perhaps things were about to change.

Without realizing she was doing it she took her mother's hand as they reached the quay and went down the granite steps. At that moment, the police cars forgotten, mother and daughter were thinking the same thought: that the steep sea-washed steps to the ferry were a vast improvement on the crowded escalators of the London Underground.

'Coffee's ready!' Wearing her customary jewel colours in an amethyst velvet top and emerald pants, Chrissie was waiting at the kitchen door. She pulled out a chair and, standing behind it, asked, 'Did you hear anything in Falmouth or on the ferry?'

'About the police cars, you mean?' Helen eyed her friend curiously. She seemed a bit on edge, pulling at her fingers as if removing invisible gloves, and with her springy grey hair standing on end like a halo. 'I haven't heard a thing,' she said. 'What about you?'

Chrissie filled two mugs with coffee and got out the cake tin. Then she sat opposite Helen. 'Nothing definite,' she said quietly, 'but people are saying there's been a murder.'

'Murder!' Helen clasped both hands around her mug. It was hot but she kept hold of it. 'Not in Pengorra,' she said in disbelief, 'don't say that!'

'Drink your coffee,' the older woman said flatly. 'The grapevine round here can be pretty accurate, you know.'

'But Chrissie, it can't be true, can it? What's being said?'

'That a dead body's been found not far from Trenoon.'

'*What?* Whereabouts? When?'

5

'This morning, I think. Biddy in the mobile shop said it was at Menna Cross.'

'But that's only a few hundred yards from the house! Katie and I saw nothing except that one police car in the village.'

'Yes, but you didn't come by way of the Menna to get here, did you?'

Helen was on her feet, knowing she had to get home, but Chrissie was reciting more details, her expression adding weight to her words. She looked wary, uncomfortable; the way people look when faced with something unpleasant and unexplained. 'When Jackie brought the post he said the police had got tapes across the road, stopping traffic in all directions, and they've put a big white tent over the actual crossroads.'

'But has there been anything on television, or local radio?'

'No. Perhaps it's too soon for that, but Jackie says there are men in white overalls everywhere.'

'That doesn't mean murder though, surely? There could have been an accident.'

'That's not what they're saying, but I suppose it could have been talked up a bit, what with the stone being there since the year dot and all the tales about the gibbet.'

Helen relaxed a little. That would be it. The Menna – the local name for that particular crossing of the roads – was the site of a prehistoric standing stone, one of many to be found in unexpected places around Cornwall. As for tales of a gibbet, she didn't know if they were true or simply colourful folklore. It seemed to her that all this talk of murder was over-dramatic and out of proportion, but the back of her neck was feeling cold again . . .

She left the coffee untouched and gave Chrissie an apologetic kiss on the cheek. 'I've got to go,' she said, picking up her shopping, but hesitated when she reached the door. There was something else that seemed over-dramatic in the light of what she'd just been told, and who better to share it with than an old friend? 'Chrissie,' she said uneasily, 'I was up at the Menna myself last night, on my way home from yoga. I was there and I stopped the car right next to the stone.'

Chrissie flopped back in her chair. 'Did you see anything?'

'No, of course I didn't. Well, yes, I did see *something* – a plastic bag. It was pretty windy, you know, and as I was driving along before reaching the Menna a big white plastic bag blew across the windscreen. I had to brake – hard. I got out to move it but it blew away again, like a low-flying kite. I was surprised it flew at all because it must have been a bit wet. I thought I'd better get hold of it so it wouldn't cause an accident if anyone else went that way.' How far-fetched do I sound, she asked herself in exasperation, 'So I followed it – in the car. It landed on the brambles – you know, at the side of the stone.'

'So you got out? Did you see anything suspicious?'

'No, but I wasn't expecting to, was I? It was dark, it was windy, it had been raining. I thought it would be muddy and I was wearing my good suede boots. There were brambles and the bag was in the middle of them. Then a massive gust of wind came and blew it away again, high into the air. I got back in the car and went home.'

'Well,' said Chrissie matter-of-factly, 'you'll have to relate all that to the police if they ask you any questions.'

Helen wriggled her shoulders. 'I think I'll have to relate it even if they don't ask questions. If I saw nothing going on just after ten, it could help them fix a time for what happened after that.' Their eyes met, but neither of them said out loud that she might have missed being mixed up in something awful by a matter of minutes. 'Come to me for coffee whenever you like, Chrissie. Right now I feel I must get home.'

'Off you go,' agreed the other heavily, 'and Helen, I don't want to pry, but I can't help hoping . . . Does Steve being down here again mean that things are a bit better between you?'

7

Helen stared at her. 'Steve isn't down here. Whatever makes you think he is?'

'I saw him yesterday,' Chrissie said blankly, 'upstream from here. We passed on the road near Trelissick, but he didn't see me. It was raining and you know there are trees on either side as you go down to the water. I was on my way to see Mabel over at Philleigh, and I thought Steve had just come across on the King Harry.'

Helen shook her head. The King Harry Ferry ran across the middle reaches of the Fal, and for Steve to have used it meant that he'd been on the Roseland for some reason. 'I can't see him having been on the other side,' she said in puzzlement, 'nor being down here without calling at Trenoon. What was he driving?'

'Not his Merc. It was dark, sleek, soft top; could have been a different Merc, I suppose. I simply caught sight of him as we passed, but he's not easily mistaken, is he?' She gave an awkward little laugh. 'Forget it, Helen. Obviously I *was* mistaken. Off you go. What about Katie? Are you picking her up?' Once again she left something unspoken – this time that a twelve-year-old shouldn't be alone, on foot, in an area that might not be safe.

Helen felt resentment rising inside her, sour as acid. She could do without all this – police and roadblocks and feeling worried because she'd stopped the car to chase a plastic bag. She was trying to rebuild a life without a husband, for goodness sake; to create a permanent home from a beautiful house that had been rented to strangers for years, to ensure a solid, secure life for three teenagers, to make sure they knew they were loved.

With a simple clasp of the hands the two women parted, and Helen headed the car over the sunlit uplands leading to the village of Pengorra and on to Trenoon.

Detective Chief Inspector Channon stood on rising ground above the Menna crossroads, observing the careful bustle of men outside the protective tent and knowing that nothing would escape the scene-of-crime team inside it. They would be collecting samples of blood and body fluids, of grass and mud and gravel, of leaves and brambles; they knew their job just as he knew his, and he was keenly aware of what helped him succeed in it. He needed fingertip searches and routine analysis, of course he did, but he also needed something intangible, he wasn't even sure if he could name it. All he did know was that he must snatch this time of silent contemplation. In minutes someone would speak to him, distract him, and he would lose the *essence*, the atmosphere of the murder scene.

Body and face immobile, only his eyes moved. If it were not for the police presence and paraphernalia this would be an idyllic spot. Behind him lush green fields rose on either side of a narrow road that climbed and curved out of sight; in front of him the same road crossed another and then dipped between trees towards a boatyard at the water's edge. To the left of the crossroads a field was cornered by a stone wall, its surface laced with autumn-bare vegetation; and the fourth side, where the road continued to Pengorra, was the site of the murder – because murder it was. He hadn't needed the forensic physician to certify death, though he'd been eager enough to hear the pathologist's first assessment of the timing of it.

The victim was dead – very dead. A young man, slimly built and apparently fit until death. There were several knife wounds to the upper torso, and the throat had been slit with such force that blood had gushed over the top of his outstretched legs, giving him the appearance of some way-out young craftsman taking a break while wearing a red leather apron. He'd been sitting – no, he'd been propped in a sitting position against the standing stone, brambles still in dark leaf on either side of him. That was how he had been; right now, hours later, he was in a van being taken to the mortuary.

Dark eyes blank, one corner of his mouth tucked in, Channon was inhabiting his inner world, opening himself to instinct and intuition. All he could sense at this early stage was a sickness overlying the scene. In spite of the bright sunlight, the sparkling water within view and the time not yet noon, he had the feeling that darkness was descending over this crossing of the roads. There was the brutality of the killing, the excessive amount of blood, the deliberate placing of the body against what could only be described as a pagan monument, because of course the stone pre-dated Christianity.

He recalled that in a recent case of murder it had been his sergeant, Bowles – yes, hard-bitten, feet-on-the-ground Bowles – who had said it was the work of the devil. He sighed. The devil, or one of his associates, had been at work again. He shook his head and breathed out heavily. Back to practicalities: had the victim been on foot? If not, where was his vehicle? Had he been followed here and killed on the spot, propped like a sacrifice in front of this ancient makeshift altar? Or had he been attacked elsewhere, maybe knocked senseless, then brought here to be finished off?

There had been no identification on him: no papers, no wallet, no keys; not even any money. Was it a robbery, or was it meant to look like one? If a vehicle had been used, either by him or to transport him, there would be tyre marks. Without a vehicle there would still be clues: footprints, fibres and blood ... blood by the pint. The killer couldn't have escaped it. Things would soon fall into the grooves of laid-down procedure, but the routine stuff was always easier if they had a positive identification. He needed to know who it was who'd been left wearing that sticky red leather apron.

He could see the lanky figure of Bowles standing under the signpost at the crossing and talking on his mobile. Channon lifted a hand and the sergeant finished his call and hurried over. 'That was the mortuary, boss. They can start at one thirty.'

'Good. What about the SOCOs?'

'They say they need the rest of the day here, and probably much longer.'

'They can have as long as they like, but they'll have to attend the post-mortem. Ask Fred to sort himself out for one thirty, will you?'

'Ask', not 'tell', noted Bowles. The bloody SOCOs were getting too big for their boots. Could nobody else see it? Even Channon was joining the bowing and scraping brigade, but at least he'd come back to earth after doing a Sherlock and gazing into space. It always seemed creepy when he did that. 'Boss,' he said, 'while we're here do you want to talk to the chap who found the body? He works at the boatyard just down the road. I know the place.'

Bowles could be a pain, thought Channon, but he was hot on saving time and effort. He nodded. 'Let's go and have a word with him, then before we head off to the mortuary I could do with a spell in the office to clear up loose ends. We don't know at this stage how long we'll be tied up with all this.'

Bowles merely shrugged. It would take as long as it took. A rapid result might look good on his record, but another spell as the DCI's right-hand man would look even better. Everyone knew that Channon cracked his cases like a chef cracks eggs.

Helen drove back to Trenoon by the route she'd used on leaving. Whatever was happening at Menna Cross she didn't want to see it. She would get to know soon enough if murder had been done. For now, all she wanted was the warmth and safety of home.

There was nothing unusual going on in Pengorra itself, but then, it was never exactly a hive of activity. Everyone called it a village, but in fact it was no more than a hamlet: no church, no shop, no pub, just three big houses and eight smaller ones gathered around the green with its ancient oak tree, its bench and its pillar-box. The police car they'd seen earlier was no longer there; in fact all was still, all was silent, the scatter of boats on the water far below only adding to the tranquillity of the scene.

Once back at Trenoon she took her shopping indoors. The beat of indie music came from upstairs and there was a smell of burnt toast and what might be burnt scrambled eggs. That would be Jaz's doing. He was apt to wander off when he'd put toast under the grill. Heaven only knew what had made him try to cook eggs.

Just then Jasper himself strode into the kitchen. Sixteen years old and already six feet two, her only son was wearing his Saturday morning gear of pyjama trousers and a menacing black hoodie, which was brought into regular use to flatten his hair when he washed it. 'Mum!' he said hoarsely. 'We've got to do something!'

Helen stifled a sigh. 'Good morning, Jaz.'

'What? Oh, sorry – morning. I say we've got to do something.'

'What about?'

'Me. I'm going to work out a diet and I want you to deal with it.'

'What sort of diet?'

'One that'll add flesh and muscle.'

'Eighteen months ago you were after something to increase your height – remember?'

Dark eyes defensive, Jaz peered at her from under the hood. 'I know I was, but now I've got taller I'm simply a joke – a freak. I can't go through life like this, I'm just skin and bone. My arms are like sticks.'

'You're sixteen,' Helen said patiently. 'You eat voraciously of a good mixed diet. Let nature take its course. You'll adjust, you'll put on more flesh and your muscles will bulk up. Eat well, exercise well and get enough sleep. Maybe you should work on the last one.'

Jaz emerged from the wet hood. 'You reckon I'm eating OK, then?'

'Yes, I do reckon, in fact I'm sure of it. Jaz – have you heard from any of your friends this morning?'

He grabbed an apple and bit into it. 'Yeah. Sinbad says a bloke's been knifed.'

Helen let out a disbelieving breath. 'Someone's been knifed and all you can talk about is your lack of muscle?'

Jaz shrugged. 'Well, I don't know who it is, do I?'

'Do you know where it happened?'

He shrugged again. 'No, he didn't say. Mum – what's bugging you?'

'I've heard that somebody's been murdered just up the road,' she said evenly.

'No way!' He shuffled uncomfortably. 'Sinbad didn't say anyone was – you know – actually dead. Do they know who it is?'

'No. I need to find out a bit more. Where's Lucy?'

'In the studio. I heard her on her mobile. D'you think she'll know?'

'I'll ask her. Then we'll all have a coffee, and maybe some toast – unburnt.'

'Oh – yeah – sorry about the blue smoke and everything.'

Helen escaped up the stairs. One of her children was aiming to be a second Ellen MacArthur and sail round the world single-handed, another wanted the physique of a weightlifter, but at least the third was normal – most of the time. She found her eldest offspring in the studio with its big, north-facing window. As always, Lucy greeted her mother with a hug, then leaned back and looked at her searchingly. 'Mum – which way did you come back home?'

'Not past the Menna,' Helen told her soberly. 'Have you had phone calls?'

'Yes, everybody's talking about a murder, but nobody knows very much.'

'We'll find out soon enough, I expect. Come down for a coffee and we'll have a chat. Lunch can be a bit late.'

Minutes later the three of them had coffee and hot buttered toast in the big room with the many-paned windows overlooking Carrick Roads. Lucy sat with her hands cupped around her mug, much as her mother had done in Chrissie Boon's kitchen. 'It's too lovely here for anything as horrible as murder,' she said sadly.

13

Chapter Two

'Let's move!' said Channon, heading for the car. 'There's plenty to do before one thirty.'

Bowles obliged by leaping into the driving seat. 'It's Heaney's boatyard, boss, and the man who found the body is Tresillian – Luther Tresillian. He rang us at 7.55 a.m.'

'On his way to work?'

'I think so. Uniforms dealt with him. They've got the recording of his call and notes of their interview with him at the murder scene, but no statement so far.'

Once down at the water he pulled up with a squeal of brakes. The yard itself was an orderly jumble of vessels, some of them afloat between wooden walkways and a few up on hard standings. Chains and ropes snaked over sandy shingle towards a group of white sheds, where a man stood watching them, eyes narrowed in a leathery face.

Before Channon could open his mouth the man declared, 'You'll be wanting Luther. He's coming.'

'Are you the owner, sir?'

'Yes, I'm Amos Heaney. This is my yard and Luther's my man. He kept vomiting earlier on, but he's a bit better now.'

There was a hint of accusation in his tone and Bowles gritted his teeth. Why did people always feel hard done by when they came close to violent crime? They'd have something to gripe about if they had to give up their free time to deal with it.

Channon, unperturbed by Heaney's tone, was correct as always with his introductions, and went through them a second time when a workman in a blue jersey emerged from a moored boat and came along a walkway. Luther Tresillian – the name sounded like an honest, salt-of-the-earth type and it suited him exactly: solid, fortyish, with weather-beaten skin, brown curly hair and very direct blue eyes.

'I'll leave you to it,' said Heaney gruffly, and went into one of the sheds.

'Just a word, Mr Tresillian,' began Channon, 'before we go back to headquarters to set up a full enquiry. I take it you were on your way to work when you discovered the body?'

'That's right.'

'You were on foot?'

'Yes, I live less than quarter of a mile away – up the lane at the other side of the crossroads.'

'The body was half obscured by brambles, wasn't it, so what drew your attention to it?'

Tresillian gave a half-embarrassed shrug. 'I had to acknowledge the stone,' he said. 'Every time I pass, I acknowledge it.'

'In what way, sir?'

'You won't understand if you're not from round the Fal. My father used to doff his cap whenever he passed the stone. It's a local custom – among the older folk, that is. I don't wear no headgear but I give a nod when I pass – a mark of respect, I suppose you'd call it.'

Bowles looked down at his hands. This guy was nothing but a weirdo. Everyone knew there were oddballs along the estuary, but this was something else!

Next to him Channon was clearly intrigued, but deadly serious. 'So you always acknowledge the stone – shall we say you greet it? And in greeting it, you saw the body?'

'Yes – at least, I saw the head and shoulders. If it was the middle of summer I'd have thought it was somebody who'd slept the night there after a drop too much, but winter's nearly here. And then I saw the blood. Nearly black, it was, but there was no mistaking it.' Tresillian had lost colour as he relived those moments of horror.

'You saw a terrible sight,' said Channon gently. 'Believe me, it will fade from your mind with the passing of time. Did you touch the body?'

'No – your men asked me that. I didn't go closer than a coupla' feet. It – I mean he – he just looked dead. I dialled 999 right away on my mobile – the first time I've seen the value of it, to tell you the truth.'

'You did well,' said Channon warmly. 'Thank you. Did you tell anyone else what you'd seen?'

'Yes, I rang my wife and told her to watch the children. I felt unsafe, sort of, and we have three young lads.'

'Mr Tresillian, you're a local man, you know the area and you know the standing stone. Would you take your mind back and tell me exactly what came into your head when you realized you were looking at a dead body?'

'I thought, God in heaven, this is murder,' said Tresillian simply, 'and then I thought, why have they set him against the stone?'

'Ah, so it's a good stone?'

Tresillian knew at once what he meant. 'I've never known it used for evil purposes,' he said shaking his head. 'No black magic, nor nothing of that sort.'

'And is it true that a gibbet stood there many years ago?'

'Yes,' admitted the other, reluctantly. 'My grandpa used to say his mother told him of it. That's no reflection on the stone, mind. The gibbet was put there by modern man – modern in comparison to when the stone was laid, at any rate.'

Channon nodded. 'Mr Tresillian, you say you thought, why have they set him against the stone? Why did you think "they" had done it rather than one person?'

'I don't rightly know,' said Tresillian in puzzlement. 'It must have seemed clear to me that more than one had put him there. The stone's a few feet up from the road, so he'd have had to be lifted, then there's the brambles and such. I don't know why I thought it, but I did.'

'Thank you,' said Channon. 'That's what I'm after – the reaction of the first person to see him.'

'Not the first person,' contradicted Tresillian, 'no, not the first. Whoever put him there was the first to see him against the stone. But, inspector, I did have another thought, you know.'

'And what was that?'

Tresillian shook his head, as if surprised that Channon hadn't asked the question himself. 'I thought, who is he?'

'You had no idea?'

'None, but then, he didn't look like a man – he looked more like a thing – a puppet, or a rag doll.'

'He looked bad,' agreed Channon sombrely. 'So far we haven't got his identity, but we're working on it. Now, Mr Tresillian, we need an official statement from you. Are you at work all day?'

'Usually I'm here all Saturday – it's a busy day with the weekend sailors coming and going – but Amos says I'm to have the afternoon off, so I'll be at home.'

'Somebody will be round to see you later. It's purely a formality for our records.'

They left him standing among the ropes and chains, with the purposeful flow of the water behind him, and Bowles headed for the Truro road, with Channon deep in thought at his side. When the DCI was in thinking mode Bowles usually left him to it, but now he simply had to know. 'Boss,' he said in bafflement, 'what was all that stuff about the stone?'

'I wanted to clarify that there was no local knowledge of it being used for occult purposes.'

'What? You mean like Tresillian said? Black magic and so forth?' The sergeant couldn't help his voice rising.

'The dead man had his throat cut, Bowles. That could be interpreted as a sacrificial act. I wanted the spontaneous reaction of a down-to-earth local man, that's all.'

Bowles wriggled in the driving seat. Every officer in Cornwall – in the British Isles, come to that – must have heard some tale or other about black magic or witches and warlocks, but that didn't say the tales were true. As for Channon taking it seriously – that was what came of all that staring into space.

Once parked in Truro, they went on foot to the mortuary, Bowles taking notes as they walked and Channon giving orders at speed, already in the intent, obsessive state that was usual with him at the start of a new case.

Bowles would have been equally keen, but he couldn't help thinking that he could do with a bit of nosh before the post-mortem. It was one thing to feel a bit peckish out here in the fresh air, but another to have an empty stomach while old Hunter was examining a corpse on the slab.

'Even when the SOCOs have finished at the crossroads,' the DCI was saying, 'I want the site itself to stay taped off and under guard.'

'You think it's going to be a tough job, boss?'

'I don't know yet, but even if the powers-that-be decide against giving us more men and an incident room at the scene, I still need an office manager for admin and deployment. Inspector Meade is off sick, so I've told Inspector Savage to keep herself free.'

Bowles merely grunted and kept his mouth shut. John Meade was bad enough, he thought sourly; tied up with tradition and given to blunt criticism of a mere sergeant, but Inspector Addie Savage was worse. For a start she was a woman, though these days you couldn't hold that against her; you couldn't make the mildest criticism, even if it was true.

Oh yes, Addie the baddie was another of the old school, hot on protocol, tough as an old boot *and* looking like it; with a brain like a razor and a clear compulsion to live up to her name – Savage was her own family name, because needless to say she'd never married.

'Bowles, are you listening?' Channon was on edge as they reached the mortuary. 'I want no delay in passing stuff that's

18

their concern to Forensic. You must list everything simply as an extra check to ensure that nothing is missed.'

'Right,' said Bowles, outwardly submissive but thinking, yes sir, no sir, three bags full, sir – reach me, fetch me, carry me. Life was going to be a laugh a minute when he had Addie the baddie on his back as well as the DCI.

George Hunter was waiting for them, his assistants ready to remove and bag the dead man's clothing. The cameras clicked and Hunter watched intently over his glasses, but even he had to give way to Fred Jordan of the SOCOs whenever the younger man called a halt to retrieve a scrap of evidence.

When the body itself was ready for examination Channon, as always, avoided looking at the face. Once, as a sergeant observing a post-mortem with his DCI, he had found himself looking straight into the eyes of a dead eighteen-year-old girl. Blue, they had been, wide open and absolutely lovely. It was weeks before he could get them out of his mind, but he had done his best for her. The work he put in on her case, and the results of that work, had been what secured his promotion to Inspector, but since then he had never again locked eyes with a corpse.

'Give me the essentials, George, if you will,' he said now, 'then I can leave you to it with the detailed technical stuff.'

Hunter waved a delaying hand at the camera and sound man, then spoke in verbal shorthand to the detectives, while Channon watched and listened with close attention. 'Time of death, subject to confirmation, fourteen to sixteen hours ago. Cause of death, massive blood loss from the severed veins and arteries in the throat. Damage to the trachea. Three stab wounds to the chest before the throat was slashed –'

'George,' interrupted Channon, 'how easy would it have been to cut through the throat so deeply?'

'Not easy at all. This young man isn't heavy with flesh and muscle, but he's lean and tough and sinewy. The right blade would have helped, of course – you haven't got it, I suppose? Well, you're looking for a very, very sharp knife;

blade slim and firm and fairly long – five to seven inches. I'll have to work on the angle of the attack, but at first sight it looks as if the killer was standing above and behind the victim, pulling the head back to expose the throat.'

'No defence, then?'

'A little, though weak.' Hunter turned over the man's left hand, where the inside of the fingers was scored by a single cut. 'This is a reflex defensive action, probably.'

'Do you see the killer as strong? Male? Did he know about anatomy? Was he cold-blooded or in a frenzy?'

'You're the detective,' retorted Hunter drily, 'but I'd say strong, almost certainly male or possibly a fit and determined woman. There are scratches on the forehead, perhaps from the brambles that have been mentioned. See, the wrists and ankles are also scratched, where his trousers and sleeves rode up and exposed his skin. Bruises on the torso and upper arms – possibly from dragging him to the site of his death or transporting him there.

'But to get back to the head: the lobe of the right ear is damaged – can you see it? An earring was taken off, pretty roughly.' Hunter peered at it through a lens. 'Yes, this ear had been pierced to hold an earring, which must have been wrenched off, probably seconds before death, from what I can make of the bleeding. Pretty rough by normal standards, but a mere nothing compared to what else has been done.'

Channon exchanged a look with Bowles. 'Surely to God,' he said quietly, 'nobody would slit a man's throat in the middle of nowhere, in deepest Cornwall, just to steal his earring?'

Bowles shrugged, but his mind was racing. Would somebody slit a man's throat for a *diamond* earring, a very large diamond earring? Pale eyes inward-looking, he leafed through the files of his memory, then studied the bruised, chalk-white face, comparing it with one he'd seen a couple of months earlier. He took Channon's arm and turned him away for a moment. 'Boss,' he said quietly, 'I think I know who he is.'

'Stomach contents later,' Hunter was saying, 'also sexual health, recent sexual activity and, hopefully, orientation. Analysis of organs, blood group, etc. – no probs getting DNA of course – you'll have everything in absolute detail ASAP but can't promise an exact time. Then it'll be up to your lot in Forensic to deal with the usual swabs and scrapings and all the stuff Fred's got lined up.'

Channon wasted no time. 'George,' he said, 'I've seen what I want to see. The sergeant here thinks we have a lead on identity. As much as you can as soon as you can – right?'

'Right, oh master.' Hunter turned back to the slab and began his formal post-mortem examination.

Once outside Channon said briskly, 'Who do you think he is, and why?'

'I think Paul Stradling from down the Carrick Roads. His old man's loaded. Ronald – no, I think it's Richard – Richard Stradling, something big in the City, as they say, but spends all his spare time down here.'

'Is there a mother?'

'If there is I never saw her.'

'So what was the contact?'

'Paul made a complaint of criminal damage to their beautiful boat, diddums do. Les Jolly and I interviewed him. He was nice enough but so would I be if my daddy-oh was a millionaire. He was young, lean, dark, and he had a massive diamond earring in his right ear. Not a fly-boy, more of a low-key stylish type, except for the earring.'

'Face?'

'I was trying to match the two, but the guy on the slab looks different to what I remember. Young Stradling had similar hair colour – wavy, I think, and just a bit spiked up. Good teeth – oh, I didn't check on them.'

'Do it,' ordered Channon. 'I'll wait.'

Bowles went back and said politely, 'The DCI wants me to look at the teeth, Mr Hunter.'

The pathologist parted the lips to reveal a mouth full of clotted blood thrown up from inside the throat. Obligingly

21

he wiped the teeth with tissues. They were perfect: completely symmetrical and probably dazzlingly white when unbloodied. 'Thanks,' muttered Bowles and made his escape. 'Brilliant gnashers,' he reported. 'Boss – I think it's him.'

'If so, you've saved us time and effort, sergeant.'

'And money,' agreed Bowles. 'What now?'

'First we check that nobody, including the Stradlings, has reported anyone missing. Then we contact his home to ask whether he's there. Look – come in here for a minute.' He took Bowles into a small room that was used to accommodate anyone brought in to identify the dead. Soon they might have Stradling senior in here, thought Channon bleakly. 'Bowles,' he said, 'where exactly is the Stradling house?'

'Less than quarter of a mile from Pengorra, in fact, it's called Pengorra Court, and it's some pad, boss. Amazing views if you like that sort of thing. This boat – it's a very swish ocean-going yacht with every luxury you could think of. It was damaged by an axe, of all things – a pretty basic bit of vandalism. The guilty party was a local yobbo who'd been sacked after skimping a job on the boat. No big drama – it was all done and dusted in a couple of days.'

'Sentence?'

'Slapped wrist from the magistrates – a fine and community service. The Stradlings seemed satisfied. End of story.'

'The end?' asked Channon thoughtfully. 'Maybe not. Now, have you got a note of the nearest local constable to the Stradling place and Pengorra?'

Bowles brought forth an expression of brisk competence. 'Better than that – I've got his mobile number!'

Channon almost smiled. The sergeant had his virtues. 'First, we'll check with headquarters that nobody's been reported missing, then ring this local PC and let me talk to him. He can make a preliminary visit and then report in while we're driving over there.'

But for Bowles at that moment something was more important even than the phone calls. 'Boss, will there be time for me to get a sandwich or something from the canteen?'

Channon let out an exasperated breath. 'I thought you'd started eating a decent breakfast? What was all that bragging you were doing about making an omelette with crispy bacon?'

Good God, the man had ears like bugging devices. The 'bragging', as he put it, had been a remark, a mere observation to Mary Donald, who at least had the decency to acknowledge that people needed to be fed if they were to remain efficient. 'I did have an omelette for breakfast,' he said with dignity, 'along with wholemeal bread and a pot of tea. But that was at seven this morning and it's now two in the afternoon.'

'All right, all right!' said Channon, flapping a hand. 'Get something in the canteen, if you must, but first the phone calls. Do it here, where it's quiet.'

So in the little room where people waited to identify the dead, the two men made their phone calls; and in the stainless steel expanse of the mortuary, George Hunter continued his examination of a young man whose head had been half severed from his body.

They were on their way to the Stradling house with Bowles at the wheel and Channon constantly on his mobile, but in a quiet moment the DCI asked, 'So who's this lad who was charged with damaging the boat?'

Bowles examined the orderly files of his memory. 'Goodchild,' he said, 'Martin Goodchild, though I recall his mum being a doting type who called him Marty.'

Before Channon could reply his mobile rang again. 'Well done,' he said to the caller. 'We'll be there in a few minutes, so wait for us in your car and the three of us will talk to him.'

He turned to Bowles. 'That was PC Cloak. He says Paul Stradling left home yesterday evening and hasn't been seen since. His father is demanding to know what's going on, but hasn't heard about the murder and has no idea that his son might be the victim.' Channon stared grimly through the windsceen and told himself that a difficult interview lay ahead. He had asked for DC Mary Donald's support but she'd been up on Bodmin and had only just started back. 'So,' he went on, 'are they hard up, the Goodchilds, or comfortably off? How old is Martin? Is he of average intelligence?'

'He can't be all that bright to use the axe from their own garden shed to vandalize a palatial yacht when everyone knows he had cause to resent the owner. As for his age, he'll be just about eighteen, I think, and no, they're not exactly rolling – the mother's a barmaid and he does odd jobs on people's gardens and knows a bit about boats. He helps out at the local yacht club and Heaney's boatyard. It was Heaney who fired him when something went wrong with the boat.'

Channon grunted. This was following an all-too-familiar path. 'What had he done to warrant losing his job?'

'Something about not checking what he'd been told to check on the boat. Paul went out in it and realized that something was wrong. He turned back before there was real trouble, but Heaney knew what must have happened. He lost his cool and gave Marty the sack.'

Channon thought of Heaney's long, leathery face and shrewd eyes. He didn't see him as a man to lose his cool in a hurry, but maybe the Stradlings were a source of income who must be kept sweet. Whatever the truth of it, things were moving at breakneck speed even before the body was formally identified. 'Could it have been deliberate on Marty's part?' he asked. 'A first, failed attempt to kill Paul for whatever reason?'

Bowles kept his eyes on the road and concealed dismay. He didn't want this to be an open and shut case. Stradling had money, he carried weight; this could be an important, possibly national case that would look good on his record. 'It could have been an attempt, boss,' he admitted reluctantly, 'but there was nothing to suggest it at the time. It seemed to be mere negligence on Marty-boy's part.' At that moment they topped a slight rise and instinctively he slowed the car. 'Pengorra Court,' he announced, 'second home to the Stradlings.'

To their left lay a huge, cream-walled house, set against the wooded hillside that ran down to Carrick Roads and facing the autumn-dark fields of the Roseland. Channon surveyed the scene with his sombre gaze. Earlier Bowles had said of the house, 'Amazing views if you like that sort of thing.' He did like it, very much, but had no liking whatsoever for what he had to do next.

Slowly he got out of the car and joined the waiting constable. Then the three of them made for the entrance to Pengorra Court.

'Detective Chief Inspector?' Richard Stradling shot an impatient look at the burly PC Cloak. 'Well, that's an improvement on dealing with underlings.'

Stradling had come to them in the hall, listening impatiently to Channon's careful introductions and waving a hand in refusal when he suggested they went further indoors for a chat. Now Channon said mildly, 'PC Cloak was merely acting on my instructions, sir.'

Light flashed on Stradling's glasses as he looked from one to the other of them. 'All right, all right. So what's the problem? Do you want me or my son, because he's out somewhere.'

'Are there any other members of your family at home, sir? Perhaps your wife?'

'No, there aren't,' the other said shortly. 'My wife died six months ago.'

'I'm sorry to hear that, sir. This visit concerns your son. I believe you haven't seen him today.'

'That's correct. What *is* this? He went out last evening, I'm not sure where. I'd taken it that he was in bed after a very late night when this constable called and asked us to check. My housekeeper reported that his bed hadn't been slept in.'

'Was that a cause for concern, sir?'

'No. Paul is twenty-six years old, inspector – a grown man. I don't lay down rules for his coming and going, either here or at our house in London. When we're here he sometimes sleeps on the boat or stays the night elsewhere. He doesn't need me to hold his hand.'

There was a hint of ridicule in the words, causing Bowles to look carefully at the tall broad frame, the well-cut silver hair, the expensive casual clothes. Clever or not, he thought, millionaire or not, this one was heading for a fall . . .

Channon fixed Stradling with his straight dark gaze. 'I'm sorry to inform you of this, sir. We suspect that your son has been the victim of a brutal attack.'

Stradling blinked and then shook his head in bewilderment. 'An attack? Who would do that? A drunk? Someone deranged?' Then he became still, staring intently at each of them in turn. 'What are you saying? Is he badly hurt? Is he in hospital? Where is he – at Treliske?'

'Mr Stradling,' said Channon gently, 'I would have thought you might have heard this by now. I'm very sorry to tell you that a young man was murdered last night at the crossroads known as the Menna, less than a mile from this house, and we have reason to believe that the young man could be your son, Paul.'

Stradling lifted his hands, palm upwards. 'It can't be! We had a meal together last evening. We spent time together.'

Channon sighed. It was more common than anyone would believe for families to see a routine occurrence as proof positive that nothing unpleasant could have happened. 'That may be so, sir, but you haven't seen him since, have you?'

'No – no, I haven't.'

'Mr Stradling, when we set off to come here we left pathologists starting the post-mortem examination of a young man's body. That procedure is still under way.

26

When the preliminaries are completed, I want you to go with my sergeant to view the body and tell us whether or not it is your son. Do you think you could prepare yourself for that?'

'What? Yes – yes, I suppose I could.' Stradling's face was taking on a blotchy look. The clear, tanned skin of a healthy older man became mottled with greyish patches at the side of his nose and along his jaw. Behind the rimless glasses he was blinking incessantly. 'This young fellow – had he no papers on him? No identification?'

'None whatsoever, sir.'

'So what makes you think – oh, very well. I'll go with your men. I'll be ready.'

'Thank you, sir. You'll be picked up in about an hour's time.'

Silently the three of them left Stradling standing in the hall of his beautiful old house, while pity descended on Channon like a weight across his shoulders. It hadn't sunk in with the man – not by a long way. Privilege and wealth would be of no help whatsoever when he saw his son on the slab. But no matter how sorry he was for Stradling, he couldn't face taking him to see the body. It would only revive memories that were slowly being put to rest ... Bowles would have to do it.

Katie leapt from the little ferry boat and climbed the steps to where her mother was waiting. 'It's been a great day,' she announced, and in the same breath, 'have you decided about the sleepover?'

'I've talked to Holly's mum and she's cancelled it,' Helen told her. 'Some of the other mothers wanted their children at home. Everybody's a bit worked up, you see – have you heard about the murder?'

'Yes, people were talking about it when we all had a pizza at lunchtime.' Katie slammed the car door and sat next to her mother, aware that she'd been wanting something exciting to happen, but not, she told herself resentfully, anything as bad as murder, and certainly not near Trenoon. 'What do you know about it, Mum?'

'Only that it happened at the Menna, and that by late morning Sinbad had heard that a man had been stabbed, because he rang Jaz and told him. There might be something on the regional news on TV, or local radio, I suppose, and the police are already going round the houses in Pengorra.'

'Have they been to our house?'

'Not yet, but I imagine it won't be long.' Helen didn't say anything about the message she'd left with the local constable about being at the Menna before it happened. Right now she wanted to emphasize something quite different. 'Listen, Katie – until this murder is sorted out, or solved or whatever, I don't want you going anywhere *at all* on your own.' With a determined air she switched on and they headed along the narrow street towards the uphill road and home.

Eyes wide in consternation, Katie was squirming inside her seat belt. She loved wandering the paths down at the water's edge and sailing her own little boat in the narrow stretch of water where she was allowed to practise. Her mother's implacable expression told her that it was no use arguing. 'Can't Jaz and I even walk to the school bus?'

'Only when the police can assure me it's safe,' said Helen. 'Until then, I'll drive you both into Pengorra in the morning and meet the bus in the afternoon.'

Katie pushed out her lips. 'Marvellous! Have you told Jaz?'

'Yes, I have. He's no happier about it than you are.'

Katie gave a world-weary shrug. 'If it's murder it must be to do with drugs.'

'We'll know soon enough,' replied Helen, then asked herself how many times she had used that phrase since she called at Chrissie's.

At Trenoon they found Lucy in the kitchen with her mobile on the table in front of her. A single glance told Helen that something was wrong. 'What's the matter?' she asked, instinctively putting her hand over Lucy's and pulling Katie close to her side. 'Where's Jaz?'

'He's gone out on his bike – just for a minute, he said, to see Sinbad.' Lucy's tone was oddly wooden, her eyes wide and still fixed on the mobile. 'The police are all over Pengorra, asking things, and Rilla's just been on. She was worried that the first I knew would be when the police called here.'

'The first you knew about what?'

Still Lucy didn't look at her. Then she said, 'It's Paul who's been murdered.'

In that instant Helen's world tilted. Later it was to turn upside down, but just then she was too stunned to think straight. It was Paul who'd been murdered? Paul Stradling? But they knew him – all the family knew him, each in their own way. He was only in his twenties.

She let go of Katie and tried to put her arms round her eldest child. Unbelievably she shrugged her away and stood up. 'Tell us about it then,' demanded Katie, but Lucy looked at her blankly and walked out of the kitchen.

Chapter Three

Was this what it felt like to be old, Helen asked herself; when the brain became sluggish and couldn't take things in? It was as if her mental awareness was groping around in a half-light, unable to evaluate what was happening.

The four of them were in the dining room for their main meal of the day, with curtains drawn, lamps lit and a log fire burning in the grate. It should have been a cosy family meal, but incomprehension swirled like mist around the table. They were having chicken casserole, a favourite with them all, but it seemed that only Jaz had an appetite. Helen watched him eating. Clearly, it would take more than murder to put her son off his food.

Then Katie, who had been shifting restlessly on her chair, announced, 'I might as well tell you – Dad's on his way.' Her tone was matter-of-fact, but the alert dark eyes were swivelling from one to the other, assessing their reactions.

They all stared at her. 'How do you know?' asked Jaz through a mouthful of rice.

'He said he was setting off at once.'

Her brother swallowed. 'When did he say that?'

'When I rang him soon after Mum and I came in and we'd talked about everything. I didn't tell you before in case one of you tried to stop him coming, but it's too late for that now.'

Helen let out breath. What was this? Of the three of them Katie was the most upset about the break-up because she and her dad were so close, and now because murder had been done she'd summoned him, no doubt believing he could make everything right just by being here. Or had she? Maybe she'd simply told him what was going on and he'd decided he must come . . .

She looked across the table at her youngest. You knew where you were with Katie. There were no subtleties, no evasions; she simply said what she had to say and you either liked it or lumped it. 'Why did you ring him?' she asked. 'It's awful about Paul, it's terrible, we don't know what's going on, but I can't see we're in any danger inside the house. I was going to tell him about it, anyway, as soon as we know a bit more.'

Lucy was twirling her fork around. 'Rilla didn't wait until she knew more before she told me,' she said tightly. 'She'd heard it from somebody whose auntie works at the house and thought I should know. Maybe Katie just thought Dad should know, as well.'

Katie gave the defiant toss of the head that was an exact replica of Steve's reaction to criticism. She eyed her mother coolly and came out with one of her rapid, multi-subject sentences. 'I just told him that Lucy's all upset and that the police are going round the houses and that they took Paul's dad off in a police car and we think it was to identify his body and that the police are coming to talk to you because you were at the scene of the crime.'

'Only by coincidence,' said Helen shortly. 'I'm not exactly suspect number one.' She shot a glance at Lucy, who was pushing food around her plate. 'Try to eat just a little bit, love. You'll only feel worse with an empty stomach.'

'Suspect number one?' Jaz repeated. 'I reckon they'll have Martin lined up for that, don't you?'

Helen stared at her plate, all at once unable to take her own advice about trying to eat. This was all getting too close to home. Martin Goodchild wasn't exactly part of the family but he was here twice a week helping in the gardens, and sometimes she asked him into the kitchen for a mug of tea and a bite to eat. He worked hard, showing knowledge and even a touch of flair; he kept an eye on

31

Katie's little boat and sometimes did other odd jobs around the place. Only yesterday he'd taken her urgent mail right into Falmouth. He was extremely useful and they'd all decided that the affair of vandalizing the Stradlings' yacht had been a one-off.

But Lucy had turned on Jaz. 'Why Martin? Because of what he did to the boat? He couldn't have hated Paul enough to murder him.'

'Maybe he didn't actually hate Paul,' said Katie. 'Perhaps he was just jealous of him. He knows you've been out with him and that you went to that party at his house.'

Lucy looked blank. 'So?'

Jaz had been helping himself to more chicken and now he banged the lid back on the dish. 'Hey,' he said, 'let's not get heavy.'

'I'm not getting heavy,' said Lucy doggedly, 'but what do you *mean*, Katie?'

Helen held up a hand. 'It's no use us all getting at loggerheads. What Katie means is that Martin likes you, Lucy – he fancies you. We're all aware of it so I can't believe you've never seen it for yourself. For goodness sake, though, whatever he thinks about you it doesn't make him a murderer. Jaz had words with Paul last week but that doesn't make him a murderer, either.'

'Glad to hear it,' said Jaz, taking more salad. 'Can we change the subject, Mum?'

'Yes, when I've said one more thing. Paul seems nice enough – seemed, I should say – but he was a businessman just like his father, and to be frank, I don't see either of them as a tender-hearted philanthropist. What I'm saying is they've probably made enemies in business, either down here or in London. Now, as soon as we finish our meal I want the three of you to clear away and load the dishwasher while I go and check on the spare room ready for your dad.'

Later, alone in the long attic room facing the water, she sat on the bed and thought about the man who would soon be sleeping there. Something was pushing its way through the tightness of her chest and she recognized it as relief – yes, she was relieved that Steve was coming. It didn't take away the pain that had been with her for the past six months, but he was the other parent to their children and she needed him here when they were all close to murder. It was as simple as that; she was glad he was coming all the way from London to be with them. Then a cold little voice in her head asked a single sentence: 'All the way from London for the second time in two days?'

Suppose Chrissie had been right and it *had* been him she'd seen near the King Harry? Why had he been down here in Cornwall without letting them know? Jumping up from the bed she headed back downstairs. She would think about it later. Right now she had to get her mind in gear for when the police came. She needed to remember the exact sequence of last night's events: where she saw the plastic bag, what time it was, exactly where she stopped the car . . .

Even to herself it sounded weak that she'd been at the site of a murder simply because, on a dark and stormy night, she'd been mad enough to chase a plastic bag.

Pengorra had never seen such activity. Police cars ringed the green and a bank of floodlights showed lorries bringing electronic equipment and workmen carrying tables and chairs into a heavy-duty tent attached to a huge caravan.

Short, thin and dynamic, hair and uniform immaculate, Inspector Adelina Savage was directing operations. She had to admit that the caravan wasn't exactly the incident room of her dreams, but it was the best she could come up with at short notice. The important thing was that the place would be up and running within twelve hours of the finding of the body, with everything to hand for what might or might not be a lengthy case.

Ticking off her priorities one by one, Addie Savage couldn't help wondering how she would get on with the senior investigating officer, Bill Channon. It would hardly be like old times. The days were long gone when they worked together as young officers. She was now thirty-six years old and had reached Inspector years ago; Channon must be forty-three or -four and a DCI.

Was that why for the first time in ages she felt uncertain of her own capabilities; because she would be working under Channon, who had earned himself a reputation for detection? If he had, what of it? She had her own reputation in admin. She could organize, she could manage people, get things done. She was seen as tough and she *was* tough – years of hard grind had seen to that. Bill Channon wasn't the only one with a reputation.

At that moment his sergeant, Bowles, was picking his way towards her across a tangle of cables, his complexion greenish in the glare of the lights and his hair flattened against his skull. She hadn't got the measure of this one yet. She knew he wasn't well liked by the rank and file, that he was known to be difficult, but clearly he had ability or he wouldn't be working hand-in-glove with Channon.

'Ma'am,' he said politely. 'The DCI said he'd see me here when I got back from the mortuary. Do you know if he's arrived yet?'

'I've just heard he'll be here in five minutes. The father identified his son, I take it?'

'Yes,' answered Bowles briefly. He was feeling annoyed with himself. He always said he could handle anything apart from weeping and wailing, and when that happened he simply ignored it; yet taking Stradling to identify the mutilated mess that had been his son had been just about as much as he could cope with. By the time they reached the mortuary Hunter and his minions had cleaned the body and covered up the chest and throat, thank goodness, but he told himself that even so the dead man had looked very different from the healthy, laid-back young yachtsman with the zonking great diamond in his ear.

'He identified the body at once,' he told Addie Savage soberly. 'Yates and I took him home and he refused the offer of a family liaison officer. He won't be alone – there's a housekeeper and other staff there. We're going over tomorrow to take statements from everybody and to examine the place.'

Still scrupulously polite, he excused himself and went to find a table where he could gather his wits and check his notes. Channon had been busy liaising with London for info on Stradling's business affairs, but now, with formal identification made, Bowles knew he would be eager to get moving. Not only that, he would want the low-down on Stradling's reactions, his manner, his actual words.

Having gone through his notes, the sergeant let his thoughts drift back to Addie the baddie. He had to admit she didn't mess about; everything was going like the clappers and the makeshift incident room was almost ready for use. Maybe she wouldn't be all that bad to work with, but the fact remained that he didn't like taking orders from a woman.

There was something else, though, and he knew it would sound mad if he told anyone – it was her eyes. They got to him. Very steady and intent, they were, and clear as blue glass. They gave him the weird idea that she could see inside his head – read his mind. All right, that was imagination, but one thing at least was certain: no matter how she provoked him, he wouldn't be tempted to say a word out of place. Unlike her predecessor she wasn't yet ready for retirement; therefore it made sense not to antagonize her . . .

A minute later Channon joined him, carrying a bottle of water. He plonked it on the table, ran a hand through his hair, and said, 'Well?'

'It's him, boss.'

Channon nodded. 'So, did you take Yates? How did it go?'

'Yes, I did take Yates. Stradling was a bit stiff and unbelieving on the way over – you know how some of them are. I put him with Yates in the relatives' room and checked with old – with Mr Hunter, then we took him in. By that time the body was a bit easier on the eye than when you and I saw it. Stradling took one look and simply nodded.'

35

'Did he change colour?' asked Channon. That, at least, couldn't be faked.

'Not noticeably. He was a bit grey-skinned from the time we set off.'

'What was his reaction? What did he say? Can you recall his exact words?' There was no need to spell out that a family member was always the first suspect for murder.

Bowles didn't need to look at his notes. 'He nodded at once, but didn't speak right away. He simply dabbed at his mouth with his handkerchief, as if he'd been sick. Then he jerked his head at Yates and me and with a sort of surprise in his tone, he said, "You're right. All of you are right. It's Paul."'

'Did he mention the earring?'

'Yes, almost as an afterthought when we were leaving. He said, "My son always wore an earring, but I didn't see it. That can't have been a motive, can it?" I said we knew about it, that I remembered it from several weeks ago, and that it wouldn't be overlooked.'

'He didn't say anything about Goodchild?'

'No. He was very quiet. As I say, he just seemed in a daze. He said more than once that he needed to go to bed. I thought it a bit odd as by all accounts he's a pretty forceful type in everyday life.'

Channon looked at him and said quietly, 'It isn't everyday life when your only son is killed, though, is it?'

Oh, no! Channon's only son – his only child – had been killed, hadn't he? In an accident, *and* his wife. 'No, of course not,' Bowles muttered awkwardly. He changed the subject. 'I arranged for statements to be taken tomorrow morning.'

'Good. Did you mention the cars?'

'Yes, I said that they might be needed for purposes of elimination, and that they weren't to be touched until we gave the word.'

'What did he say to that?'

'For the first time he showed a bit of spirit. He said, "Wouldn't you be better occupied finding who killed my

36

son than taking statements and poking around in cars?" I just said it was routine, and that was it. We got back here five minutes ago.'

'Thanks, Bowles. That was a grim task.'

You can say that again, Bowles thought, but merely replied, 'All in a day's work, boss.' He looked back on the last few hours and told himself it would have been even grimmer if he'd been on Stradling's wavelength, if he'd liked or even respected him, but he hadn't managed to do either. The man was too confident, too dismissive of police procedure; he thought the sun had shone out of his son's backside and boy, was he loaded! Oh, and he saw himself as God's gift to Cornwall. He might not have said as much but it had all been there in what he *didn't* say. You didn't need a degree in psychology to fathom it out.

Then Channon asked, 'Could you do with something to eat?'

Bowles tried not to goggle. The DCI asking him if he was hungry? Was it simply his way of saying thanks for dealing with Stradling? 'I'm starving,' he admitted, and for an instant real friendship flared between the two very different men.

Channon smiled. 'Inspector Savage has had several volunteers from Pengorra and round about. She's arranged for someone to provide tea and hot pasties for those working late, but by tomorrow we'll have our own food laid on. Right now there are two local women serving stuff up in the tent.'

The mere thought of nourishment made Bowles feel more energetic. What he could do to a cuppa and a pasty! But first he had to know what Channon was planning. 'I'll eat something in a minute,' he said, 'but boss, what's next?'

'The inspector and I will be working late, making arrangements and setting things up for tomorrow,' Channon told him, 'but there are interviews that can't be left until then. Did you contact Goodchild?'

'I sent Yates to the house in person to tell him to be available all evening, but he rang me to say there was nobody at home. He's just been on again to say that Martin's in Falmouth for the evening and Sue – that's the mother – can be found behind the bar at the Yardarm. That's where she works. It's an old pub about half a mile upstream on this side of the water.'

'If they didn't know already, they'll have heard of the murder by now,' said Channon, 'so they'll be expecting us. Have your food, then go to the Yardarm and tell the mother we want to talk to them both. Say Martin isn't to leave the area and set a time for early tomorrow morning.'

'I haven't checked yet if he's eighteen. If he is, do we need the mother?'

'Yes, we do. For back-up, alibi and general impressions. We don't have to see them together.'

'At home or at the station?'

'Don't get carried away, Bowles. At home, to begin with. Also you'll have heard that Cloak had a message from a Mrs Pascoe just up the road? She says she was at the Menna crossroads last night.'

'What, before it happened, or after?'

'Before, presumably. I think she might possibly have brought herself to report a dead body, don't you?'

'Not if she was the one who put it there.'

'You see her as covering herself by admitting she was at the scene?'

'It's been known,' said Bowles.

'If she put him there she's some weightlifter. We'll deal with her this evening, before we get bogged down with other stuff. Ask somebody to give her a ring to say we're coming, and again before we set off to make sure she's in. It's been quite a day and I don't want a wasted journey.'

Bowles went off in search of sustenance, leaving Channon to settle himself in his makeshift office – a table and a chair, separated from everything else by a wooden screen. Every luxury, he told himself.

* * *

38

At last Helen was alone with Lucy. She'd dropped Jaz off at Sinbad's house for the evening, Katie was watching a video of *The Perfect Storm* and their father, presumably, was somewhere on the road from London to Trenoon.

It was the ideal moment for a heart-to-heart, so she'd been weighing her words ready to speak when a brisk policewoman had rung to check that Mrs Pascoe was at home as a detective chief inspector was about to call at Trenoon to talk to her.

That in itself was weird enough; there hadn't been a policeman in the house since a constable called at the family home in Highgate after an attempted break-in, and that had been seven or eight years ago. But if a visit from the police seemed weird, more unsettling still was her own deep unease, almost a sense of guilt, about Lucy – or to be more precise, Lucy and Paul Stradling.

The unpleasant truth was that she didn't really know what the dead man had meant to her own daughter, not because she didn't care, but because they'd never discussed it. Lucy, who had confided in her about every crush, every boyfriend since the age of fifteen, had said very little about Paul Stradling.

Of course, she'd known that her mother had reservations about him. Helen had thought him too old, too sophisticated, too materially privileged for her gentle, unspoilt daughter; and Lucy, sensing disapproval, had kept quiet, maybe playing down what she really thought and felt.

For her part, Helen hadn't interfered, reassuring herself that there wasn't an actual relationship to interfere *with*, just a couple of dates and an invite to a swish party. What was more he worked in London with his father and only came down to the Fal for a weekend every two or three weeks. Hardly the basis for a sizzling romance – or so she'd thought. Now, it didn't seem quite so clear cut. All she knew was that there was a void inside her because she didn't know what Lucy was feeling.

Her eldest child had always been emotional, given to showing her feelings, to crying if she was upset or talking non-stop if she was on edge; but she had shed no tears for Paul, nor said anything of importance about him apart from repeating what her friend Rilla had told her. Right now she was sitting in silence with the lamplight making silver of her blonde head; her shoulders tense, her lips folded tightly together.

Play it gently, play it cool, Helen warned herself; you've got to start communicating on this, the same as you do on everything else ... 'Lucy, my love,' she said quietly, 'do you think we should get in touch with Paul's dad? Send a message of sympathy or support, or ask if there's anything we can do? Or maybe,' she braced herself at the mere thought of it, 'or maybe ask him round here for a meal, or something?'

Lucy looked at her. 'Is that what people do when someone's been murdered?'

'I don't know,' Helen admitted, 'I really don't, but it seems wrong to do nothing at all.'

Lucy gave a jerky little nod. 'All right, shall we send a note from the family? What can we say?'

'How about we're deeply shocked and grieved, and – and that we don't want to intrude, but that we're here if he needs anything.'

'Paul's dad isn't the needy type.'

'Perhaps not, but he's never been in this situation before, has he?'

'No.'

'Listen, my love, I feel bad because we've never said much to each other about Paul, and I'm pretty sure it's my fault. You knew, didn't you, that I wasn't too happy about you seeing him? I thought he was too much of a City wheeler-dealer for you, too money-conscious, but that doesn't mean I'm not devastated that he's dead – I'm absolutely staggered. Can we talk about him now, Lucy?' she asked urgently. 'Do you think you could tell me how you felt about him? Whether you were close? Whether either of you wanted a – a more serious relationship?'

'How serious can you get?' asked Lucy quietly.

'What?'

She was stunned to see open hostility in her daughter's eyes. 'I say, how – serious – can – you – get? For your information we loved each other. We were a real couple. We were sleeping together and he wanted to marry me!'

Helen gaped at her, pain pulling at her heart like chains on an anchor. 'Lucy,' she said brokenly, 'my little love – you never told me.'

'Maybe I thought you wouldn't want to know.'

'Oh, my pet, of *course* I wanted to know! And when did you manage to sleep together, anyway? You've only been out with him twice.'

'No I haven't. We've seen each other a lot, but I always told you I was going somewhere else. Several times he came down midweek and stayed in Falmouth rather than at their house, and so we met at his hotel. I loved him, Mum, and now he's dead, and I don't even know if they'll let me see his body!'

There was a rasping sound in the room. With a shock Helen realized it was coming from her own open mouth, so she closed it with a snap of her teeth. She was recalling how, during the meal, when they'd talked about Martin, she had told herself that things were getting close to home. *This*, she thought bitterly, *this* was close to home! Her good, sweet little Lucy sleeping with the smooth, big-spending son of a millionaire! If he hadn't been murdered already she would have throttled him herself!

Lucy was quite still but gnawing at her lips. Arms open, Helen went to her, but at that instant the doorbell pealed and seconds later Katie leapt into the room. 'It's the police, Mum,' she said, eyes wide. 'Can I let them in?'

Chapter Four

Some house, thought Bowles, and some women: two luscious blondes from the same stable. In spite of the tearstains, the younger one was drop dead G; but he had to admit that the mother was more his type – he liked them well-upholstered. As for the kid – well, she was just a gremlin, but she might grow up with a bit of style. She had personality, judging by the way she was standing guard over her mother.

He watched as Channon went through his usual painstaking introductions, noting how the mother grew more relaxed when faced by his calm, unhurried manner. Bowles always thought him long-winded and over-polite with witnesses, but he had to admit that he could gain their confidence and calm them down. His own preferred method was 'don't stand any messing and go for the jugular', but just lately he'd been asking himself whether he would rather be known as tough or clever – or, of course, both. No prizes for guessing which.

They were being ushered into a big warm room with curtains drawn against the night and a log fire glowing dull red in the hearth. 'Please, make yourselves comfortable,' said Helen, but they continued to stand; Bowles from force of habit in his customary position behind the DCI's right shoulder.

Channon was responsive to atmosphere, and after a day that had encompassed a grisly death, a traumatized finder of the body, a post-mortem, a bereaved father, the taking over of a village green and literally dozens of phone calls, he had the sensation of the room enveloping him, comforting him, like a soft luxurious sweater round cold and aching shoulders. But this wasn't the time to get fanciful; it was late and the refuge of his own house and bed was hours away.

By now Helen and the girls were on a sofa, facing him, and before he could speak she asked, 'You don't need to talk to my daughters, do you?'

He could see that the older one seemed stunned, while the younger one was watching him curiously, her manner almost belligerent. It was abundantly clear that all three were on edge, so why waste the opportunity? 'As we're here, we may as well have a word, with your permission, of course,' he said calmly. 'How many of your family live here, Mrs Pascoe?'

'My three children and me.' She put a hand on the knee of each of the girls. 'This is Lucy and this is Katie, and there's my son, Jasper, who's out for the evening. My husband lives and works in London – we're separated.' It was getting easier to say that, she thought; would it ever get easier to live it?

'Is he in London as we speak?' asked Channon.

'No, he isn't, as a matter of fact. He's on his way here.'

'Why is that, Mrs Pascoe?'

'It's becoming known about the murder, inspector, so people round here are upset. They're worried about the safety of their families. My husband feels he should be here.'

Channon nodded. 'And did any of you happen to know the younger Mr Stradling?'

Things were moving fast, thought Helen – too fast. This was supposed to be just a few questions about last night at the Menna. But what she had said to herself earlier still stood: 'Tell it how it was – the plain, unvarnished truth. No more – no less.' She couldn't do any other – she didn't want to do any other. Quietly she answered, 'We all knew Paul – all five of us. We simply can't believe what's happened.'

Well, well! An entire family connected to the dead man. Was Bowles right? Was this woman's admission of being at the crossroads simply a whitewash job? He observed Helen Pascoe carefully. No – he thought not ... 'Our talk may take some time,' he said, 'so I think we'd better have it in the morning. If I can't get here, my officers will ask you for details of how well each of you knew the deceased, and they'll need you to give your whereabouts at the time he died. Also, you'll be asked to make an official statement for police records.'

Helen let out breath. With a single sentence she had embroiled the whole family, but what this detective had said in reply was fair enough. She nodded. 'That seems reasonable.'

'I'm glad you see it like that. For now, though –'

Katie interrupted him. 'Do you mean we're all suspects?' She liked things to be exciting, but this was starting to be horrible.

Channon focused his attention on her. Evidently she was keen on sailing, judging by her sweatshirt. 'No, you're not, Katie. None of you are suspects at this stage. All this is simply part of the routine enquiry.'

She liked this man; he was strong, he knew what he was doing; she could imagine him at the helm of a boat in dangerous waters. She wasn't aware of it but she was beaming at him in full approval.

Bowles watched with increasing irritation. For crying out loud, he had the gremlin eating out of his hand! How did he do it? And did he know the time? At this rate they wouldn't be home before midnight.

But Channon was giving Katie a benign little nod before turning back to her mother. 'For now,' he repeated, 'I need to know about last night. Mrs Pascoe, I believe you told PC Cloak that you were at the Menna crossroads? Can you tell me why, and when?'

Helen leaned forward. How mad would she sound? 'The reason why is that I was on my way home from yoga. A few of us, all friends, meet at each other's houses every

44

Friday. We practise yoga and then have a drink and a chat together. Last night it was at Julie Chenoweth's, so I had to drive past the Menna, both going and coming back. As for when I was there – I usually leave at about ten, so it would be around ten past, maybe quarter past. I'm sorry I can't be absolutely precise.'

So am I, thought Channon, but merely said, 'We'll need the names and addresses of all your friends, of course. Now – your vehicle. Were you driving the red Freelander that's parked outside?

'Yes, that's mine.'

'And was it still raining as you drove home?'

'No, but it was still windy.'

'Did you stop at the crossroads?'

'Yes. You see, about a hundred yards before I got there, a big plastic bag blew against the windscreen. I had to brake hard because I couldn't see a thing, but there was nobody behind me. I got out to move the bag but it blew away again – it was sort of flying – a bit like a kite.'

Bowles broke in. 'Wouldn't the bag have been too wet to fly?'

'I would have thought so, but the fact remains, it flew.'

'So what did you do then?' asked Channon.

Helen swallowed. 'I chased it – in the car.' She saw the sergeant curl his lip and said evenly, 'I thought it might land on someone else's windscreen.'

'Very public-spirited,' said Channon, straight-faced. 'So what happened next?'

'It landed ahead of me at the Menna – on the brambles round the stone. I stopped the car and got out.'

If this was true it was a godsend, thought Channon. 'You stopped at the crossroads? How close to the stone?'

'Well, I was driving in this direction, so I was on the opposite side of the road from it. I walked across and got to within about five or six feet. The road is lower than the base of the stone, of course.'

'And the bag? Where exactly was it at that point?'

'As I said, in the middle of the brambles.'

45

'Did you try to reach it?'

'I hesitated. I didn't know if I could get to it and in any case I was wearing good suede boots. I thought it might be wet and messy. But before I could decide what to do a massive gust of wind came and blew it away again in a – a sort of upward spiral. I gave up and drove home. That's all I can tell you.'

'Oh, I think you might manage rather more than that, Mrs Pascoe. What was visibility like?'

'I don't remember a moon. My headlights were on, but shining in the direction I was going.'

'So – and this is very important – did you see anything unusual near the stone?'

'No, I just recall it gleaming. I thought it was still wet, but you know how granite always has a sort of glow? The leaves were all shiny, as well. It was a bit creepy, actually. I was glad to leave the place.' Remembering, she shivered.

'Was there anyone nearby? Did you see a parked car? Did anyone pass you on the road?'

'No, no and no,' Helen said steadily.

'Now, this bag. How big was it?'

'Pretty big, no pattern or design on it, and white – or at least, very pale. It wasn't a supermarket bag for groceries – more the size for holding a new pillow. I'm pretty sure it wasn't flimsy, but it flew around as if it was as light as a feather. I think the wind got inside it, or something.'

'When you left the Menna, you came straight home?'

'Yes.'

'And you didn't see anyone between the Menna and this house?'

'No, not that I recall. I just got back, parked the car and came in.'

'And what time would that be?'

'I suppose about twenty-five past ten.'

'Have you used your car today, madam?'

'Yes, several times.'

'Mm, a pity. What about your boots? Have you worn them since last night, or cleaned them?

'Neither.'

'Right. We'll need them for forensic tests, Mrs Pascoe – and I'm afraid we'll have to take the Freelander, purely for the purpose of elimination and comparison – tyre marks and so forth.'

Helen stared at him. Living at Trenoon made transport pretty vital, though she could always use Lucy's car, of course. 'How long will you keep it?'

'Twenty-four hours should do it. You won't be without a vehicle if your husband is here, and I presume the Fiat is your daughter's?'

'Yes, yes,' she agreed. Everything was moving at top speed – getting complicated. She hadn't had time to gather her wits about what Lucy had told her, she hadn't even held her close. Her daughter had lost the man she loved, yet now she was having to listen to her mother being questioned about the scene of his death. She should have sent her out of the room. More, she should never have opened her mouth to the police about last night. If she'd kept quiet about the Menna she could have been sitting with Lucy at this very moment, listening to her, trying to talk to her, and – yes – handling her own dismay about her sleeping with Paul Stradling and wanting to marry him.

Feeling at a disadvantage with the detectives looking down at her, she got to her feet, resentment sharpening her tone. 'Is it usual to commandeer the belongings of witnesses so early in an enquiry?' she asked.

'Not usual, madam, but in this instance necessary, and, I assure you, perfectly in accordance with the law. Where forensic evidence is concerned, the earlier something is examined and recorded the better. The sergeant here will give you official receipts for the car and your boots. They will be well cared for and returned to you undamaged.'

For seconds there was silence, and then for the first time Lucy spoke, her voice low and quite without expression. 'Have you found out how Paul was killed?'

Channon eyed her with compassion. Clearly, this one

47

had known Paul Stradling very well . . . 'Yes, we've found out,' he told her, 'but I can't discuss it, I'm afraid.'

She was jerking her head at him. 'No, no, I realize that, but do you – do you think it was quick?' The obvious question 'Did he suffer?' lay heavy and unspoken between them.

'Yes, I think it was,' he answered very gently. 'I don't think he suffered much.' That might possibly be true, he told himself; and even if it wasn't, did it matter? At least the girl looked slightly less bereft. 'We'll be on our way, Mrs Pascoe, as soon as we have your car keys, and of course, your boots. We'll be in touch first thing tomorrow. Please make sure that all five of you are available for interview.'

The three of them were at the door as they left the house. Channon saw that Katie had taken hold of her sister's hand. He found himself looking back for the smile of approval that had captivated him just minutes ago, but all he could see was a perplexed frown beneath the curly black hair.

'No time now for discussion,' he said, handing the keys of the Freelander to Bowles. 'Take it straight to Forensic and I'll tell Eddie Platt it's on its way. He'll have people still there, working on the SOCOs' stuff and the odds and ends from the mortuary, so all that will have priority. I'll let him know I'm in a hurry for anything he gets from the car, and I'll ask one of the uniforms to run you back to Pengorra. Wait a minute! No I won't – it's ten o'clock!'

Bowles was unlocking the door. 'Tell me news,' he muttered.

But Channon was stopping him from getting in. 'Sergeant! What are you doing? You're the last one I expect to leave loopholes for a clever brief.' He delved in the boot of the police car and unearthed a new pack of protective gear. 'Get it on!'

Bowles concealed a sneer. If there was one thing that irritated him it was having to dress up like a dog's dinner to protect every possible clue. He started to put on the white overalls and meanwhile Channon was still talking.

'Forensic is close to your place, isn't it? Right – finish for the day when you've delivered this lot and I'll see you down here at seven in the morning. No later!'

'Yes, boss,' said Bowles. You lucky devil, he told himself mockingly; the first night of a case and you'll be home by ten thirty! He moved the driving seat further back and switched on, observing the dash with narrowed eyes. The Pascoes – with or without a father – didn't exactly stint themselves. The house alone was worth a bomb, and as for this set of wheels, it was new in the last six months, with every extra in the book. It was clear that money wasn't a problem at Trenoon. He rather hoped that Channon wouldn't be present in the morning. It might be interesting to make them all sweat a bit over their statements.

They drove separately up the road behind Trenoon, one aiming for the Truro road and the other for Pengorra village. A Mercedes passed them going downhill to the house, with a dark, shadowy figure at the wheel. In the beam of his lights Channon caught sight of the driver's head and registered black hair with streaks of white at the temples. Daddy Pascoe, presumably, all the way from London. So that was where little Katie got her colouring . . .

Martin Goodchild arrived home and stared in surprise at his mother. 'Why aren't you still at work?' he asked in puzzlement. 'It's only half past ten.'

'If it comes to that,' she retorted, 'why aren't you still in Falmouth with your mates?'

Both edgy, mother and son eyed each other and Martin was the first to look away. She knew he didn't like to see her dolled up for behind the bar: make-up put on with a trowel and her hair round her shoulders, but she'd told him often enough it was the landlord, Reg, who wanted her to look like that; in fact, he'd have had her cleavage on view as well if she'd had one worth showing.

Martin made for his room, then at the foot of the stairs turned with one hand on the newel post. 'I came away early,' he told her reluctantly. 'The others kept taking the piss about the murder and I got fed up with it.'

Sue Goodchild rushed to his side. 'Taking the piss?' She puffed a disbelieving breath. 'The man's dead, Marty. People are saying he was hacked to pieces. What's there to take the piss about in that?'

He shook his head. 'No, Mum, they were taking it about *me*. You know – because of the boat thing. They didn't mean it, or anything.'

'Oh, they pulled your leg about being a murderer, is that it? Just for a bit of fun?'

'Sort of.'

'Well,' she said heavily, 'if you must know that's the reason I'm here instead of behind the bar. Reg said some of the regulars were asking questions and he thinks it's bad for trade.'

'Questions? About me?'

'Marty, of *course* about you! When you vandalized that boat you might as well have shouted from the rooftops that you had a grudge against the Stradlings.'

'Not both of them. Just Paul. I've told you that before.'

It was true. He'd told her, quite calmly, that it wasn't fair for Paul to have so much: brains, money, an amazing job and a devoted father. It was Paul who brought the boat back and Amos Heaney, no doubt weighing a valued customer against a part-time mechanic, had given him his marching orders; so Marty, her Marty, had seen that as justification for damaging one of the most beautiful boats on the Roads. And to cap it all, he'd been convinced he was being victimized when the police were brought in.

Sometimes she wondered if he could be her own flesh and blood. Oh, it was obvious he *was* – he had inherited her brown eyes and thick brown hair, her pale skin, even her teeth: beautifully regular with very pointed canines. It wasn't his appearance that made her wonder – it was his mind. It didn't run on the same lines as hers, or anyone else's, for that matter. He had the weirdest ideas and said the strangest things just as if they were ordinary and acceptable – it had always been the same. 'All right,' she said now, answering him, 'your grudge was just against Paul, and now he's dead.'

'Yes, and the first I knew of it was when Biddy told us at teatime.'

'I know,' she said, 'I know, son.' She could never, ever tell him that just for one dreadful moment, she'd wondered . . . Hastily she looked away from him. He might be a bit different, but he had a knack of knowing what she was thinking.

His next words showed that she needn't have worried, because he was still dwelling on what had happened at the Yardarm. 'So what were the customers saying?' he persisted.

She always tried to give him the truth, but this was one of the times when it would be easier, and maybe kinder, to give a watered-down version. She thought rapidly and decided to stick to the facts. 'Some of them were asking why I was still serving drinks when at any minute my son would be taken in for questioning.'

Martin lifted a shoulder and stuck out his bottom lip, as he always did when he felt unjustly treated. 'Do *you* think I'll be taken in?'

'No I don't, for the simple reason the police are coming here first thing in the morning, to question us both. The sergeant we dealt with last time came to the pub to tell me. They'd been trying to ring us but of course we were out.'

'Is that why the customers were saying things? Because the sergeant was there?'

'Only partly. Some of them had passed remarks before he even showed his face, but it was after he'd been that Reg said I'd got to go.'

'He didn't give you the sack?'

'No, he told me to take a few days off on half-pay.'

'Oh.' He eyed her doubtfully. 'That's not so bad, is it?'

'No,' she agreed, 'it's not so bad. I've got a bit put by that'll help make up my wages, but with your gardening earnings coming to an end for the winter, we'll be a bit tight.'

Tight, she repeated to herself wearily, when had money *not* been tight? It had been tight since long before Marty was born. At that time she must have been the only married woman along the Roads, if not in all Cornwall, to have worked full-time right through a pregnancy until the moment she started in labour. She thought: not so bad, eh? Tell me about it.

She looked at her son. She didn't always understand him, she didn't really know what made him tick, but the ties of blood were deep and abiding. She loved him. As for the man who fathered him – in wedlock, what was more – he had never even seen his son, so he could burn in the fires of hell as far as she was concerned.

Rain was blowing in by the time Channon parked the car by the village green in Pengorra. For a moment he stayed behind the wheel, watching the scene under the floodlights. He thought back to a murder case in the village of Porthmenna on the Lizard – a triple murder, admittedly – where the incident room had been palatial compared to this mish-mash of caravan and tent and prefabricated sheds. Still, it wasn't the premises that mattered, it was what went on inside them – or so he liked to tell himself.

When he opened the car door the smell of hot pasties wafted to him and to his own surprise hunger wrenched at his innards. What on earth? If there was one thing that years of police work had done for him it was to train his digestive tract to accept irregular meals, but evidently tonight was an exception. He decided to eat on the job – something so rare as to be almost unheard of.

Inside the tent staff were preparing for morning, while in one corner two local women were still cheerfully offering food and drink to anyone who needed it. He went across to them and chatted for a minute. One of them was Cornish to the marrow and the other cut-glass Home

Counties, but in this instance they were working together good-naturedly, as colleagues. He wasn't sure if that was always the case in the local seafaring communities, where the population was often a mix of native Cornish folk and second-home owners. To an onlooker, it was a case of moderate incomes living cheek by jowl with astronomically high ones, in mutual respect and harmony. Would the killing of Paul Stradling uncover an uglier side to the mix, such as envy and frustration?

He took his pasty and tea to his own table and chair, blessing whoever had provided the wooden screen. At least his officers would be spared the sight of their DCI slumped in total exhaustion, wolfing a pasty from a paper napkin. His solitude was short-lived. No sooner had he taken his first bite than Addie Savage came round the screen. 'Oh, sorry, I didn't know you were eating,' she said. 'I just wanted a word before I go home.'

Mouth full, he waved her to the other chair. 'It's a long time since you and I worked in harness, Addie.'

'I know – water under the bridge and all that,' she said lightly. 'Everything you asked for has either been done or is under way. Everyone knows there's a briefing in the morning at eight o'clock sharp.'

'Have you had any reports in from the first enquiries?'

'Several. I've had them typed out in narrative format with sources listed and numbered. I remembered you like to have local info from the word go.'

'It sounds as if I made an impression,' he said, striving for a lightness he was too tired to feel.

'And not just on me,' she answered, laughing. It was still there, she told herself, ready and waiting to be called into play; the work-based banter that had lightened many an hour of hard slog. The days were long gone when she'd wondered if their friendship would ever evolve into something more personal, and of course it hadn't. Bill had found the love of a lifetime, while she had taken a transfer to north Cornwall and found that work could make a very good reason for living.

53

For his part Channon was thinking that Addie had always been efficient. Maybe with her as office manager he wouldn't miss his old friend John Meade as much as he'd thought. But that reminded him. 'One thing you can do for me, Addie. Get Les Jolly down here, will you? He's a zero on people skills but he was damn good at analysing family background and local history on that triple killing on the Lizard.'

'Will do,' she agreed. 'Anything else?'

'No – just give me the reports and then get off home. Do you still live alone?'

'Yes, I do. And you?'

'The same,' he said, and with a nod he went back to his pasty and prepared to spend time on the day's findings.

Quietly Addie Savage went away, cleared her table, checked on the night staff and then set off for home. Sabbath or no Sabbath, she thought, tomorrow would be a busy day.

Chapter Five

It was 7 a.m. and all was quiet at Trenoon. The kitchen was warm from the Aga and Helen sat next to it in her big wicker chair, drinking tea and recalling the previous day.

Guilt marched back and forth across her mind, pushing aside regret and confusion and the new, sick horror that had come with the murder. How could she not have seen Lucy getting so involved with Paul? Seven months ago she would have known – she would have sensed it. Had she been so sunk in misery that she'd been blind to her own child falling in love?

Once the police had interrupted her and Lucy, there had been no chance to go back to their talk. She would have to tackle her soon – this morning – before they made their statements. Steve had agreed that Lucy must tell the police that she and Paul had been close. Last night when the young ones had gone upstairs she'd talked it over with him, sitting in front of a dying fire in a welter of questions and answers and supposition, almost like they used to do before the split-up if something was causing them concern.

He had been tight-lipped about Lucy sleeping with Paul, but said grimly, 'She was likely to do it sooner or later, and these days waiting till the age of eighteen is considered restrained, I suppose. What I can't understand is the secrecy. She always told you everything. You were so close.'

In the way of families, that was how it had been: Lucy was closest to her mother, Jaz was equally at ease – and sometimes at loggerheads – with both his parents, while Katie, true to her temperament, had been her daddy's girl.

And it had worked; they'd been a warm, loving, ordinary family. What a mess it was now, Helen thought; what a wreck of the framework in which they'd lived and loved.

She and Steve had been on neutral terms, discussing Lucy. There had been none of the falseness, the awkwardness that usually weighed down the rare times they were alone together. In front of the children it was different – she could dredge up a sort of normality. She might feel lost and betrayed but she had vowed that nothing on God's earth would make her say or do anything to cause them to doubt that their father loved them.

Replying to him, she had said, 'Lucy knew, Steve. She knew I had doubts about her seeing him – that's why she kept it secret. You've had dealings with both him and his father. What did *you* make of him?'

She thought she saw something glint in his eyes, like a blade, sharpened and then put safely away behind the flicker of his eyelids. 'I found him tough in business,' he said carefully, 'every bit as keen as his father. They drove a hard bargain about financing the new premises for the practice, and – and there were a few other things. I never really got Paul's measure – he wasn't a show-off, in spite of the earring, though I'm pretty sure he liked the high life. But Helen, from what I saw in London he had girls queuing up for him.'

She swallowed. This was getting worse. 'Do you mean he wasn't serious about Lucy?'

'I don't know, maybe we'll never know, but if she believes he wanted marriage, why disillusion her? Let's just be here for her until we can see how she's handling it.'

'How long can you stay?' The question just came out of its own accord. She hated herself for wanting him in the house, but all at once he seemed the embodiment of all that she needed: strength, parental concern, a reliability that was completely at odds with his adultery.

'If you want me here I can stay for a week,' he said. 'I've brought some work with me that I'd been doing at

56

home. I'll need to use the studio for a couple of hours a day, though.'

'Right,' she agreed promptly. The studio was where she herself worked from home, designing textiles and wall-paper and working on a new paint range for the same firm who had employed her part-time in London. Ever since she and Steve met at university, design had been their working bond – Steve in architecture and her with colour and fabrics and now the revival in wallpaper. She crushed a yearning for that old sharing of interests, and said, 'Have I told you that the police want statements from all five of us?'

'Yes, but I think it's just a matter of routine. We'll tell them the truth – all that we know.'

She looked down at her hands, clasped tightly on her lap. 'Inspector Channon said they'll want to know where we all were at the time of Paul's murder,' she said carefully. Now, she thought, he'll tell me if he was down here yesterday – and if he was, he'll tell me why.

But he told her nothing of the sort. 'We'll go through it with the three of them in the morning,' he said, 'so we'll all have it clear in our minds what we want to say. The police won't have time to listen to us waffling and contradicting ourselves.'

Minutes later they had parted for the night. 'I'll see you in the morning, Helen,' had been his polite farewell. Hers had been a stiff, 'Goodnight, Steve.' She'd watched him climbing the stairs and thought: the end of an awful day in an awful year.

But now, sitting among the cushions by the Aga, she reflected on that. Yes, it *had* been an awful year, but a year in what, after all, had been a lovely, lovely life ... She dragged her mind from the bright years of their marriage to the grim, unreal present and the murder of Paul Stradling.

At two minutes past eight Channon was in full flow, outlining the basic facts of the case. He liked briefings, believing that to keep all ranks informed made them feel involved, and that if they felt involved they worked harder and better and sometimes delivered a gem.

Bowles had obtained a picture of Paul Stradling. Blown up in size and picked out by a spotlight it showed a good-looking, blue-eyed young man, smiling at the camera and wearing a peaked nautical cap and striped sweater, with sunlight glinting on his earring. Hardened as he was to violence, Channon felt slightly sick to think of that tanned young throat being sliced from one ear to the other.

'Right now we have nothing,' he was telling the assembled company. 'No weapon, no transport for the body, no wallet, no contents of pockets; as yet no forensic, no DNA, and so far no suspects – apart from a youth who may or may not have an alibi. All we do have is Paul's body, stabbed in the chest and with the throat cut – and left propped, for reasons unknown, against a three-thousand-year-old standing stone.

'You'll all be given a list of the most important questions to ask on the doors. Inspector Savage here will answer your queries and allocate the area each of you will cover. I want full reports on each visit you make, but – and this is vital – anything that you consider urgent, or even significant, must be phoned in right away, rather than simply included in your report.'

Standing to one side, pale eyes intent, Bowles watched and listened, admitting to himself that Channon could always get the rank and file behind him. A picture came into his mind of a new constable back at the station, listening dutifully as he was given a bawling out over a minor slip-up; respectful with his 'Yes, sarge,' and 'Right, sarge,' but face set, eyes deliberately blank, resentment oozing from him like acid.

He observed all those who listened as Channon gave them their orders. It was Sunday morning, a time when most of them would have been off duty and at home, but not a single one looked other than motivated. And why not? Because this was murder and there was a sort of prestige in working on a murder enquiry? Because Channon so rarely pulled rank or cracked the whip, because he was a good communicator, or because they all knew that as a detective he was in a class of his own?

Bowles shrugged impatiently. OK, so Channon was a good detective. He was still a softie and he was still a pain in the backside, but when a man made it to DCI maybe he was entitled to be just what he felt like being. When *he* got his promotion to Inspector he'd be what he wanted to be, and would it matter if he saw resentment on the faces of the lower ranks? Well, would it? To his own amazement he wasn't sure of the answer to that one, so he brought his attention back to Channon. This case was going to be no pushover – he could feel it. So there was work to be done, starting now.

Heading for the Goodchilds' house along a road that was now open to traffic, they passed two SOCOs still working outside the white police tent at the Menna. 'Old Jordan's making a meal of the search, boss,' observed Bowles.

'*Mr* Jordan is an acknowledged expert on scene-of-crime examination,' said Channon in mild reproof. 'He's respected throughout Cornwall and no doubt elsewhere.' They drove up the lane where Luther Tresillian lived, until Bowles stopped at a pair of whitewashed cottages, both with neat, autumn-bare gardens. A big green van was parked on a stretch of gravel at the side of the left-hand one.

Bowles waved a hand at the van. 'Mobile shop,' he announced. 'A tough old bird does the rounds in it all along this side of the water.'

Channon consulted his notes. 'Bridget Stumbles – spinster,' he read aloud. 'Word came in from yesterday's enquiry that she knows the area as well as anyone and better than most. Also, she's next-door neighbour to Martin and his mother . . .'

For seconds he stayed in his seat, remembering a woman who ran a shop on the harbour front in Porthmenna on the

Lizard. A good woman – he'd thought of her as the eyes and ears of the village, and she'd been useful to him. Maybe this Stumbles woman would prove useful as well? 'We'll have a word with her later,' he said as Martin Goodchild opened the door.

Before they crossed the threshold he knew that Bowles's description of a local yobbo with a barmaid for a mother had led his imagination on a downward spiral. He had a squeamish streak on domestic matters and had half expected a grubby house with dirty coffee cups hanging around and a smell of fried food. But here – he gave the place a quick, all-seeing glance – here was a cosy, spotlessly clean little cottage. And here was Martin's mother . . .

In the flurry of introducing themselves he observed them both. Martin was a big lad, well made but not overweight. He looked perfectly normal considering he had rampaged over the Stradlings' boat with an axe: no outward signs of learning difficulties, no visible antagonism to the police, he appeared to be an ordinary if slightly withdrawn teenager.

The mother was probably in her late thirties, a slim, almost skinny woman with shiny brown hair drawn back from her face in a coil that was fastened by an old-fashioned velvet bow. Politely she offered them seats on a small sofa in the living room.

'Mrs Goodchild,' began Channon, 'we're here to check on what you and your son were doing when Paul Stradling was murdered. I expect you can see that we have no choice but to investigate Martin in particular, in view of the court case for criminal damage some weeks ago.'

He saw her eyes swivel to look at her son and then return to meet his. She seemed taken aback by his approach. 'You have your job to do,' she agreed, 'but we didn't expect nobody no higher than the sergeant here to come and see us.'

'I'm in charge,' Channon admitted, 'and as you can see, I like to do the important interviews myself. Now, the sergeant and I want to check your movements on Friday evening.'

'Movements?' echoed Sue dubiously, as if the word was synonymous with guilt.

'Yes,' said Channon patiently. 'What both of you were doing.'

'Both of us?' Lord, she thought; her wits had flown out the door as this top man walked through it. She was repeating everything he said!

Martin spoke up. 'My mother is a lady of good character,' he said. 'She knew nothing about what I did to the boat.'

'I'm sure she didn't,' agreed Channon mildly, 'but you see, this is a routine enquiry. Now, you first, Mrs Goodchild, if you please.'

'I work six nights a week behind the bar at the Yardarm,' she said. 'Monday's my night off. I drive over there in my little old car. I start at six and finish at eleven. On Friday I was there for my five hours, as usual.'

'We have to check what people tell us,' confided Channon, as if such a thing was an embarrassing necessity. 'Will your employer be able to back you up on that?'

'Of course he will. He always says he can set the clock by me arriving.'

'Really? And by your leaving?'

'What? Well . . . no. I don't always get away on the stroke of eleven.'

'Can you remember if it was the stroke of eleven on Friday?' he asked intently.

'I've been thinking about it,' she admitted. 'We'd been busy with it being a Friday, but I was well on with clearing up, even before last orders. It might have been ten past. I'd have reached home about half past.'

Channon nodded. 'So what time would you have come through the Menna?'

She stared at him. So that was it! All this meek and mild stuff was leading up to her being at the Menna. 'I didn't pass through the Menna at any time,' she told him with satisfaction. 'Going to and from work I always use the top lane. If you carry on the way your car's facing when you leave here, you'll come to a different, smaller crossroads. That's the way I go to work.'

'I see,' said Channon. 'We'll go back by that route, then, to see for ourselves. Mrs Goodchild, did you notice anything at all that seemed unusual while you were coming home?'

'No,' she said, 'nothing. Nothing at all.'

'And was Martin at home when you got here?'

'Yes. He stays in on Fridays and goes out with his mates on Saturdays.' She couldn't help sounding a bit pleased about that. His mates might be a bit – well, a bit rough – but for years he hadn't had a mate at all. Not a single one.

'Thank you, Mrs Goodchild.' Channon turned to her son. 'Now, Martin, you do realize that you're in an unfortunate position with having been on bad terms with the Stradlings?'

Oh, no, thought Sue. In a minute Marty would be pointing out that it was just Paul he was on bad terms with. She flashed him a warning glance, but to her relief all he said was: 'I know I must be under a bit of suspicion on account of what I did, but that was just an impulse because I was annoyed that Paul had cost me my job at the boatyard.'

'Oh yes – the job. Could you tell me why Mr Heaney sacked you?'

Now he'll shrug and push out his lips, thought Sue, but her son kept perfectly still. 'I was told to check the engine. It was immaculate, like it always was, so I skimped on it and didn't empty the water separator filter. Water carried over into the engine and it stopped when Paul went out in the boat. He queried it with Mr Heaney who knew right away I'd cut corners. So he sacked me.'

'How did you feel about that?'

Martin shot a look at his mother, and said, 'I wasn't surprised. Mr Stradling's a millionaire – I was a part-time mechanic. Now I just do my gardening and a few odd jobs.'

'I see,' said Channon again, and thought he did see a small part of the picture. Martin was young. He lived in modest circumstances. He could only have envied Paul

Stradling his money, his lifestyle ... but was envy motive enough to deliberately inconvenience him at sea, to maybe endanger him; or worse – unbelievably worse – to slit his throat? And if it had been motive enough, how could he have transported the body to the Menna? Hardly on the pillion of his motorbike. No, it was too difficult a crime for Martin, too horrific, too big a gesture. He was sure of it – at this stage.

Bowles could contain himself no longer. 'Were you alone here?' he asked Martin. 'How did you spend the evening? Did you have any visitors, did you make or receive any phone calls? Did you leave the house?'

Martin stayed quite calm. 'No, I didn't. I was on my own. Nobody rang me and I didn't make any calls. I watched a bit of telly and played computer games and listened to music.' Then he looked from Bowles to Channon and said loudly, 'They have high performance computers in the City of London, did you know that?'

Bowles looked blank, so Channon took over. 'I don't know much about it, actually, Martin. I suppose the Stradlings use that sort of computer in their business?'

'Oh, yes, Paul has one on board *Daphne.* It's brand new, and he uses it just for finance. Do you know that he buys his sweaters in France?'

Sue cleared her throat. She'd been expecting it! He was starting with his odd remarks. She watched Channon intently. Would this top man think he was backward? Not that anybody had ever said as much. All she'd been told was that he might have mild Asperger's – which as far as she could see meant he was a bit odd – and that he'd be fine if she simply loved him and looked after him. God only knew she'd done that since the day he was born.

But Channon was getting ready to leave. 'We'll need statements from you both,' he said. 'Someone will telephone you shortly to make arrangements. We must be off now. Thank you for your time.'

Once outside, Bowles faced him on the grass verge before heading next door. He was put out at what he considered lax questioning. 'You never asked about the TV programmes, boss,' he protested.

'No,' agreed Channon, 'I didn't. Bowles, if someone is lying about watching TV, they'd have to be a moron not to check what was on.'

'I know, but he is a sort of moron, isn't he? He hasn't got a proper job and the things he comes out with are a bit weird, surely?'

Channon's mobile shrilled. 'Sir,' said a female voice, 'the incident room here. Mr Richard Stradling has rung asking to see you in person.'

Channon's heart plummeted. Bereaved families were so difficult – and so sad . . . Stradling senior was on his list for a visit, but not until later. 'Tell him I'll be there in half an hour,' he said, and to Bowles, 'Stradling wants a visit. It might be important, or he might simply be too distressed to cope.'

Bowles almost said, 'Count me out,' but stopped himself in time.

Channon jerked his head towards the next cottage. 'We'll leave Miss Stumbles until later. Take me back to Pengorra now and I'll pick up my car and go to see Stradling on my own. That'll leave you free to deal with the Pascoes. Sort out two good lads, warn the Pascoes you're on your way and then get statements from all five of them. Cover everything. Now – do I need to say it?'

'No, boss, but I'm sure you will.'

Channon grunted. 'I shouldn't have to! Be gentle with them, be polite, tread softly.'

Behind the wheel again, Bowles's eyes glinted. Things were going his way. He had escaped a visit to Stradling senior, and been given a free hand (apart from the warning) with the Pascoe clan. So . . . he wouldn't take good-boy Yates, he was too squeamish. Soker would be better, and maybe one of the uniforms. That decided, he slowed as they approached the crossroads mentioned by Sue Goodchild.

'I suppose she'd turn right here to go to the Yardarm,' said Channon thoughtfully. 'Get someone to check with the landlord that she was actually on the premises all evening, will you, and ask him to confirm when she set off for home.'

Sun was breaking through patchy cloud as they headed back to Pengorra. To their left was sloping pasture, dark and damp; but below and beyond it was the glint of sun-kissed water. They turned into the road and Channon stared down unseeingly at a skim of white sails as a boat sped down Carrick Roads. Deep in thought, he was preparing himself to face Richard Stradling.

Eyes puffy, nose red as if from frequent blowing, the bereaved father was at the door as Channon stopped his car. 'I can't be left high and dry like this,' was his greeting, 'I must know what's happening.' He jerked his head backwards to indicate that Channon should follow him, then turned on his heel and marched indoors.

He led the way to a small room, perhaps once a writing room, but now fitted out as its modern-day counterpart, a home office – but of some magnificence. In addition to computers there was every electronic aid imaginable and, looking almost primitively old-fashioned, a huge blackboard on one wall, presumably used by father and son to make their calculations and list stock market prices.

Stradling waved to two deep armchairs in the window recess. 'We can talk face to face here,' he said. 'Take a seat.' He moved his own chair so that his face was, indeed, only two or three feet from Channon's. 'I can't remember much that you said yesterday,' he admitted, 'but I take it you're the top man on the case?'

'Yes. I'm Channon – Detective Chief Inspector. We'll do our very best to keep you informed of what's going on, Mr Stradling, but my sergeant did tell me that last evening you refused the offer of a liaison officer. These men and women are specially trained to help the victims of crime and also to assist bereaved families. They can be the link between the family and the enquiry, as well as dealing with their queries and concerns.'

'Keeping the man in charge free of distractions?'

'Yes, but that's not their main function.'

Red-rimmed blue eyes looked into his. 'I don't need anyone to hold my hand, Channon. I simply want to be kept informed about progress and procedure. My personal secretary is on his way down here from my firm in London. He knows how I like things – he can do my liaising.'

'As you wish,' agreed Channon, observing the other closely. This was a man used to being in charge – to giving orders and making decisions; a strong character, but with traces of a father's tears clearly apparent, and what might be his natural aggression simmering.

Long ago Channon had realized that there was no norm for the behaviour of bereaved families. Some were stunned beyond speech, some wept for hours, days, weeks; others talked non-stop, apportioning blame, justifying, explaining. Some were hysterical, others silent and dignified, many outraged and resentful. A few, like this man, concealed grief behind a thirst for action and retribution. He used to think that a violent death in the family revealed the true character of the bereaved, but he was no longer so sure of that.

Leaning forward with his face close to Stradling's, as the other so clearly desired, Channon felt the urge to get on the other man's wavelength, to communicate at every level. 'Mr Stradling,' he said quietly, 'many of my officers have worked through the night and many more are at work on this case right now. Forensic tests are still being done on your son's body, on his clothes. These tests are important, even vital, but they are preliminaries. We haven't yet found out where he spent the evening, why he wasn't in his car, if he was with anyone, and where, precisely, he was killed.'

He thought Stradling to be less tense, but hostility still simmered beneath what he had to say. 'When I told you last night that I don't lay down rules for my son's coming and going I meant it. There was only one exception – he would tell me if he wanted to go out in *Daphne*, that's our boat, our Hallberg-Rassy, named after my late wife. She was still alive when I bought it for our thirty-fifth wedding anniversary. Apart from using the boat Paul never reported his whereabouts to me, or to the staff. My household budget isn't so tight that a missed meal is seen as a catastrophe.'

For a man so evidently wealthy to so much as mention a household budget revealed an interest in money that could only have helped to make his millions, thought Channon, but he merely replied, 'I never imagined that it was, Mr Stradling. Are you saying you lived such separate lives here that you seldom knew where Paul actually was?'

Stradling's lips tightened. 'No, I am not saying that. We were close, not separate. I *am* saying that he was twenty-six years old, not a teenager.'

'Do you know his friends and acquaintances here in Cornwall?'

'Some of them. As soon as he arrives I'll get my secretary to list them for you.'

'What about girlfriends? Did he have anyone special?'

'Not that I know of. Paul was a young, healthy male. He's had several girlfriends, partners, lovers, whatever you want to call them.'

There was a strange air of bravado in the words, Channon told himself, but no mention of Lucy Pascoe. He thought for a moment, then said, 'Mr Stradling, is there anything in particular that you want to know about the case? I'll try to answer your questions – within the constraints of my job, of course.'

'Yes!' answered Stradling promptly. 'What's being done about finding if anyone had a grudge against Paul?'

'For a start, my colleagues in the City of London are investigating Paul's activities within your firm and on his own account, trying to ascertain whether he has made any enemies in high finance.'

'Oh!' said Stradling blankly. 'Well, I'm glad to hear that, of course, but Paul wouldn't sail close to the wind in his dealings at work, you know.'

'I'm sure he wouldn't,' said Channon gently, 'but we check everything.'

'What I was meaning when I spoke of grudges was the situation down here. You sound like a Cornishman – you must know that among local communities there's sometimes envy of outsiders with money.'

'Yes, I do know that. I also know that most Cornish folk accept that people like yourself boost the economy of the county – even if you do raise the price of property beyond the means of some of them.'

Stradling shrugged. 'I'm on a committee that works to protect Cornish housing for the Cornish-born, but market forces always rule. Look, Channon, I'm pointing no finger of blame, but I suppose you *have* checked what that odd lad Goodchild was doing last evening?'

'He is being investigated,' said Channon. 'I can't say more than that. One point – your son's earring. My sergeant thinks it was valuable. Is that correct?'

'Yes. Paul was good at the job, you know. He would have taken over Stradlings when I retire. He had expensive tastes, but even when he'd pulled off a good deal or made a packet he never asked for a present or a bonus – maybe because he had more than enough money for whatever he wanted.

'But he did once admire an earring worn by some celebrity or other. Just a single stone, though very large – I think that particular one was an emerald. Then Paul pulled off a deal that I'd have been more than proud to have masterminded myself. I talked it over with – uh – with my wife and bought him the earring. It was a fine white, set in platinum as a decoration for the ear. He must have liked it because he always wore it.'

'Could you tell me its value?'

'I got it at trade, of course, but at the time, because of its size and the quality, it was valued at over a hundred thousand. Do you think someone knew its value and killed him for it?' Stradling's mouth twisted, as if he tasted something bitter, and Channon thought he saw a hint of tears. 'For what was a present from his mother and me? Do you think that?'

'I don't know, but I hope to find out. You must trust that I'll do my best for you. We all will.'

Stradling fished out a damp handkerchief and blew his nose. 'I'm having a hard time getting to grips with this. It's only six months since my wife died, and that nearly finished me. You see, Channon, all my money – my hard-earned money – couldn't buy her a death without pain and loss of dignity. I loved her more than my life . . . and – and now Paul! I can hardly believe it.' Impatiently he snatched off his glasses and wiped his eyes. 'I'll tell you one thing, though. Money will help to find who killed my boy. I'll put up a reward that'll have criminals throughout the West Country grassing, or whatever they call it.'

'We're not quite at the stage of putting up rewards,' Channon warned. 'It may help enormously, of course, when we've assessed what we're up against.'

'And what about television?' asked Stradling with a bewildering change of subject. 'It had less than thirty seconds last night. I've spoken to the regional people about it. Publicity can only help, surely?'

'It usually does,' Channon agreed, 'but not inevitably. It can bring you more attention than you want, don't forget. There'll be more about it on today's news, though bulletins are scanty on a Sunday. I'll have to go now, Mr Stradling. Will you bear in mind that my officers will be here to search where they think fit, and to take full details of your vehicles, paying special attention to Paul's, of course. Possibly, they may need to remove them for forensic testing, purely for comparison and elimination.'

Stradling blinked behind the glasses, all at once a devastated father rather than a razor-brained financier. 'Your men can come whenever they like,' he said quietly, 'and do whatever they want when they're here.'

'Thank you,' said Channon, and meant it.

Chapter Six

Steve closed the door on Bowles and the other two and went back into the sitting room. For seconds there was silence, until Helen said, 'That was awful. It was as if we're all suspects.'

Steve was tight-lipped, but pointed out, 'We have no experience of police procedure during a murder enquiry.'

Katie went to sit on the hearthrug in front of the fire. For once she was silent, but Jaz was pacing back and forth by the windows, resentful at what he'd seen as being treated like a child. 'It was a load of hassle,' he burst out angrily, 'just to find out how well we knew him and what we were doing at the time of the – the –' He shot a guilty glance at Lucy. 'Uh – you know – the time it happened.'

When his sister spoke it was in her new flat, expressionless voice. 'You can use the word murder, Jaz. Paul was murdered. The sergeant thought I was an attention seeker when I told him we were close.' She looked at her parents. 'I wish I'd never listened to you both when you said I must tell them about it. He made me feel like some sort of man-hungry exhibitionist!' She turned and headed for the hall. 'I'm going out!'

'No!' It was said before Helen knew it. 'I mean, don't go outside the garden, love. Your dad and I have decided that none of us must go out alone until they've caught the – that is – well . . .' Like Jaz, she didn't know what to say. She couldn't use the word murderer – not to Lucy, not here in the sitting room of Trenoon. This house had always been her safe haven, her favourite place in all the world, where only good things happened – until now.

But Lucy was opening the coats cupboard. 'Let her go,' said Steve, 'as long as she stays near the house.'

Helen sank down on a sofa. She wished they'd both been there when Lucy made her statement, but she was eighteen, technically an adult, and they'd thought she would want privacy when she talked about Paul. Jaz and Katie now knew that the relationship had been serious, but not how serious; they knew nothing about them meeting secretly in Falmouth to sleep together.

When she and Steve made their statements one thing at least had been clarified: he had been in London on Friday evening, so Chrissie was mistaken in thinking she'd seen him at the King Harry. As for the two younger ones' statements – she and Steve had had to be present, of course. Jaz had been precise and matter-of-fact. He'd told how he and Sinbad and other local teenagers were sometimes invited to use the gym and the games room at the Court. He had said nothing of his recent disagreement with Paul. They had all discussed it beforehand and decided it was pointless to mention it – it had been trivial, over in minutes.

As for Katie, she'd had remarkably little to say about Paul, apart from relating how one day when she'd been admiring *Daphne* from the bank he'd shown her over the big boat and explained the chart sat-nav to her. When the sergeant asked, 'So would you say you were friends with Paul, Katie?' she had answered with her usual directness, 'Not really. I didn't like him much. He pretended he knew all about sailing, but he didn't.'

Now, Helen thought that her youngest looked like a worried little elf, sitting cross-legged on the rug, her hair in its wild tangle, her eyes wide, and she was grinding her teeth again. She was going to have to stop her doing that before she damaged them – or wore them down to stumps.

As always, Steve was on Katie's wavelength. 'What's up, Katie?'

'That sergeant was horrible,' she said tightly. 'Mum, did you mean it when you said we're all suspects?'

'No, love. I just meant that with so many questions it had seemed at the time as if we were.'

But Katie had turned back to her dad. 'I shouldn't have said I didn't like Paul, should I?'

'Stop worrying, pet. Perhaps it wasn't the most tactful thing to say as he's just been murdered, but we'd advised you to tell the truth, so why shouldn't you have said it?'

Katie writhed around like she always did when asked a difficult question. 'Because they might think I killed him,' she muttered.

'Don't talk drivel!' That was Jaz, still by the windows. 'The biggest thicko in the entire police force wouldn't think a midget could lug Paul around and cut him to pieces!' He shot a look at his mother and then at his father, his face stretching as his thoughts clarified. He didn't need to say that at well over six feet *he* was no midget.

Anger was building up inside Helen at this disruption to the family. Weren't they in enough of a state without all this? She said, 'We're all getting a bit on edge, aren't we? I think the sergeant was just trying to be tough. We've told them what we were doing on Friday evening,' including Steve, she thought, 'so we'll have to leave it in their hands. There'll be dozens of statements taken – maybe hundreds. Look – who wants a coffee?'

'Not me,' said Jaz, all at once sullen. 'I'm going to Sinbad's.'

'What have we decided, Jaz?' asked Steve impatiently. 'I thought we said no going out alone, even in broad daylight.'

'Not even if you're a suspect?' asked his son mockingly. 'Anyway, you don't live with us any more. You can't tell me what to do!'

'That's enough,' snapped Helen. 'Your dad may not share this house but you're only sixteen, so he *can* tell you what you can and can't do. If you want to see Sinbad ask him to come over here.'

'I can't. His parents don't want him to go out.'

'There you are, then,' said Helen wearily. 'Your dad's right.'

Then Katie jumped up from the rug and glared at her mother. 'It's all your fault!' she shouted. 'It's you who said you couldn't live with him any more. I'd never have left him on his own in London if you hadn't said we could come and live here!' Like a whirlwind she rushed out and they could hear her feet on the stairs.

Jaz shuffled his feet and flattened his hair with his hands. 'I'm sorry, Mum,' he said hoarsely and, ignoring Steve, left the room.

This was a nightmare, Helen told herself. She must be fast asleep, dreaming it, but she only had to look at Steve's face to know it was no dream. 'I didn't use the house to tempt her to stay with me,' she told him wretchedly. 'It was just that I knew I could cope if I was here. It wasn't a ploy to keep her – really it wasn't.'

He looked down at her. 'I never thought it was. And for the record – I think I deserved to lose her – and her brother and sister. Oh, Helen, how can I –'

'Don't!' she said. 'Don't say it!'

His eyes were black as night. 'Say what?'

'That you're sorry.'

'Not even though I am?'

'No, not even then. We've been through it all, Steve. There's nothing more to say. I must go down the garden now, to talk to Lucy.'

'Are you going to find out how we can help her?'

'I'm going to try.' But she knew that even in turmoil there was no respite from feeding the family. 'It'll have to be soup or hot snacks for lunch,' she said. 'I'll cook the roast tonight.' Without looking at him again she went to put on a jacket before going outside to talk to their daughter.

With Addie Savage in charge, the makeshift jumble on the green had become a hive of orderly activity. By common consent and usage, the big tent with its computers, telephones and constant bustle was being referred to simply as 'the room'. The caravan had separate sections, two of which were now earmarked for interviews and admin, while another one, complete with door, was for the DCI. Addie smiled at the prospect of Bill Channon finding he no longer had to use the table and chair behind the screen – that would now be her domain. The caravan's main room and kitchen were ideal for drinks and light meals, and as for the prefab sheds – the smaller would be a holding cell, if needed, the other used for storing and recording evidence.

Not quite as immaculate as usual after a hectic morning, Addie gave a thumbs-up of thanks to her team of helpers. Sometimes she surprised herself by the speed at which she could get things done. She knew that her nickname was Addie the baddie – it had come with her from north Cornwall. When she first heard of it, it had hurt, because she knew she was no baddie – she always played fair with everyone, from the newest officer to the loftiest of her superiors.

Then, slowly, it had dawned that to have a reputation as a strict, demanding inspector got things done, and when things were done, and done well, respect followed. With the respect of colleagues, life at work was good. And what about life at home? Well – it was just life – sometimes good, sometimes empty. What was new?

She turned to find that Channon had come back and was eyeing what she'd accomplished. 'How's it going, Addie?' he asked.

'Under control. There's a detailed report from George Hunter on your desk.' She wagged a finger. 'Please note – real desk in real room with real door! George stressed that what's in the report is correct as far as he's concerned, but not yet complete. The SOCOs' stuff is still being assessed by Fred's team, and Eddie Platt in Forensic rang to tell you he's finalizing several things himself and will be in touch shortly.'

Well, well, things were moving. Channon looked around him and then at her. 'Your promotion must be about due, Addie.'

'Overdue,' she said shortly, 'but not through lack of effort on my part.' Then, as her gaze fell on the blow-up of Paul Stradling smiling under his peaked cap, she asked quietly, 'How did it go with the father, Bill?'

'The poor devil's still grieving for his wife, so the only way he can deal with losing his son is to get aggressive – you know how bereaved parents can be. Anything more on where Paul spent the evening?'

'Somebody's at the yacht club now, checking the times we were given. He often went there, apparently, and to the the Yardarm and the Pandora.'

He shook his head. 'He wasn't at the Yardarm or Sue Goodchild would have seen him.' And as for the Pandora, he thought, who along Carrick Roads *didn't* visit that legendary inn at some time or other? But it would be checked, like everywhere else. 'We need to account for every minute of his evening,' he said grimly. 'I'll see you, Addie.'

'What about a drink?'

'A drink?' he repeated blankly.

She concealed a smile. He hadn't changed much over the years. 'Would you like a tea or coffee?' she said very slowly and clearly.

He replied with equal deliberation, 'No, I would not, thank you,' then with a nod went off to inspect his room and George Hunter's report.

Fifteen minutes later he leaned back in his chair and shook his head. Accustomed as he was to violence, he had still felt nausea rising as he read the report. As Hunter had stated, it wasn't final, but it was detailed, calm and factual, which only seemed to make the brutality of the killing more shocking.

There was a lot to absorb, but for now the key fact was that the dead man had been taken to the Menna whilst still alive. According to the pathologist he had been knocked senseless – a heavy blow to the head by the proverbial

75

blunt instrument – then almost certainly transported to the Menna before death.

Right now it was a priority to establish Paul Stradling's movements on Friday evening. Equally vital was to find out how he had been travelling around – was it in his own car, or his father's, or someone else's, or even on foot? More vital still was to find out how he'd been transported to his death. A healthy young man, even a lean one, couldn't simply be dumped in a bin bag and carted around willy-nilly, then lifted up from the road to the stone. Channon recalled Luther Tresillian's words: 'Why have they set him against the stone?'

Hunter had stated as certain that the dead man had been stabbed at the Menna, first in the chest and then the cutting of his throat. The amount of blood-flow from the neck had confirmed that that had been the fatal wound. The chest stabbings, though bad enough, had been preliminaries. Subject to confirmation, the earring had been pulled off in the final moments, before or immediately after the throat was cut. Blood had still been circulating, if sluggishly, when Paul gave up his diamond.

To Channon at that moment, the theft of a stone worth a hundred thousand pounds seemed of small importance compared to the manner of Paul's death . . .

Helen was wiping the kitchen table after a snack lunch, moving the cloth in smooth, precise sweeps back and forth across the wood. She was starting to go over it for the third time when she stopped and stood up straight. What was she *doing*? The table didn't need it!

Then it dawned. The table didn't need it, but she did. She needed to bring a sense of order from somewhere; she craved it as an antidote to the chaos in her family. She slumped down on a chair. Chaos was the word. Lucy was refusing to talk about Paul; Katie, self-possessed little Katie had clearly been crying but wouldn't admit it and was now down the garden, forbidden to board her beloved boat;

while Jaz was constantly on his mobile to Sinbad and his other friends, and had come to the table minus his usual obsessive eagerness to eat.

As for Steve, almost as if they'd agreed on it he had taken his lunch up to his room. He was angry about something, she could tell by the set of his mouth, but he'd shrugged it off when she tried to get his feelings on the police visit. Now he'd gone out in his car, saying he needed some air, and she'd felt she could hardly question where he was going.

She was yawning again, and told herself it was ridiculous. How could she feel sleepy when her mind was racing in all directions? She should be taking action to make sure her daughters were all right. She should be insisting that Lucy discussed Paul with her, but how could she? She didn't even know this new Lucy, who spoke in a flat little voice and looked at her with open hostility.

Amongst the turmoil there was only one thing that was good, and she might as well admit it. Steve was with them. It had been bitter-sweet relief to talk with him last night about Lucy and Paul; deep comfort to have him here with them when the police came.

The police ... guiltily she made herself think about the murder. It seemed so unreal, so bizarre, that it was taking second place in her mind to the upset in the family, to the fact that her daughter had been in a serious relationship of which she'd known nothing. The fact remained that Paul wasn't right for her – *hadn't been* right, she corrected herself hastily. Just a minute, she thought in dismay, what am I thinking? Surely I'm not glad he's dead? If only her brain would stop this mad question and answer.

'Hello!' somebody called, and with a quick tap on the door Chrissie Boon came into the kitchen, grey hair on end, a ruby-red scarf looped around her neck. 'Helen, my love,' she said breathlessly, 'I know I should have rung to see if it was OK to come, but I didn't, and here I am – hey, what's the matter?'

'Chrissie.' In that one word Helen revealed how she valued their friendship. 'Thanks for coming,' she said, and burst into tears.

A mug of tea in one hand and a chicken sandwich in the other, Bowles was reflecting on his morning. If it was possible to feel both satisfaction and unease about the same event, then those were his feelings about the visit to Trenoon.

The unease was because he had ignored Channon's warning about treating the Pascoes gently. He hadn't missed Soker shifting in protest when he gave them a grilling, but oh, he'd enjoyed it, especially with the father. Why should one guy have so much? Not only living free of his kids, but driving a one-year-old Merc and with a posh pad in London; then to cap it all, looking like a cross between a male model and a pantomime demon king. One thing, if Pascoe had been up to anything he'd have had to cover that black and silver hair. Without knowing it, Bowles ran a hand over his own lank, ginger locks.

Not far away a group of young detectives and uniforms were chatting noisily. No actual laughter – Channon discouraged merriment when working on a murder – but Bowles was aware that the men shared something that he himself rarely experienced: a kind of togetherness, a comradeship, maybe even real friendship. Thoughtfully he drank his tea. When he got his promotion he wouldn't need friends, or even comrades. If he cracked the whip they wouldn't just jump, they'd ask how high . . . As for Channon, at that moment he was shut away in his new office studying Hunter's report. No doubt in the fullness of time he would condescend to share its contents, and then ask him what he'd unearthed at Trenoon.

'Hey, sarge!' It was Soker, one of the group. 'Guess who's just gone in to see the DCI? Pascoe. He was looking a bit tense. I wonder why?'

'Wondering is for fools, Soker,' retorted Bowles. 'Certainty is what it's all about. Evidence, proof, confessions.'

Soker answered submissively, 'Yes, sarge. Absolutely, sarge,' but one of the others smothered a snigger. At once Bowles knew they'd been talking about him. So much for taking Soker to the Pascoes' rather than good-boy Yates. The lot of them were too soft. What they needed was a spell in the Met.

In his office Channon eyed the lean figure of Steve Pascoe. The man was angry; he was also wary. 'Take a seat, sir,' he said politely. 'I'm sorry to say my time is limited by the pressure of work.'

'I realize that,' said Pascoe shortly. 'I won't take up more than a few minutes. I'm here on two counts. The first is to make a complaint about your Sergeant Bowles. On his visit to Trenoon this morning he was abrasive, uncaring, and at times barely civil. He upset my entire family.'

Channon seethed beneath a calm exterior. He'd warned Bowles, warned him because he knew his methods, just as he knew how wealth and privilege affected his fragile ego. 'My sergeant is perhaps over-keen at the start of a new and distressing case, Mr Pascoe, but I assure you he's an experienced and dedicated officer.'

'Is he indeed?' said the other man between his teeth. 'Then let me tell you that my younger daughter – aged twelve, please note – was left believing that she could be a murder suspect. My elder daughter was made to feel that she was some sort of sex-mad exhibitionist because she and Paul Stradling had been in love!'

Channon lowered his eyes. Well, well! Confirmation of what he'd suspected, and no doubt Bowles was champing at the bit to pass it on to him.

'As for my wife,' Pascoe went on, 'she was left with the impression that she could be an accessory after the fact because she'd chased a plastic bag!'

'And what about your son and yourself?'

'What? My son happened to know Paul, that's all, but even he said he was made to feel like a guilty child.'

'And you, Mr Pascoe?'

Dark eyes looked into dark eyes, and Channon told himself that this was where the wariness came in. 'Uh, that's my other reason for being here. I knew I'd be a fool not to mention it, but I couldn't bring myself to tell the sergeant. The fact is, I was down here on the Fal on Friday, and not in London, though as yet my family don't know about it. I've been thinking about renting a place near here in order to work from home, and I wanted to view a converted barn that's just come up to let across the river. I was hoping it would make a combined home, office and studio.'

Channon studied the other man. Maybe it was reluctance to tell Bowles that had kept him quiet about being down here, maybe it was reluctance to tell his family, or perhaps he'd been up to no good and wanted to come clean before they found out about it in general enquiries. 'Could I ask if this is purely a business venture, Mr Pascoe?'

'No, not entirely. It's feasible for me to work from home because on most of my commissions I don't need to interact with my colleagues, and anyway I can contact them online. The real reason for the move is that I want to be near my family.'

Pictures dropped into Channon's memory, as clear as if the events had happened only days ago. Pictures of another husband who had found out too late that his wife and family mattered more than a sexual fling with a young girl – a girl who was brutally murdered. Where was the Baxter husband now? Was he back with his good – his truly good – wife?

He dragged his mind back to the man facing him. 'The reasons for you wanting the move are your own affair, Mr Pascoe, but thanks for telling me. I expect we would have got to know about it from our general enquiries and our door-to-door checks. We do try not to miss too much, you know.'

Pascoe was still looking edgy, so Channon said, 'I do understand you being upset about the sergeant's visit. Leave it with me. I'll deal with it.'

Reassured, but not clear exactly why, Steve Pascoe nodded. 'Thanks. One more thing – I don't want him near my family again.'

'I can't promise that,' said Channon, a shade wearily, 'but if he does have to have more dealings with you, I don't think you'll be given cause for another complaint.' Once alone again, he reached for the phone. 'Send Sergeant Bowles in,' he ordered grimly.

His demeanour deliberately jaunty, Bowles strolled in and faced his superior across the desk. Channon eyed him coldly. 'Do you want to stay on this case, Bowles?'

'What? Of course I do!'

'I'm surprised to hear it. Did I, or did I not, warn you about how to treat the Pascoe family?'

'You said, "Tread softly,"' agreed Bowles reluctantly, 'and I think I said, "That's not my style."'

'And what was my response?' persisted Channon.

Bowles swallowed. 'You said, "*Make* it your style, sergeant."'

'So you heard me?'

'Yes.'

'And ignored me?'

A pause. 'Yes.'

'Bowles, your treatment of them has upset the entire family, and the father has made a complaint. Not only that, he had a piece of useful information, but couldn't bring himself to give it to you.'

Bowles's lips thinned. 'But he's given it to you, of course?'

'Yes, he has. Because I treated him with respect, as I did his wife and children when I saw them. How many more times do I have to tell you that we need the public on our side? Treat them well and they'll help us. Do the opposite and they won't. As well as being for our own benefit, common decency demands fair treatment rather than a rough ride simply to massage your ego.'

Bowles shrugged and Channon's mouth tightened. 'From now on, sergeant, you treat everyone, under suspicion or not, with courtesy and respect. If I find you've done otherwise, you're off this case and every future case of mine. Not only that, you'll have to look for promotion without any backing from me. That's my last word on the matter. Have you heard what I've just said?'

'I've heard,' agreed Bowles sullenly. He sucked his teeth. He was right and the DCI was wrong, but he could hardly say so, not if it would affect his promotion. In any case, Channon's eyes had taken on that metallic look, a sure sign he was livid. The words were sticking in his throat, but he managed to bring them out. 'Sorry, boss,' he said awkwardly. 'I'll watch it in future.'

'And I'll be watching you, Bowles. Now go and get on with organizing the once-over of the Stradling place.'

'But what was this information from Pascoe?'

'You blew your chance of getting it at Trenoon, so you can wait for it!'

Right, thought Bowles, and you can wait to hear that the Pascoe girl had the hots for Paul Stradling – unless Daddy-oh has already revealed it. 'As for Heaney,' Channon was saying, 'I'll go to the boatyard to see him myself while you're at Pengorra Court. See you get a good team together.'

'Right away, boss,' said Bowles, and made a rapid exit.

Chapter Seven

Wearing her sailing jacket and her *I Love Ellen* sweatshirt over ancient jeans, Katie was sitting between her two favourite boulders at the water's edge. Sometimes she thought that the best place in all the world must be this very spot; at other times she believed it to be the window-seat in her bedroom with its amazing view of Carrick Roads, but in the end she always admitted that the place she loved most was simply anywhere on the water – the sea for preference, and failing that, the river.

Right now, because everything else was so awful, she was drawing comfort from being in a good place, this particular one being as far as it was possible to be from the house without actually leaving the garden. Her little boat was tied up nearby and the water itself was only inches from her boots – she could smell it: salt, earth, a whiff of crab from somewhere, all mixed up with wet rope and timber. It was heaven, and there was something else she loved – the strip of damp, silver-gold sand that lay at the foot of Trenoon's garden. She dug cold fingers into it and shivered, partly with pleasure and partly because she was so mixed up she didn't know what to do next and that was scary.

Her mouth turned down as she reflected on the last six months. It had been the hardest act of her entire life to leave her dad in London while the rest of them came to live at Trenoon. She'd missed him so much she'd felt guilty if ever she found she was enjoying herself. Life should have been better now he was back, but it wasn't – it was worse.

She wriggled her thin shoulders. Another thing – why did her parents think she didn't know about sex? Anyone with half a brain, eyes to see and ears to hear *had* to know about it – it was on TV, in books and magazines, with everybody talking about it and going to bed with everybody else. It was a complete and utter *bore*! OK, it had to be special in some way, or her dad wouldn't have done it with someone else besides her mum.

Actually, the situation they were in was her mum's fault. She'd told her so earlier, when she lost her temper and shouted at her. Couldn't she see that Dad was sorry, that he only wanted to be with her and the family again? Couldn't she forgive him for messing about with that woman at work? They'd all met her last year at the firm's family barbecue; she was awful – tall and thin, with red hair and very shiny lips and the sort of eyes that are always watching, watching.

Without realizing it she started to grind her teeth, and when she heard the noise of it in her head it made her thoughts seem clearer. Now she told herself that the situation with her dad was quite bad enough without Lucy having changed. She was being really weird since Paul was murdered, so she must have been in love with him. Had she been to bed with him, because everybody did it, didn't they? Ugh! Was she going to have a *baby*? Lucy had always been the big sister who loved her; she'd been fun, really cool, even if she wasn't much good at sailing, but all at once she was this – this stranger. And what about Jaz? He was different as well. If he wasn't worrying about having no muscles he was hunched over his mobile to his friends, because they were all obsessed with the murder.

Uneasily she thought about when she'd told the sergeant that she didn't like Paul. Her dad had tried to reassure her about it but she shouldn't have said it – she knew she shouldn't. Children had been convicted of murder in the past, she'd read about it, though of course the police would have had to produce evidence. They'd never get evidence against her because she hadn't done anything, but people were sometimes wrongly accused – worse than that, wrongly convicted . . .

'Katie, my love – I knew I'd find you here!' Chrissie was clambering over the rocks and down to the sand. Katie breathed out in relief that it wasn't her mum. Though she'd been rude to her she wasn't ready to say sorry, not yet, and in any case, she liked Chrissie. When she was younger she used to call her Auntie Chrissie, but now she called her just Chrissie, like everyone else. Could she ask her what she should do? Could she tell her about her life being so terrible?

And then Chrissie's kind, familiar face was bending close to hers, and Katie felt tears come – again! She hardly ever cried, but this was twice in one day. Was she having a breakdown, or something? One of the teachers at school was away ill, and somebody said *she'd* had a breakdown. 'Chrissie,' she demanded, jumping up and wiping her cheeks with her fingers, 'can people have a breakdown if they're very upset?'

Chrissie gave her a squeeze and they stood together at the water's edge. 'Sometimes they can,' she answered cautiously. 'Why? Are you thinking of Lucy?'

'No,' said Katie, her lips trembling again, 'I'm thinking of me. Everything's going wrong, you see. I asked Dad to come home but he's acting like a visitor and sleeping in the attic. Mum pretends everything's all right but she's really worried about something and I don't think it's just the murder, and Lucy's gone all different and Jaz is on the phone all the time and . . . and . . .'

'Slow down, my precious. And what?'

'And the police might think I've murdered Paul.'

Chrissie nodded thoughtfully. 'I think we need to talk this through.' She delved into her patchwork bag and pulled out a thermos flask and two china mugs. 'What about a drink of hot chocolate? Your mum's just made it for us.'

Katie cheered up slightly. 'Are we going to drink it here?'

'It's a bit breezy, I suppose. Shall we go into the summer-house, even though it's winter? Then we can talk without anyone hearing.'

Katie heaved an enormous sigh. Perhaps things would seem a bit better after a talk with Chrissie and a mug of hot chocolate. Together they climbed back over the rocks.

Quiet descended on the village green as the cars left for Pengorra Court, and Channon watched them from the door of the tent. The officers were well briefed, they knew their jobs, and Bowles would behave himself after being warned.

Addie Savage was watching as well – watching Channon, and thinking that other DCIs she'd known would have gone along and been on the front row examining the murdered man's room and grilling the house staff. But then, other DCIs weren't Channon. He had his own way of doing things. He would follow laid-down procedure, but only so far, and right now the look on his face was one she remembered from their younger days. He was groping, working to get into the case in his own way, to feel at one with it, to *know* it.

'I've got Les Jolly coming to us like you wanted,' she told him. 'He's been on that garage fraud near St Just, but his sergeant knows you need him this side of the river. He'll be here first thing in the morning.'

'Good,' he said. He was staring at the houses circling the green. Apart from a scatter of dwellings along the lanes this small cluster constituted Pengorra. In all there couldn't be more than there were fingers on two pairs of hands, yet every single household had offered help, either with catering or searching the riverside fields for whatever needed to be found. He had even been offered a room and bed should he need it.

It was a close-knit little community, part of the greater seafaring community of Carrick Roads, where native Cornish folk lived in harmony with second-home owners.

Or did they? Appearances could be deceptive – in his job he couldn't forget it. Resentments and frustrations could simmer and seethe on the banks of this famous waterway.

'Addie,' he said, 'we've got maps and charts by the cartload, but I need to talk to someone who knows the people who live along this bank, rich or poor. As soon as I can I think I'll go and talk to Bridget Stumbles.'

'The mobile shop lady? You've read the notes from last evening's house-to-house visits?'

'Of course I have. They've listed times and facts, I know that, but –'

'What you want is what's behind the facts,' she finished for him.

'Correct, as always,' he said with a small smile, 'but there are other things more pressing at the moment. I'm off to see Amos Heaney at the boatyard.'

'About the Goodchild boy?'

'Yes. I want to know whether his negligence with the engine could have endangered whoever took the boat out. And maybe Heaney can give me a bit of background on Martin himself.'

Addie observed him with her glass-clear blue gaze. 'Do you reckon he's a possible?'

'They're all possibles,' he said heavily, 'until they're eliminated. Martin's an oddity, but even if he'd hated Paul enough to kill him how did he get him to the Menna? George Hunter is sure he was knocked out elsewhere and then finished off at the crossroads. I suppose it's possible that the first attack took place really close to it – maybe within yards.'

'If it did, could Martin have carried him there?'

'I should think so. He's a big young fella.'

'But if he did, why was he intent on putting him against the stone?'

'Why indeed,' he echoed drily. 'The fact is, we won't make much headway until we know exactly how Paul spent Friday evening.'

'It's in hand,' she assured him. 'You'll have details as soon as there's anything definite.'

He nodded. 'Hold the fort, Addie. I'll be back as soon as I can.'

'Will you be all right without your sergeant?' she asked, tongue in cheek.

The look he gave her held no humour. 'Bowles is watching his step,' he said. 'In fact, he's treading on eggshells.'

'Nothing like a change,' she replied. 'I'll see you.'

Amos Heaney was in the white-painted shed that served as an office, wearing a neat dark cardigan over a shirt and tie. Channon surmised that such clothes were in deference to the day of the week, and Heaney's greeting confirmed it. 'A visit from the man in charge,' he said, pulling out a chair. 'You have no choice but to ignore the Good Book, then, same as me?'

'Six days shalt thou labour, and on the seventh . . .' quoted Channon, glad he'd caught the cue.

The other's leathery features creased in an approving smile. 'I'm past retiring age, but not as comfortable as I'd like to be,' he confessed. 'I can't afford to let the big marinas steal my trade because I'm closed to business, so though it galls me I open on the Sabbath. I mainly do my paperwork and such, but I'm here and available for enquiries and new customers.'

It was clear he was dealing with a staunch churchgoer, so Channon rose to the challenge. 'Much of my work is based on the Ten Commandments,' he said gravely, which was true enough. 'At present I'm working on "Thou shalt not kill".'

Heaney jerked his head towards the crossroads up the lane. 'It's a bad do,' he said soberly. 'You might say it's the handwork of the devil.'

Mention of the devil again. Channon merely nodded. 'I have a few questions, Mr Heaney. They may seem random, or peculiar, but please bear with me. First, regarding Martin Goodchild . . .'

'I knew somebody would be asking me more about Martin. *He's* no devil, inspector.'

'I'm not saying he is, but we need to eliminate him from enquiries, and these questions are a start. Tell me, do you know if Martin had a grudge against Paul Stradling, for any reason?'

'I wouldn't say against Paul in particular. Martin just has a chip on his shoulder about the well-off in general; but then, so does many a one, especially youngsters who haven't got much. I always thought he could do better for himself than odd-jobbing, you know. The lad's no fool – in fact, I'd say he's clever. It's just that he marches to a different drummer.'

'When he skimped on checking the Stradlings' boat that time, could his neglect have endangered whoever went out in it?'

'Endangered? No, more like inconvenienced. We were in a spell of good weather – low seas with light winds – so that wouldn't have been a factor. If the fuel line water separator filter wasn't checked and emptied, then the engine would have cut out – and that's what happened, of course. She's a sophisticated craft, safe as houses, less than a year old and with every extra in the book.'

Channon noted it was 'she' rather than 'it' with this life-long seaman. 'But could Martin have known in advance that it would be Paul who went out in her?'

'No, because both father and son liked to go out by themselves whenever they felt like it. There's hydraulic sail handling so one person could cope on their own. Mr Stradling had stipulated that.'

'Did Paul himself bring the boat back here?'

'Yes, he came back under sail as far as he could, then we gave him a tow to the yard. He knew she'd just had a routine check, but even so it was obvious something was wrong – he just didn't know what.'

'But you did?'

'I do know boats,' said the other drily, 'even the posh new ones. It's my job to know, as it was my father's and grandfather's before me. I knew the Hallberg-Rassy. I went over her when she was first delivered. Mr Stradling asked me to. I have a copy of the full specification here in my cupboard.'

'Was it normal practice to let a young part-timer do maintenance on an expensive boat such as that?'

'Yes, Martin knows his engines. I'd have employed him full-time if I'd had the work coming in and the money to pay him a decent wage. As it is I'm well placed with Luther as my right hand man. He has a family to keep and he's solid as a rock.'

'I'm sure he is,' agreed Channon. 'Now, do you confirm that you dismissed Martin because of his negligence on the Stradlings' boat?'

'Yes, I confirm it.'

'Was the reason behind his dismissal that the Stradlings are wealthy and influential and you didn't want to lose them?'

'That's what folk have hinted – said as much to my face, in fact – but I wouldn't have been all that upset to lose them,' answered Heaney. 'So the answer's no, that *wasn't* the reason.'

'Then what was?'

Heaney looked out of the window at his boatyard and waved an encompassing arm. 'This was the reason,' he said simply. He waved his other arm at the blue-grey glitter of Carrick Roads and for a second stared up at the clouded heavens. 'All this,' he repeated, 'all of it.'

Then he spoke in the clear, gentle tones of one addressing a young child. 'My family name had been risked,' he said. 'My reputation for service and fair dealing had been smirched, for no reason other than lack of care. I couldn't have it – it's as simple as that. If Martin had skimped on an ancient old row boat belonging to a pensioner he'd still have had to go.'

'I see. Thank you. What about the vandalism of the boat? Did you know about it?'

'Only what I heard after it happened. I was upset by it – in fact, I was shocked, but as I've told you, there's something in Martin that marches to a different drummer. Not to the drum of the devil, mind. I don't see him as no killer.'

Channon merely nodded. 'To Friday night. I'm trying to establish how Paul Stradling's body was brought to the Menna, if he didn't get there of his own volition. As a man of the Fal you'll know whether a body could have been transported by water, from either upstream or down – in secret.'

'It's possible, I suppose,' said Heaney dubiously. 'There's many a spot for landing a small boat and unloading what I suppose you'd call cargo. Somebody could have moored to my jetty, come to that, and took their chance on being seen. There's a bit of a climb from the water to the cross-roads, so it might have needed more than one individual to carry such a weight. On balance, I'd say easier and quicker by road.'

'Thanks. Now, to Paul himself. How did you find him?'

Heaney said flatly, 'I don't reckon to speak ill of the dead.'

'Oh. There's something ill to speak, then?'

'Nothing in particular.'

'Well, did you find him easy to get on with?'

'Easy enough. He was civil. Neither he nor his father ever questioned my bills.'

'I assure you that this is important, Mr Heaney. It's not idle gossip.'

The older man chewed his lips and narrowed his eyes. 'He had an eye for the girls,' he said reluctantly.

'That's not unusual in a young man of his age, is it?'

'No, of course it's not.'

'Well, then?'

Heaney looked away. 'Young girls from these parts,' he muttered. 'What you might call country girls.'

Steady on, thought Channon, we're not in the 1920s. Go slowly, though, take it slowly. 'I see,' he said consideringly. 'Do you happen to know any of them?'

'Yes, one was my great-niece from near Devoran. He romanced her to the skies and then dropped her after – well – you can guess what. Her mother found out there were others as well, one only fifteen.'

This was more serious. Instead of feeling pleased that a motive for murder might be surfacing, Channon's heart sank as he envisaged a throng of outraged parents to be investigated.

Almost as if their thoughts were linked, Heaney said awkwardly, 'I know this sounds like seventy years back, and I know there's young girls today who know more than I do – more than I want to know.'

'It's all right,' Channon assured him. 'Take your time.'

'I haven't seen anything myself,' the other went on, 'but Luther was mending a faulty door catch in Paul's cabin, when by accident he saw some photographs.'

'Yes?' prompted Channon, but thought wearily, no – not the old, old story of porn . . .

Heaney went on, 'They were of a young woman – well, a teenager, Luther thought. They were indecent.'

'Ah.' Motives for murder were circling busily beneath the surface, thought Channon, but please, don't let this teenager be the Pascoe daughter! 'Did Luther recognize her?' he asked.

'No, he didn't know her, but he was worried, so he told me. We talked it over and I decided to keep them on.'

'Keep them on?'

'Yes. I considered whether to ask the pair of 'em to take their custom elsewhere. But Luther and me – well – we had to admit we're a bit old-fashioned compared to London folk, so we left it.'

Channon said, 'Mr Heaney, I think I'll have to talk to Luther about what you've just told me.'

'I know. Give me a chance to mention it to him first, will you?'

'I will, but I'll need to see him by this evening.'

'Make it after eight – he goes to evening chapel.'

'I'll do that. Thanks for your help. Can I talk to you again if I need to?'

'I'm always here,' said Amos Heaney, 'even on Sundays.'

Feeling much better, Helen went indoors after waving goodbye to Chrissie. What a friend! Loyal, intuitive, sympathetic, she was always there when she was needed. It had been a comfort to confide in her and ask her to talk to Katie, who was now here at her side, intent on speaking.

'I'm sorry about earlier, Mum,' she said flatly. Contrition was there, but backed by lingering resentment.

Helen gave her a squeeze. 'I'm sorry too, my love. I know your life's been turned upside down, but like we've always told you, your dad's here for you, even when he's not under the same roof.'

Mindful of her discussion with Chrissie, Katie tried for sweet reason. 'He's under the same roof now,' she pointed out quietly, 'but things are still awful. I'd just feel better if he was back with us for ever.'

So would I, thought Helen, then at once wondered if that were true. Even if it was, there was no point in saying so, because their future was mapped out. Steve, however reluctantly, would go back to London and life for the four of them would continue here in Cornwall.

Katie was twisting one foot around the other. Things were still awkward between her and her mum, and she was getting fed up with it. She liked life to be sorted, clear-cut and definite, but she couldn't arrange it like that on her own, not if grown-ups wouldn't do what she wanted. Chrissie had made it seem a bit better, but deep inside her she knew that even when the murder was solved, even when Lucy was her old self again, she wasn't going to be really happy until her dad came back for good.

Right now it was making her chest hurt to see her mum's eyes. They were like the eyes of someone watching a sad and distant scene, rather than simply looking across the kitchen. 'Mum,' she said, 'is there something else wrong that I don't know about? Is it to do with Lucy?'

Helen observed her youngest, this odd little bundle of non-approaching puberty, obsessive organizational skills and impatience. 'No,' she lied. 'It's just that we're all at sixes and sevens, what with giving our statements to the police and the awfulness of Paul's murder. Don't worry – we'll sort ourselves out.'

Unconvinced, Katie ran her fingers through her wild hair and tried to think what she could do to please her mum. Ah – that was it! Her homework was completed, checked and in her bag ready to hand in, but she said, 'I think I'll just go and have another look at my English essay to see if I can improve on it,' and ran off upstairs.

Once out of the boatyard Channon sat in the car and rang Bowles at Pengorra Court. 'Keep a close lookout for photographs among Paul's things,' he instructed. 'Remove them and bring them in, the same with his cameras. Tell Stradling it's routine.'

Bowles was riveted. 'What's going on, boss?'

'Not a lot, but it might be significant. I'll put you in the picture when we're back at the room. I don't want to come too heavy but you must get all the computers on the premises together and under guard. Nobody to touch them except our qualified men. Stradling might not like it.'

'He won't object,' said Bowles confidently. 'He's a wreck.'

Channon thought of the decisive financier with his tearred eyes, and hoped that nothing too sick would be uncovered among his son's belongings. 'Next,' he went on, 'send a man out to the boat and put it under guard until we can give it the once-over. I don't really see it, but it's possible that the first attack on Paul took place there. Nobody to be allowed on board, not even Stradling. He loves that boat, so go gently with him – did you hear that, Bowles?'

A subdued 'I heard' came over the line.

'Right. I won't say any more, except do everything, repeat everything, by the book.'

'Absolutely,' came the reply, and after a pause, 'sir.'

Channon headed back to the village green and then slowed the car as he approached the crossroads. He was within a couple of hundred yards of the Goodchilds' cottage and that of their neighbour Bridget Stumbles. On impulse he headed there and parked on gravel behind the big green van.

A large, ungainly woman wearing a man's cap and a floral overall over trousers was emptying a bucket of soapy water down a drain. She straightened up at his approach, eyes alert amid deep wrinkles. 'It's the chief inspector, isn't it? You've come to see *me*?'

The inference 'Why me in particular?' was there, but Channon merely nodded politely. 'That's right. I'm DCI Channon. I know you've had one visit from my officers already, Miss Stumbles, but this is a quick courtesy visit as I was passing, just to say I might be calling to see you for a chat in the next few days.'

Biddy Stumbles looked at him. A courtesy visit? Did this top detective, investigating a murder, think she would see it as normal practice for a man in his position to call on somebody like her out of courtesy, or for 'a chat'? She couldn't help the hint of derision in her tone. 'About anything in particular?'

'No, just to get your views on the people who live in these parts – incomers as well as those born and bred here. I thought that in your position as a travelling shop owner you would be something of an expert on the population.'

Well, he was diplomatic, if nothing else ... 'I know plenty of folk,' she acknowledged. 'I know the parents of some of 'em, even the grandparents. But I must tell you, they're my friends as well as my customers.'

She was telling him that she wouldn't tell tales on people she'd known all her life. 'I understand,' he assured her gravely. 'I won't be asking for confidential information, just general background. I'll let you know if and when I'm coming.'

Bucket in hand, she observed him with shrewd dark eyes. 'And what's the name again?'

'Channon – Detective Chief Inspector.'

'Well, Mr Channon, as long as you know where I stand, I'll chat as much as you like.'

He shook her hand and she watched him drive off. Then she went indoors for more hot water. Sunday afternoon was her time for cleaning out the shop. With all Pengorra in a state, somebody had to keep to a routine . . .

Chapter Eight

The rain was clearing as Channon parked by the village green, but inside the tent the smell of wet canvas and damp earth hung over the duckboards and tables like fog. Eager for a spell of thinking time he walked quickly through the bustle, but Addie Savage waylaid him.

'PC Cloak's had a word and it might be useful. His wife's sister's just rung him direct to say that Paul stayed several times at the hotel where she works – a swank place called the Carrick Diamond at the other side of Falmouth. A young woman would join him there – at least twice for the night and several times during the day. She says it was the Pascoe daughter, Lucy. She's known the mother for years, but although she was concerned about the set-up, she didn't like to say anything.'

'She's saying it now, though?'

'Well, the murder was on television news earlier this afternoon, and local radio as well. You did ask for any information, however trivial.'

He sighed. 'Of course I did – she was right to let us know. I'd already gathered that Lucy was involved with Paul, and it was obvious we'd have to follow it up.' He looked across to where staff were sorting through piles of papers. 'There's probably something or other in the door-to-door reports, as well. What does Lucy say in her statement?'

'They're fishing it out now, but wasn't Bowles in charge of taking it? Hasn't he said anything?'

'Not yet, but no doubt he will. We're due to have a

mutual update when he comes back. It's becoming clear that Paul was one for the girls, so we're going to look into it.' He plonked a bottle of water on his desk. 'It's pretty grim under canvas in this weather, Addie, and there's a cold spell coming up. What's the situation about us getting better premises?'

'I'm working on it,' she said. 'In the meantime we make do – that's the word from on high. Oh, and you'll be getting a call from the City of London boys. They've got basic info on the Stradling firm's affairs, and they want to clarify who's in charge before they dig deeper.'

'I'll be here,' he said shortly. Impatience to be on his own was there beneath the words, and he knew it. 'Sorry, Addie, but I need a bit of space to sort out priorities. Just for ten minutes.'

She lifted her hands, palms upward. 'So if they ring shall I disturb you, or fob them off?'

'Give me the ten minutes, *then* disturb me and I'll clarify whatever they want.'

With a nod and a flash of the crystal eyes she marched off. She was good, he told himself, but sometimes he longed for the calm good nature of her predecessor. Right now he was in the tense, impatient state that was usual with him in the first days of a case, and John Meade used to calm him down without making him lose momentum.

He stared out at the once peaceful village green with its border of cars. Since the finding of the body more than thirty hours had passed, and what had they got? Not much. They had only two avenues of enquiry worthy of the name – Martin Goodchild and the Pascoe family. Goodchild's every move was being checked, but another visit to Trenoon was looming – and soon.

Helen heard the crunch of gravel and the soft thud of the car door. Steve was back. They'd talk to Lucy together – Chrissie had been all for it. 'Your daughter was in a close relationship with a man who's been murdered,' she'd said bluntly, 'and they'd talked of getting married. You've got to discuss it with her, Helen, both of you, or how can you help her? If he'd died a normal death you could have allowed her time to grieve, to adjust in her own way, but murder's not normal. The police will be checking on everything. By now they probably know about them being lovers.' Chrissie had talked sense – but then, she always did.

Steve came in and slung his coat on a chair, just as he used to do. 'I've made a complaint about the sergeant,' he announced, standing at her side by the sink and looking intently at the vegetables she was preparing, not at her. 'Channon was good. He apologized. He said the sergeant's over-keen.'

'He's right there,' she agreed, 'but look, Steve –'

'Just a minute,' he interrupted, 'let me tell you something. The only reason I didn't tell you before is that I didn't know if it would happen and I wanted to have it cut and dried ready to put to you.'

'Tell me what? Put what to me?'

'I wasn't in London on Friday. I was down here, across on the Roseland. If I'd got round to telling you first I would have admitted it to the police this morning, though I'm not sure if I could have made myself tell the sergeant, even in private.'

So – Chrissie had been right. 'I half knew, anyway,' she told him. 'Chrissie thought she saw you coming off the King Harry, but I told her she was mistaken. Why were you here?'

He hunched his shoulders. 'I'm looking into moving down here to be near you.'

'What about your job?'

'I'll work from home and keep in touch online, going up to London once or twice a week. I've had agents looking out for a property to rent. One came up on the Roseland and I came down to view it. I didn't want to tell you.'

'Why not?'

He had the look she'd got to know, a look that would

have been alien to him only nine months ago; it held humiliation, shame and a dogged determination. 'In case you didn't want me so near. I know you won't have me under the same roof – except for just now because of what's happening – but I can't bear being three hundred miles away. So what do you think?'

'I can't tell you where you can live, Steve. You must know that.'

'You can tell me whether you like the idea.'

She met his eyes. 'It will be good for the children – Katie in paticular.'

'Not good for you, though.'

It had been a statement, not a question, but she gave an answer that came from instinct. 'I don't know. Leave it at that, for now, and do what you feel to be right. Steve, even more important than all this is Lucy. She doesn't want to communicate, but we've got to talk to her.' She flopped down at the table and wiggled her fingers at the opposite chair. 'Let's go through what we can ask her to get things clear, because I think the police will be here again soon.'

From across the table the familiar eyes looked into hers. 'So do I,' he said. 'Helen, I feel so bad about her changing her mind and taking this gap year. But for that she'd be away at uni and out of all this.'

They both knew that the split-up had made Lucy postpone her degree course, but Helen considered it as much her own doing as Steve's. She'd been the one to set up another home. She'd been the one who was too full of self-pity to see her own child falling in love. Firmly she said, 'Her gap year's well under way. It can't be undone. Now, what can we say to her?'

'No photographs,' was Bowles's greeting when he came back, 'and no camera – at least, not in the house. The boat's off limits, under guard, and not yet searched.'

'We'll sort that out in a minute,' said Channon. He was feeling better after a concentrated think and a talk to the

City of London police, and now he waved to the one spare chair. 'Take a seat, Bowles, and let's get up to date. How's Stradling?'

'It's sunk in,' said Bowles. 'He's a wreck, but I reckon he could still be awkward as hell if he was pushed. He didn't like us taking his Bentley – you should see it, boss, a Continental GT, very dark green, I think the colour's called midnight emerald – and then the Aston Martin, a dark red, not flashy, just pure class –'

'All right, all right, stop drooling,' said Channon irritably. 'So you pacified him?'

'I explained we had no option, and that it was merely a formality. We've taken full statements from everybody and I've started on a list of important points arising from them. Stradling's secretary has arrived from London – one Nigel Nollens, a cut-glass type who seems bright enough if a bit snotty – so Stradling has a minion to run round after him. But, boss, what's with the photographs?'

'Keep calm, Bowles. They're of a young girl – one of many, I suspect, and they're naughty. How naughty? I don't yet know because they've been seen by only one man, and that accidentally.'

'Who? Have you talked to him?'

'Luther Tresillian, and no, I haven't. He didn't recognize her.'

'So it's not Lucy Pascoe?'

The DCI's dark gaze rested thoughtfully on the sergeant. He knows, thought Bowles, he knows I kept it back about Lucy and Paul, but all Channon said was: 'It's likely there are more on the computers. Two men are on their way now to bring them here, so our experts can examine them first thing tomorrow.'

'In the meantime do we go and have a word with Tresillian?'

'Not until this evening. He'll be expecting us. What he found shocking may strike us as pretty mild, of course. If it's just a bit of consensual titillation with an over-age girl then we need go no further.'

'Surely it could provide a motive,' protested Bowles.

'Yes, it could. An outraged father, maybe, or a vengeful mother, but I suspect there are other girls, in which case we'll be investigating the lot.'

'Can't we grill Stradling to see what he knows?'

Channon took in breath. 'We may find him a bit difficult, but he's a bereaved father; so no, we cannot grill him, not until such time as we have either the need or the grounds – or both. What we do need as our top priority is to find out how Paul spent Friday evening. What did you get on that?'

'Not a lot,' admitted Bowles. 'It's an odd set-up there. Stradling seems to see it as an informal weekend retreat where he and Paul could come and go as they please, and where the staff are only visible when they're needed.'

'So who exactly *are* the staff?'

'A chef – male; one maid – young and quite an eyeful; a housekeeper; a daily cleaner who lives nearby; and two gardeners, one of them female and partner to the chef, one male who's also a sort of general handyman and is married to the housekeeper.'

'Quite a retinue to run an informal weekend retreat.'

'You could say so, though the chef doubles up as the cook while they're at sea and has sole responsibility for keeping the boat immaculate. They haven't come up with much about where Paul was. They say he goes out most evenings but they never know exactly where.'

'Did he go out on Friday?'

'They don't know that either. When the evening meal's over they're off duty and in their quarters unless they're needed. They weren't required on Friday and so they did their own thing. Paul's car was there as usual on Saturday morning, so they thought he was having a lie-in after a late night. I've got everything I can on the movements of both father and son, all listed and waiting.'

Channon nodded. This was the good side of Bowles. 'Inspector Savage is in charge of collating all info on exactly where he was, minute by minute, so we'll examine it and maybe add to it. Now, to the house itself – what did you find?'

'Nothing that throws light on the killing. It's some pad, boss. Paul's rooms are those of a well-heeled young guy with an interest in sailing and sport – and women. Several glamour pictures of celebrities – very tasteful, fully clothed. A few art books – boring studies of nudes, nothing exciting.'

'His social life, then? Mobile, pager, diary, even a calendar?'

'We've brought them all back for examination, including an old-fashioned diary. No little black book, though, so maybe he didn't list his conquests.'

Bowles hadn't managed to hide a sour note, but Channon was unsurprised. Many a man besides Bowles would be envious of Paul's privileged lifestyle, of his looks, his car, maybe of his earring. 'Did you see any reminders of the mother?' he asked with interest.

'A few framed photographs and a painting. She was some looker, even when she was older.' Bowles shook his head. 'Stradling was clearly besotted.'

Channon smiled at the sergeant's bafflement. 'It isn't unknown for a man to be devoted to the same woman for a lifetime,' he pointed out 'But back to Paul – we've got to get all his contacts. We know he and Lucy were lovers, what we don't know is how serious it was, and whether in Lucy's case Paul saw a commitment – even a future together, and if that was so we don't know whether the parents backed it. So . . . we have to talk to them.'

'We're going to Trenoon again?'

'I'm going, Bowles – in the morning. You are not, for reasons I don't need to spell out. I'll take Yates or Mary Donald.'

Oh, typical! Good-boy Yates, the little white hen. Mary was all right, though. She was the only person who took the slightest interest in his attempts at cooking his own meals. But back to the salt mines – there was something he had to know. 'What was the information that Papa Pascoe wouldn't give to me?' he asked abruptly.

'That he wasn't in London on Friday. He was down here on the Fal, looking at property to rent in order to be near his family.'

'Well, well! Did they know about it?'

'Apparently not.'

Bowles kept silent. His tough approach with the Pascoes had deprived him of learning that little snippet, and was about to lose him the chance to take part in a crucial interrogation. The question was – had it been worth it?

He thought of the lovely old house with the log fire and the big windows looking across the water, of the Freelander and the Mercedes and the daughter's new Fiat, of the man he'd thought looked like a cross between a male model and a pantomime demon king. Then he recalled the tension and resentment of the family, and in particular the little gremlin, Katie, with her uncertainty turning to confusion and fear . . . All right, so it *hadn't* been worth it. End of.

The lamps were lit and fresh logs were crackling on the fire. Jaz and Katie had been asked to stay away, and with Steve at the other side of the hearth Helen was all set for a heart-to-heart with Lucy. When she came in she looked at them both, tucked her mouth into a tight little line and sat on a footstool between them. Then she waited.

'Lucy, your dad and I need to talk to you about Paul,' Helen began. 'We'd like to give you as much time as you need to adjust to losing him, but we can't do it. You told the police you were close to each other, and by now they probably know just how close. We think they'll be here again very soon to ask you more questions.'

The flat little voice said, 'If they ask more questions, then I'll answer them.'

'Of course you will,' agreed Helen, 'but we didn't know until last evening that you and Paul were so deeply involved. Could you fill us in on what you meant to each other, and whether you can imagine anyone wanting him dead?'

Steve added, 'It's possible you might need our help, pet; or at least a bit of back-up. We'd be better placed to give it if we know what's been going on.'

The lamps were casting shadows on Lucy's face, hollowing her eyes and etching dark grooves from her nostrils to her chin. Helen found it so unnerving she jumped up and switched on more lights. 'We need to be able to help you,' she said, and wanted to demand: How long have you been sleeping with him? Has he actually asked you to marry him? Does his father know? but she kept silent.

The little voice said, 'It's been going on, as you put it, since the party at their house – seven and a half weeks, to be exact. We liked each other before then, because we'd met a few times in a mixed group. At the party we arranged to see each other in Falmouth. He wanted to pick me up here,' she shot a sideways look at her mother, 'but I said you might not like it. After that first time we saw each other a lot. He would come all the way from London midweek. We used a couple of hotels – sometimes during the day and a few times for the night. He was in love with me, I was in love with him. We discussed getting married.'

'Didn't he think you were a bit young for marriage?' asked Steve gently.

'No, why should he? I'm of age. He wanted to talk to you both, but you were always in Highgate, Dad, and Mum didn't like him.'

'I didn't know him,' protested Helen wretchedly. 'It was simply a gut feeling that he was too sophisticated for you. I might have found him lovely on closer acquaintance.'

'Well, you'll never get closer acquainted now, will you?' Lucy's words fell into the warm room like winter rain. Then she said, 'And if you're worried I'm pregnant, forget it. We both had more sense than that.'

'I'm glad to hear it,' said Steve crisply. 'As a matter of fact, we didn't expect you to be pregnant. We're just worried that you might have to answer a lot of questions before you're up to it – about his friends, his social life, his interests, and any earlier relationships.'

'Oh, that's it, is it? You think an ex-girlfriend cut his throat! You think she put him over her shoulder and carried him to the Menna?'

'No we don't,' Helen assured her, 'but as nobody knows what *did* happen, it's a remote possibility. Hell hath no fury, and that sort of thing.'

Lucy turned her head from side to side, blonde hair swinging out on either side of her pale little face. 'You both seem pretty sure I wasn't the first,' she said. 'Well, I knew that. He told me about all the others. He said he only found what he was looking for when he met me.'

That could be true, Helen thought sadly, but antagonism still lay behind Lucy's every word, and it cut at her. She shot a quick look at Steve, then said, 'Listen, love, I'm so very sorry that I was too wrapped up in other things to pay proper attention to what you were doing. I'm absolutely stunned that I didn't know you were falling in love. And what about uni? Did Paul know you were in a gap year?'

'Of course he did. We often talked about it. He wanted me to take my degree after we were married.'

'And where had you planned to live?' That was Steve. Helen could tell he was shaken by the way he was holding his mouth.

Lucy hesitated for only a second, then said, 'Well, it would have had to be near his work in the City, so we'd have had our own place in London.' When they both stared at her she burst out in her old voice, 'Why are you treating it as so astounding? The only thing that makes it different from other couples is that he's dead.' The green eyes were dead as well, wide and quite blank. 'He's dead!' she repeated, as if they might not have grasped it. 'So we won't be buying a lovely apartment in London, and I certainly won't be going to uni like a good little A level student!'

Her bright, lovely daughter with her array of A stars, thought Helen in anguish. She must advise other parents who were obsessed by their children's results: just arrange a murder and it'll put A levels into perspective . . . but Steve was answering Lucy.

'Whatever you do,' he said heavily, 'your mum and I are here to look after you. We want to be with you when the police come – just to watch over you.'

'That'll be useful,' she said. 'You can hold my hand and help me deal with the sergeant.' She stood up, pressing her long denim skirt against her legs, as if to keep it from touching them. Then, holding the folds of it like an Edwardian miss, she left the room and went back upstairs.

For a moment there was no sound apart from the crackle of the logs, until Helen said brokenly, 'We didn't find out if she knew of anyone who might want to hurt him.'

Steve replied, 'More vital than that – we didn't find out if she was with him on Friday evening.'

Sunday tea was being served in the incident room, but without a lace cloth and silver teapot. It was simply hot toast and cakes, officers finding that, with a new chill in the air, food and a hot drink were good for morale.

Too busy for such comforts, Bowles was closeted with Channon and Addie Savage, sorting information on how Paul had spent Friday evening. The sergeant found it strange that even with extra manpower it had taken so long to establish the movements of a man who was well known locally, who had a doting father, a houseful of servants and a highly distinctive car.

He would have liked to blame Addie the baddie for the lack of speed, but no, she was her usual calm efficient self; handling the computer boys and the house-to-house teams with an iron hand but no sign of a velvet glove. There was one good aspect, though; as the man in charge of the visit to Pengorra Court, he himself would have an input.

'So,' Channon began, 'father and son arrived from London at around five thirty, each in their own car. Did they always come down separately, Bowles? It's a long way for a two-car drive, especially in gas-guzzlers like theirs.'

'That's how they liked to do it, apparently. Daddy-oh saw himself as the tolerant parent who didn't interfere when Paul zoomed around enjoying himself. I suspect they were happier in their own cars, because Stradling sounds a bit of a stickler about his Bentley. The handyman said he always had to give it the full Monty spit and polish within half an hour of Stradling arriving, and then quite often it stayed in the garage until he went back to London.'

'What if they went sailing?'

Bowles shrugged. 'They both walk down to their jetty through the grounds – I see it as a sort of ritual, a complete break from their life in London. It can't take them more than two or three minutes, with another minute on the water to get to the boat.'

'There's no access for a car to get down to the jetty, then?'

'Oh, yes, there is – a good gravel track from the side of the house right down to the water, but they don't use it much, except sometimes when one of them sleeps on the boat. That's more likely to be in the summer, and more often Paul than his father. The maid – the eyeful I mentioned – was a bit tight-lipped when I asked how often Paul slept on board. I couldn't tell whether she was uptight because she'd shared his cabin or because she hadn't.'

'No doubt we'll find out in time,' said Channon, 'we usually do. Now, what did Paul do after they arrived?'

'Both Stradling and the staff confirm that he was indoors until six fifteen, when he left the house in his car. They imagined it was to go to the yacht club, as that was his usual choice.'

'It was quiet at that time,' continued Addie, 'but the bar staff and three members who were there are definite that he stayed for a good half-hour, leaving soon after seven. He drank champagne, his favourite aperitif.'

'And then?'

'Back to the house. Two different witnesses saw him in his car, one near Mylor Bridge, the other minutes later, going through the village here, when he could only have been almost back at the house.'

'He was alone in the car? It wasn't stationary?'

'Alone,' she confirmed, 'and he was on the move.'

'He arrived?' That question was to Bowles.

'Oh, yes. Daddy-oh and the staff are all adamant that he returned before seven thirty. At seven forty-five staff say they served a simple three-course meal – simple by their standards, anyway – followed, as was usual in cold weather, by coffee in front of the fire in the big sitting room. After that no more details on Paul from the staff, but Stradling says they chatted for a bit about business, then Paul went up to his room for a while, he supposed to make phone calls, while he looked at his new yachting magazines. When Paul came down again they continued to talk business a bit more, then Paul went out, and –'

'What time?'

'Daddy-oh said about ten past nine. The staff don't actually confirm that. They say that everything was cleared away before nine, when they all joined together for a light supper, and then – apart from the chef and the female gardener – they watched a DVD. The handyman chap thought he heard a car about ten past or quarter past nine, but didn't take much notice.'

'What did the other two do while the rest were watching the DVD?'

'They're partners, boss. They said they went to their cottage, and heard nothing of interest. Maybe they were otherwise engaged.'

'So Stradling is sure Paul went out at ten past nine?'

'Yes, and he never saw him alive again.'

Channon sighed. He was getting no feel for the case. He hadn't the faintest idea of how Paul's mind had worked. Turning back to Addie, he asked, 'So what after nine ten?'

'Nothing,' she said flatly. 'No pub sightings, no car sightings – though don't forget it wasn't exactly a moonlight and roses night, it was wet and windy. He didn't go back to the yacht club, either.'

'He must have been in the area after leaving the house. We'll have to check if he was with Lucy Pascoe. It's crucial we place him between nine fifteen and ten thirty, because our best estimate of time of death is ten to ten thirty. Bowles, we visit the boat in daylight first thing tomorrow.'

'You think he was there, boss?'

'It's possible. Have we still got staff asking around the area?'

Addie nodded. 'For sightings at that time? Yes.'

She was chewing her lip, Channon saw. 'What's on your mind, Addie?'

'I'm just thinking it's our misfortune he was killed here,' she said.

Channon stared at her. 'His misfortune as well, surely?'

She shook her head impatiently. 'Of course. What I mean is, the greater part of his life is spent in London. Are we perhaps going overboard on local connections when there could easily be someone in London who wanted to see him dead? Father and son came down here frequently without apparent effort. The murderer could have done the same.'

She was right, of course. 'That's why the City police are on with it,' he said. 'They don't need my say-so any longer. The Stradlings aren't top of the tree, but they're big enough to warrant the City boys' own investigation. I'm still senior investigating officer, so whatever they find has to come back to me.'

Bowles asked, 'What did their prelim report show?'

'That Stradling and Son are a firm of financiers, not in the big time of stocks and shares and commodities, but still a solid firm. They back safe schemes, large and small, such as established ventures requiring more capital, firms who need temporary help with takeovers, or who need capital for change or expansion. If the amount required is beyond Stradling's range he'll act as broker to get it for them. They're facilitators.'

Bowles concealed surprise. To him it seemed very ordinary. He'd had visions of Paul glued to a phone on the Stock Exchange, risking millions on the rise and fall of shares; of Daddy-oh mixing with media billionaires like Murdoch, or in lighter moments backing theatrical gold-spinners. What the DCI was describing was so – what was the word? Prosaic, that was it – or did he mean mundane?

Channon was leaning against his desk, hands in pockets, intent on delivering a summing-up. 'The Stradlings lead a full and complicated life in London,' he said, 'but though it may be our misfortune, Paul was murdered *here*. We're the Devon and Cornwall force, and our job is to make sure we haven't got his murderer on the banks of Carrick Roads.'

And that puts me in my place, thought Addie, while, without meaning to, Bowles shot her a sympathetic grin.

'Right,' Channon said, 'leave these reports with me, will you? I'll take the diary home and read it there. Bowles, go and get yourself a cup of tea, and then make sure all your statements are being recorded. Addie – do you want to get off?'

Never one to mince words, she answered simply, 'Yes.'

'Go on, then. Bowles, we'll have a quiet hour or so before we go to see Tresillian. I have phone calls lined up.'

The sergeant took that as a hint that he mustn't sit around twiddling his thumbs, and went off to see if there was any food left. Addie put on her jacket. All at once she wasn't sure whether she was glad or sorry to be working with Channon again.

A full moon sailed the sky above the Tresillian house, and a chill in the air heralded frost. Part of Channon's mind was registering the change in the weather and thinking that mid-November was early for frost around the Fal. Were they to see the rare sight of trees still in late leaf touched by white in the morning?

He pushed trivial thoughts aside when the door was opened by Luther Tresillian. A rosy-cheeked woman and three young boys in pyjamas were playing Monopoly at a table in front of the fire. The boys stared wide-eyed at the detectives but followed their mother's lead in greeting them politely before going back to their game. Tresillian led the two men into the sitting room, where he gave them a straight look and closed the door with a thud.

'We won't keep you,' Channon assured him. 'There are just a few things we must know. First, could you tell us how you came to see the photographs?'

Tresillian stood facing them, embarrassment oozing from him like engine oil from a drum. 'Paul had reported that the door on his berthside locker wouldn't close. You wouldn't expect it on a craft of that quality, but there'd been damage as a result of young Martin's vandalism, especially in Paul's cabin, and a few things had shown up faulty even after the repairs were done.'

He took a deep breath and went on carefully, 'Amos and me always had access to the boat, so in a quiet spell I went out in the yard's dinghy to see to it.'

'You went on board? Did the Stradlings know you were going?'

'No – at least, not at that precise time. Amos had just told them we'd see to it in the next couple of days. *Daphne* was near enough, you see. She's on a swinging mooring on the Roads below the house – only a couple of minutes from the yard.'

'So how did you come to see the photographs?'

'I didn't see them at all, at first. I looked at the door and the catch was only jammed. I saw to it in no time and as I turned to go my coat brushed the foot of the berth and scattered a little pile of pictures that were there. I picked them up and – well – I couldn't help seeing them.'

'They weren't in a processor's envelope?'

'No, they were in a bundle. I think they were prints from a digital camera, done on a computer. I'd seen similar belonging to a friend of mine.'

'Right. Mr Tresillian, we have no idea whether what you saw will help our enquiry, but it *might* do, so please do your best to answer. Would you say they were a bit saucy, or shocking, or disgusting, or obscene? You can be quite frank – we're unshockable.'

'Maybe you are,' agreed the other, eyes resentful, 'but I'm not. Maybe in your job you've seen the lot, but I *haven't*. They were close-up pictures of a young woman showing her private parts. She had no clothes on – none. I'd describe them as shocking, bordering on disgusting. I don't even know what would be classed as obscene.'

Bowles was shifting impatiently. This guy was innocent as a babe unborn – or was he? Had he never, ever, flipped through a top-shelf magazine? Had his old lady never given him a thrill? But Channon was still calmly attentive. 'Mr Heaney told me that you saw the young woman's face. Did you know her?'

'No.'

'Could you make a guess at her age?'

'Mid-teens, maybe a bit older, but I'm no expert.'

'If necessary, could you identify her, either in person or from a likeness?'

'I think so, but I'd rather not meet her face to face unless it's unavoidable.'

'Fair enough. Now, did she appear distressed?'

'No, she was smiling. Showing off, sort of.'

'She was not being forced in any way?'

'Not on the pictures I saw.'

'You didn't see them all, then?'

Tresillian's weather-beaten features tightened. 'Strange to say, chief inspector, I did not. I was stunned to see them left openly on view, even on a private boat, and that's the truth of it. I was embarrassed. I put them back as I thought they must have been before I scattered them and left the boat as quick as I could.'

'And then you told Mr Heaney?'

'Yes, as soon as I got back. Then we talked it over after the day's work was done. I was calmer by then. In the end we both decided to each his own. We know we'd be out of date compared to young folk from London – old-fashioned, you might say. After that life went on and we continued doing work on *Daphne*. I didn't have to respect the man, did I? Just look after his father's boat and get paid my wages for doing it. Now is that all?'

'That's all,' confirmed Channon. 'Thank you, Mr Tresillian.'

Back in the car both men were silent for a minute. Channon had seen more images than he'd ever wanted to see when he had a spell on Vice, and he'd found Tresillian's attitude like a breath of clean air in a fetid room. Bowles was more dubious, at last asking, 'Can he really be that innocent, boss?'

'I think he can. A good man, I'd judge, who doesn't know the meaning of lechery. Somewhat naive, perhaps, but that's not a crime.'

'I'm not saying it is,' retorted the sergeant, 'but it's certainly rare in a man his age. If he's right and the piccies were taken by a digital camera it must be on the boat, because it isn't in the house, but it's a pretty sure bet that Paul has them on his computer, and maybe others besides. Harmless or steamy, a gallery of girls will give us contacts to follow up.'

'If we can recognize them.' Channon didn't see this latest development as a breakthrough; he saw it as an eater-up of man-hours, and quite possibly a complete waste of time.

Bowles, though, had reached the stage when he could see no further than his stomach. He was tired and he was hungry, and not caring if he got a put-down, said bluntly, 'Boss – I need food.'

To his surprise Channon said, 'So do I. Let's both get off home and have an early start tomorrow.'

Ten minutes later, each man was heading for home in the moonlight: Bowles for his flat in Truro and Channon for the King Harry Ferry and his tranquil, cream-washed house on the Roseland.

Chapter Nine

Frost had touched the hollows of the Roseland's gentle hills; the air was very cold and a pearl-grey sky was waiting for the sun. In his house above the beach Channon was having breakfast, relishing a spell of solitude before returning to the clamour of Pengorra's village green.

Less tense after a night's sleep, he reflected for a moment on his domestic life. His home was his refuge, the place he thought of in times of stress as balm to his spirit; he needed it to be comfortable and well run or he was miserable. Six months ago it had been neither: his housekeeper had been terminally ill, the roof had collapsed under torrential rain and the kitchen plumbing was having a major overhaul.

Things were better now. He rarely saw his new daily housekeeper, but she was good. The place was beautifully kept and there was always a meal left ready when he got in from work. His home life was solitary, his social life bordering on non-existent, and as for work – nothing new there, it was as it had always been – compelling.

His thinking session in the bath last night had brought no earth-shattering deductions; his cherished instinct was dormant, his intuition fast asleep, and the reading of Paul Stradling's diary had brought scant result: he was no nearer to knowing the dead man. The names and phone numbers would take a bit of sorting, but might reveal a great deal. At this stage, though, there was only one item of interest. Next to Lucy Pascoe's name and number, Paul had written: *This one's different* and circled the words in red. He really needed to get to grips with what sort of man Paul had been. Sometimes in the past he had felt almost at one with a murder victim, which had been good, but not as good as being at one with the murderer and solving the case.

On that thought his mind crossed over to the well-worn track of putting the day's tasks in order of priority; mentally assigning men to areas of enquiry and reviewing what he and Bowles would be handling. The visit to Trenoon – without the sergeant – was a must. He had already told Mary Donald he needed her with him there.

Then he would go to the boat. If anyone had asked what he hoped to find there he couldn't have told them, except possibly photographs, or maybe evidence that the initial attack on Paul had taken place there. And surely he would get the feel of a luxury vessel that had clearly meant a lot to both father and son. Had they seen *Daphne* as an escape from the pressures of high finance, or was it simply Stradling's last link with his wife, Paul's with his mother?

Channon was opening the car before the weather really registered. Already it was getting light. The sky was without cloud; soon the sun would rise and illuminate the stretch of pale gold sand that was the pride of the village and the delight of holidaymakers. He paused. Should he allow himself just ten minutes of pure self-indulgence before a long day's work? He made for the path that passed his garden wall and led down to the beach.

The air was very still. The grasses stood silver-tipped, something he knew was rare; the sky was warming to palest green tinged with pink. He jumped the last few feet to the sand and watched as the colourless expanse beneath his feet turned to gold beneath the rising sun. He couldn't help smiling. This was worth a few minutes of his time.

He walked on with the low cliffs at his side and the sea swirling gently, almost silently towards his feet. Then he saw that he wasn't alone. Some distance ahead a woman was walking the waterline, stepping sideways when a wave slid too close, just as he himself was doing. Her back was towards him but he could see dark hair; there was a red scarf round her neck and she wore a blue jacket and dark blue trousers.

He was still far behind her when something about the way she walked set the bells of his memory chiming. It looked like Sally Baxter, the woman who had cried when he told her that his wife and son were dead; cried for *him* – even though members of her own family were embroiled in murder. Then she had wiped her eyes on the cloth she was using to do her dishes . . .

Since the closing of that case he had seen her only once, also at a distance in a Falmouth street. But even as he remembered, the woman in front of him was leaving the beach and climbing the granite steps that led up and away. *Was* it her? She looked thinner than he remembered. And why was she here when her house was further along the coast? He stood and watched her as she turned for a last look out to sea, but still he couldn't see her face. Then she wound the scarf more closely around her throat and strode off along the frosted grasses of the cliff top.

For fully a minute Channon remained on the sands, then he turned and climbed the path back to his car. He was halfway to the King Harry Ferry before he dismissed his memories and let the demands of the coming day enter his mind.

Bowles had been at work for ten minutes and was feeling somewhat smug. Old clever-clogs had said they must have an early start but it was a quarter to eight and he hadn't arrived, so what did he class as early? Addie the baddie was already hard at it, needless to say – she was more like a robot than a woman.

He watched as she briefed four constables who were scheduled to go out on enquiries, and saw them grouped around her, listening with respectful attention. Oh, he had to admit she was good. She reminded him a bit of a teacher he'd known at senior school, where he wasn't exactly the swot of the form. She'd been the only person in his entire school life to tell him to his face that he was intelligent, and would go far if he put his mind to it. Well, he was putting his mind to it under Channon, but as for going far, he was still a sergeant.

And then the DCI walked in, already on his mobile. He nodded a greeting to everyone and beckoned Bowles into his office, where he finished his call and said, 'That was Fred Jordan. I've told him to get his lads to hurry up and not make a second *War and Peace* of his report. Now – we have a full day ahead of us, Bowles.' He held out Paul's diary. 'Read this. There are names, a few addresses and several phone numbers – it's more like the little black book you mentioned than an actual diary. I can't see why a man who must have lived and breathed electronic stuff should have had a use for such a thing. Anyway, I want you to check every detail – get as much help as you need. Making a start on it should keep you busy while I'm at the Pascoes'.'

'Do you want someone to ring them and say you're coming?'

Dark eyes met pale ones. It was clear to Channon that the sergeant was still smarting at being excluded from the visit. 'No,' he said briskly, 'I'll do it myself in a minute. Have we had confirmation of Mrs Pascoe's times at the yoga group? What about word from Forensic on the Freelander?'

Bowles hissed out a breath between his teeth. All right, all right, he thought, you come in late so everybody has to reach me, fetch me, carry me! He knew that was unfair, but it pleased him to say it to himself. Aloud he said, 'Everything confirmed with the yoga class. No news yet on the Freelander, and so far no joy on the plastic bag that Mrs Pascoe says she saw. If it's found it will go straight to Forensic, just in case it shows anything.'

'Right. Anything on Goodchild? Is it right his mother's been laid off at the Yardarm?'

'Nothing new on Martin. He's due to go and do his regular odd-jobbing at the Pascoes' this morning, and yes, his mother's laid off – on half-pay, so the landlord told Soker.'

Channon nodded and, handing over Paul's book, waved in dismissal. 'Off you go. I might need you later if I go to the boat. I'll let you know.'

With Bowles gone he rang Trenoon. It was Helen who answered. 'You're coming this morning?' she echoed uneasily. 'What time?'

Channon was calm and very polite. 'Eight thirty, Mrs Pascoe, in twenty minutes. We need to talk to your daughter, Lucy.'

Be careful, Helen warned herself, and at once felt ridiculously over- dramatic. But the situation was over-dramatic, *murder* was over-dramatic. 'She's pretty upset, Mr Channon,' she said tightly. 'Can my husband and I be with her?'

'I'm aware she must be upset, Mrs Pascoe, so I'll be bringing a female officer with wide experience of dealing with the bereaved. The fact remains that Lucy is of age, so in law she can answer questions without the presence of an adult.' He thought of the girl's expressionless face, of her tight little voice, and said, 'You and your husband can be present, of course, as it will be informal questioning, but please don't attempt to answer for her, or interrupt.'

'Thank you. We'll see you soon, then.'

'One other thing – I'm taking it that you and your husband do know the extent of Lucy's relationship with Paul?'

'Oh yes,' said Helen quietly, 'we know.'

'Good. Thank you, madam.' Keeping it strictly formal always helped if things got too emotional, and that might well be the case with Lucy Pascoe.

Calm, kindly and competent, Mary Donald was at the wheel as they drove to Trenoon. 'I'm not sure what state Lucy will be in,' Channon warned her. 'On Saturday she was stunned and withdrawn, but apart from his father she's our closest link to Paul, so we've got to talk to her. Apparently she was his latest sleeping partner, though whether she knew about all the others isn't clear.'

'What about her parents? How are they?'

'Uptight, as you'd expect, and they want to be with her while we're there. She's still only eighteen so they feel they must protect her. Keep an eye on their reactions while I'm concentrating on Lucy, will you? If they know of Paul's reputation with the girls they're likely to have had reservations about him and they just might give something away.'

'Lucy said in her statement that she and Paul had been close, but not *how* close,' pointed out Mary. 'So do her parents know the full facts?'

'Maybe not the full facts, but they know they were lovers – I checked with the mother. We'll just have to take things gently and see how it goes.'

Mary nodded. She'd heard on the grapevine that the sergeant had taken a tough line with the family, but told herself now that one thing she didn't need to worry about was the DCI doing the same.

In a bid to make things seem pleasant and normal Helen had dashed around preparing for Channon's arrival; lighting the fire in a room already warm enough and arranging armchairs in a seemingly random group of five. She had found Lucy already up and dressed and had persuaded her to have coffee and toast to give her a spurt of energy.

Now she eyed her with concern. If anything she looked worse than on the previous day: pale, drawn, and with purple shadows beneath her eyes. Helen could hardly believe that they weren't communicating. If only she'd kept it to herself that she thought Paul wasn't right for her; if only she'd pretended to like him; if only she'd taken the trouble to watch over her own child . . . If only, if only – if only she'd done just one of those things, they might still be on their old terms with each other. She would have been able to hug her and cuddle her and let her sob her heart out in her arms, instead of having to deal with this flat-voiced stranger.

120

'I think the inspector just wants to find out what you know about Paul's contacts,' she said, attempting to make light of the forthcoming visit.

Lucy's distant gaze rested on her mother's face and moved on. 'I shall tell him we were planning to get married,' she said.

'Tell him whatever you like,' agreed Helen wearily, 'as long as it's the truth. The time for hiding things has gone, my love – gone for ever. He has to establish facts, so I think he'll need to know when you last saw each other.'

'Yes,' agreed Lucy, 'I suppose he will. You know what they say about the last person to see a murder victim alive, don't you?'

'What?'

'That they're automatically a suspect.'

Helen opened her mouth to pour scorn on the idea, but to her dismay found she could make no sound, not even a gasp. She put out a hand, but Lucy ignored it, and then Steve was answering the door and letting in the grave-eyed detective and a fair-haired woman whom he introduced as 'DC Donald, an officer with wide experience'.

Helen recalled that he had said this was to be an informal questioning, and yet he was being very punctilious with his 'sir' and his 'madam'. He did accept a seat, though, and so did the woman. Helen struggled again with an overpowering sense of disbelief. Could this be happening? she asked herself for the hundredth time. It was less than forty-eight hours since Chrissie told her that murder had been done, yet here they were with the police in their sitting room questioning Lucy – her little Lucy – who was about to tell this detective that she and the murdered man had been planning to marry. It simply wasn't credible. She tried to meet Steve's eyes, but he was intent on Lucy.

The preliminaries over, Channon addressed himself solely to Lucy, who was composed, but tense. 'I realize you may not feel up to this, Lucy,' he said gently, 'but we have to sort out a few things. We're trying to check all of Paul's contacts here in the Falmouth area, while our London colleagues are working on his connections there. Do you think you could make a list of all the people he knew down here?'

Lucy stared at him. 'I don't know them all,' she said woodenly, 'not by a long way. But yes, I'll make a list of those I do know.'

'Thank you. As soon as you can, please, and then perhaps you'd get someone to drop it in at the incident room for me. Now – and this is simply a routine question – do you know of anyone who was on bad terms with Paul? Anyone who had a grudge against him?'

'No,' she said, 'everyone liked him.' She flashed a glance at her mother and folded her lips together.

Helen missed it, but was thinking sadly, not 'everyone', my pet. There must have been someone who *didn't* like him, because they cut his throat ... Channon merely nodded. 'Yes,' he said mildly, 'from what we've heard he was a likeable man, but for various reasons we don't see this as an attack by a stranger. If you'll let us have that list of names – however distantly connected – we'll cross-reference them and add them to those we already know about.' He leaned forward in his chair. 'Now, to your relationship with Paul, Lucy. You've already told us you were close. I have to ask you, how close?'

'Close enough to plan marriage. We were a real couple, inspector.' She lifted her chin and in a voice with slightly more feeling, said defiantly, 'We made love almost every time we met.'

Steve shifted in his chair, and Helen sent him a warning look. God above, she said to herself grimly, two days ago I thought they'd only had a couple of dates on their own ...

'I know you stayed at the Carrick Diamond,' Channon agreed. 'Anywhere else in particular?'

'Yes, we went to the Moorings a couple of times, and once to a sort of motel place the other side of Truro.'

'What about the boat, Lucy? Did you and Paul ever go there?'

Lucy's iron composure wavered. Her lower lip wobbled and she dug her teeth into it. 'Yes,' she said unsteadily, 'several times.'

'I see. Now, this is important – did everyone know you were in love with each other, or did you keep it secret?'

'We kept it secret.'

'Why was that, Lucy?'

'I wasn't sure if Mum would approve.'

'Ah, of course. This question is important, as well, Lucy – very important. When was the last time you saw Paul?'

At that her mouth stretched wide and she gritted her teeth in an effort not to cry. Fists clenched tight, she held them up on either side of her chest with her forearms rigid. 'Friday night!' she said, her voice rising in anguish. 'We were on the boat – on *Daphne*!'

Faster than Helen could move, Steve leapt across the room and bent over his daughter, circling her with his arms. Eyes wide, he faced Channon. 'That's enough!' he said. 'You'll have to leave it for now!'

'I'm sorry, but I can't,' Channon told him, and nodded to Mary.

The policewoman went and knelt in front of Lucy. 'We need to know this,' she said gently, taking hold of her hands. 'What time did you and Paul meet each other, and what time did you leave him, Lucy?'

Lucy's control was disappearing. 'I knew you'd ask me that,' she managed. 'I can remember exactly. We'd arranged it earlier, you see, on the phone. I drove across and met him at their jetty. It was about nine fifteen when I arrived. We went out to the boat and – and I stayed for about half an hour. Then we went back across the water, which only took a couple of minutes. It must have been nine forty-five when we said goodbye.'

A last goodbye, thought Channon bleakly. A final goodbye.

Mary asked, 'How can you be so sure of the time, Lucy?'

123

'I knew Mum would be back from yoga soon after ten. I wanted to be home before then so I wouldn't have to lie about where I'd been.'

Still on her knees, Mary looked at Channon, who asked, 'Did Paul seem any different than usual? Was he upset about anything, or angry?'

'Not really, though he was a bit tense, as if he had something on his mind. I thought it was because he wanted to tell Mum about – us, and I didn't want to. We just talked about me taking my degree, and getting married and stuff.'

'And when you left, did you see him getting back in his car, or did he head back to the house on foot?'

'Neither. He just stood in the light of the lamp at the end of the jetty, watching as I drove away. I could see him in the driving mirror. He was blowing kisses.' The words, 'I never saw him again' hung unspoken on the warm air of the room.

'Thank you, Lucy,' said Channon, getting to his feet. Turning to Helen and Steve he gave an odd little bob of the head. 'Sir, madam, I may have to call on you again. If so, I'll try to give you notice.'

It was Steve who showed them out, clearly relieved to see them go. Before the house door closed behind them a sound came from the room they'd left – a howl of pain, harsh and ugly. Channon knew at once that it was Lucy, still emerging from her state of shock. He wondered how her parents would handle her.

'Poor little girl,' said Mary when they were back in the car. 'Poor, passionate little girl.'

'Poor little girl,' agreed Channon, 'but as for the passion, I think she had an expert tutor. Did anything strike you in there?'

'Two things. One – when you asked if she knew anyone who had a grudge against Paul, Lucy didn't mention Martin Goodchild, though she must have known about him vandalizing the boat; and two – when she told us that everyone liked Paul, she shot an odd look at her mother. Did you see it?'

'I saw,' said Channon grimly. 'I think Mrs Pascoe didn't like Paul, and that Lucy knew and resented it.' He stared down at the sunlit water for all of thirty seconds, then said, 'Right, let's go.'

'Where to, sir?'

'Take me to Pengorra Court, then get back and ask Bowles to join me at the jetty there. Before that I need to speak to Richard Stradling, it's nearly nine so he should be up and about. Oh – and ask Bowles to make sure he has a couple of protective suits in the car – that won't please him because he hates wearing them.'

'So you're going to the boat?'

'I am indeed, and the sergeant can share that pleasure with me. Thanks for your help with Lucy, Mary. Off you go.'

At the Court a curvaceous young woman – presumably the 'eyeful' mentioned by Bowles – showed him to the office where he'd talked to the financier the day before. 'Mr Stradling isn't very well,' she announced, 'but I'll tell his secretary you're here. He's in charge of interviews – he's dealt with reporters already.'

Channon nodded. 'I'm not a reporter,' he pointed out pleasantly, 'I'm Detective Chief Inspector Channon, and I'm in charge of this enquiry. I know he must be distressed, but I want a brief word with Mr Stradling. Please tell him I'm here.'

She looked at him uncertainly, eyes wide in her pretty young face. 'Detective Chief Inspector Channon,' he repeated, and she hurried away.

A minute later Stradling walked in, followed by a younger man wearing a business suit and carrying a clipboard. The bereaved father was looking terrible. Cheeks sunken, eyes puffy and bloodshot, he was moistening lips that were cracked and sore. There seemed to be nothing wrong with his mental processes, however; his speech was still clear and incisive. 'Channon,' he said briskly, 'I told

Jasmine to keep visitors at a distance, but that didn't mean you, of course. Meet my secretary, Nigel Nollens.'

Channon greeted the young man with interest. Low sunlight shone through the window and flashed on the fashionable glasses, obscuring his eyes, but Nollens nodded and politely shook hands. As if remembering their previous meeting, Stradling directed Channon to the same two chairs as before and turned them to face each other closely, leaving his secretary standing patiently in the background. Then he sat down and leaned forward with a hand on each knee. 'So what's the latest?' he asked keenly.

It seemed to Channon that he was expecting a daily bulletin. Well, he was entitled to one, but as the man in charge he himself wouldn't always be able to deliver it, and now was the best time to say so. 'I'm here to clarify a few points, Mr Stradling. First, we'll keep you as informed as we can, but I may not always be free to talk to you. In that event, one of my staff will be in touch.'

The bloodshot eyes narrowed, the puffy lids all but hiding a look of consideration. Not for the first time, Channon saw that his fitness was being assessed as the man in charge of solving the murder of a cherished son. 'All right, all right, I'll put up with underlings,' the other agreed impatiently. 'What's your next point?'

'My sergeant no doubt explained that we're checking your computers for any links to your son's personal life here in Cornwall, and in London, for that matter, while our colleagues in the City are doing the same at their end. I believe Paul had a digital camera? Do you know if he used it much?'

'Oh, he's always taking shots of something or other – why?'

'We haven't found it so far, but we're hoping to check it for his current photographs, and also we want to find any that he put on a computer.'

'We've got computers all over the place,' said Stradling, waving a hand, 'but I daresay you'll find something, somewhere. I've worked with Nigel on that list you wanted, by the way. I don't know all Paul's friends, of course, because he leads – led, I mean – such a busy social life, but I've listed all I can think of.'

'Did you have much contact with his girlfriends, Mr Stradling?'

'Some of them came here from time to time for parties and so forth. The ones I know, we've listed.'

'Were you aware that he had started a serious relationship with one of them?'

'Serious? What's serious, Channon? Paul's motto has always been Variety is the spice of life.'

'Maybe not all that serious a relationship, then,' conceded Channon blandly, 'but did you know he was seeing a lot of the Pascoes' daughter, Lucy?'

The red-rimmed eyes widened. 'What? From that lovely old place along the bank? The blonde girl? I know he likes her, but I don't take much notice – I don't interfere with his conquests.'

A doting father, Channon thought, maybe an admiring father, who was mixing his tenses between past and present when he spoke of his son. Was it just the usual muddle of the recently bereaved, or a refusal to accept his death? He went on, 'The reason I mention Lucy Pascoe is that I think she may well have been the last person to see your son alive.'

'*What*?' Channon could have sworn he saw the glint of tears as Stradling chewed his sore lips and muttered, 'The last person to see him . . .' Then he was back in incisive mode. 'When was this, precisely?'

'After nine on Friday evening.'

'Oh, yes, he'd gone out by then – or had he? I mean yes, yes, he – oh, I don't know. But Channon – uh – Channon – what . . .'

There was something unutterably sad in seeing this capable, intelligent man being reduced to such confusion. For seconds he sat there muttering disjointedly, while Nollens hovered uncertainly. All at once Stradling took a deep breath and gathered himself together. 'The Pascoe girl wasn't the last one to see him alive,' he said with certainty.

'Oh? Who was, then?'

The bloodshot eyes glittered with vengeance. 'The murderer saw him last, of course. The murderer, Channon!'

'You're right, Mr Stradling, and you'll be the first to know when we catch him. My sergeant is on his way here as I speak, and the two of us are going out to your boat. Don't worry – no harm will be done to her. If we find anything that needs further investigation our scene of crime team will take over, which will mean the boat could be out of use for a couple of days.'

Suddenly vacant again, Stradling peered at him. 'Have I told you I love that boat? She's named after my wife, you know.' He gave a little smile, which sat oddly on the cracked lips. 'Did I tell you that?'

Channon got to his feet. 'Yes, Mr Stradling, you did tell me,' he said. 'I'll be in touch.' He looked at Nollens, who led him out of the room and to the main doors. 'What about my list, Mr Nollens?' he asked.

There was no sun shining on Nollens's glasses now. Channon saw bright hazel eyes that were blank and unrevealing as he lifted the clip on his board and extracted two sheets of paper. 'Here you are, chief inspector.'

The accent, as Bowles had noted, could only be described as 'cut glass'. The tone, however, was faintly condescending. Channon walked away from the house with lips pursed in amusement. Evidently Mr Nollens saw a DCI as a mere servant of the public. And he was right, of course.

Chapter Ten

Channon walked through the grounds towards the water, knowing that in different circumstances he would be enjoying it. The sun was shining, the air was sparklingly clear, and a faint breeze was drifting across the manicured lawns. But for the frost it could have been mid-September.

He rounded a bend and saw the jetty, reached from the bank through an ornamental arch covered in autumn-dark rose foliage and topped by a lamp. Beyond the jetty itself, looking very near and surprisingly low in the water, *Daphne* was rocking gently at her mooring. The constable on deck lifted a respectful hand when he recognized the DCI, who stood waiting under the lamp, deep in thought as he stared at two late roses, their petals edged brown from the frost.

Then Bowles drove up, crunching over the gravel and stopping with a squeal of brakes. He leapt out and called, 'Came as quick as I could, boss!' Carrying the sets of protective gear, he joined Channon and looked edgily at the water. This was not his favourite element, but he gave a seemingly careless shrug. 'How do we get across?' he asked.

'In this little boat,' said Channon. 'Don't worry, it will only take a minute and I'll row. We'll put the suits on first.' Dressed in their white gear the two men crossed the narrow strip of water to *Daphne*, landing at the small rear platform that was used by both boarders and bathers, but even as they stepped on board Channon's mobile was shrilling. Not many people rang him direct unless he asked them to, so he knew it must be answered. He fumbled awkwardly under the white suit, and grunted, 'Channon.'

'Hey, hey,' boomed Eddie Platt's powerful baritone. 'How long have you been on the go, Bill? An hour? Two hours? I'll have you know I took your message to heart and worked all last night, though I did have a kip round here at Regional – on my new inflatable mattress, please note. You wanted me to let you know if we found anything of interest in the Freelander.'

'What? Yes – yes, I did, Eddie.'

'Well then, the answer's yes, there is something of interest – great interest, though I can't say it's exactly clear-cut, black and white, knock-your-eyeballs-out sort of stuff.'

'What is it, then?'

'Traces of blood matching that of the dead man. Definite enough without a DNA check, because of freshness, rare grouping, cell count, etc; though I've put the DNA match in hand, as well. Not only that, there are fibres from his sweater – also an exact match.'

Channon was so surprised his mind went blank for long seconds. Then he said, 'So why do you say it's not clear-cut and so forth?'

'Because there were, literally, just traces – possibly residue from a rapid or incomplete cleaning up. They're inside the vehicle at the rear of the seats.'

'What about the floor covering?'

'Almost clear, except for one faint trace.'

Bowles had heard who was calling and deduced what about, but didn't know which vehicle was involved. He was so curious he had stopped with one leg raised to climb the step to the deck, and looked like a player in the childhood game of statues. Above him, also motionless, the constable was gazing impassively into space.

'The boots, Eddie,' said Channon. 'Is there anything on them?'

'Clean as a whistle,' Eddie replied cheerfully, 'at least clean of anything apart from normal outdoor debris and a few carpet fibres, presumably from inside the lady's home, but I can check them against anything you like. Right, I've been a good boy. Can I go home now for a spot of proper shut-eye?'

'You've earned it,' Channon told him, 'but can I have it in writing at your earliest?'

'Already done, and I'll send it over by messenger – how's that?'

'Brilliant. I still need stuff on the other two you've got there – you know, the Bentley and the Aston Martin. Thanks a million!' He turned to face Bowles, who had hurriedly lowered his leg to a standing position, and was agog to hear more. 'You've gathered who we were talking about?'

'Yes. You mentioned boots, so it must have been Mummy Pascoe's Freelander. Don't say Forensic have found something?'

'They certainly have. Traces of Paul's blood, possibly remaining after an incomplete clean-up. The boots though . . . they're clean apart from normal wear. What do you make of that?'

'She took them off and wore something else for doing the dirty work?'

Channon was dubious. 'It's possible, but I could have sworn she was in the clear. If she'd been up to something why contact us in the first place?'

Bowles concealed a smile. 'Like I said on Saturday, she might have put the body there, then reported she'd been at the scene in case we found traces of her.'

'I don't see it,' said Channon, 'but we've got to look into it – and how!'

'So are we going back there, then?'

'To Trenoon? Not just yet. I want to see what's in the other reports – SOCOs, forensic from the body and any more details from Mr Hunter before I go tackling Mrs Pascoe. And don't object to that, Bowles – I simply can't see her doing a runner. If she was uneasy about her car being examined she'd have bolted when we first took it away.'

131

'She wouldn't be uneasy if she'd cleaned it.'

'Maybe not, but look, we're here now, so we'll give this boat the once-over as we'd planned. Then we go back and check all our facts before descending on Mrs Pascoe.'

'Can't we take her in? We have grounds, surely?'

Channon hesitated. Bowles was right, they did have grounds. The only reason he didn't want to do it was that his instincts were screaming against it. He was so glad to feel them he would have said 'Welcome back' out loud if he'd been alone.

Doubts pushed aside, Bowles was standing obediently at the ready, raring to go. Action always stimulated him. 'Ready when you are, boss,' he said.

Sue Goodchild was emptying the washing machine with one eye on her son in the hall. She saw him putting on his working jacket and went to him, her arms full of wet bedding. 'You're going to Trenoon, then?' she asked blankly.

He looked at her. 'Why shouldn't I? You know I do ten till one on Mondays.'

'I thought it might be an idea to stay away from there,' she said, 'seeing as it's so close to the Stradlings'.'

'So are other houses on this bank. What are you getting at, Mum?'

'You need to keep well away from where Paul lived,' she warned, 'and well away from those he was friendly with. People are saying that the Pascoes all knew him.'

'All? What do you mean, all?'

'Young Jaz has been at the Court, playing games with the local lads, and little Katie – somebody said she'd been on the boat with Paul . . .' She saw that Marty was absolutely still. When he looked at her like that it made her feel a bit funny; not scared, just sort of surprised that he was her own flesh and blood.

'That's two of a family of five,' he said, in the odd, sing-song tone he used when he talked of numbers. 'Two-fifths of a family of five, that's a decimal of 0.4. What about the other 0.6?'

'If you mean Mrs Pascoe, I don't know about her, but don't you think it's likely that Mr Pascoe knew Paul in London?'

'London's a big place,' he said. 'Several million people live there; so no, I don't think it's likely.'

'All right,' she conceded, 'the other daughter, then, that lovely blonde one.'

Martin looked down at his fingers as if he'd never seen them before. 'Her name is Lucy,' he said quietly. 'What about her?'

'I've heard she was friendly with Paul.'

He was still examining his hands. 'Maybe she was. So what?'

She hesitated. It was a mad idea, but it had been in her mind for weeks – ever since the cleaner at the Yardarm had told her she'd seen Paul and the Pascoe girl together in Truro. She said gently, 'I just got the idea, Marty, that you liked her yourself.'

A dull flush rose up from his neck and covered his jaw line. In a minute, thought Sue, he'll start to move his neck all jerky. Sure enough, he gave a twitchy lift of the shoulders and shook his head very quickly. 'Why shouldn't I like her? She's beautiful, she's kind and she's intelligent. Last week we had a coffee together in the kitchen at Trenoon.'

Sue's heart sank. She was right – he fancied Lucy Pascoe. Poor Marty – her poor, poor Marty. Why couldn't he set his sights on somebody who wasn't quite so – out of reach? Some nice girl who worked in a shop in Falmouth, or did the rooms at one of the hotels? He said again, 'Why shouldn't I like her?'

'She seems really lovely,' agreed Sue, 'but that's not the point. Listen, Marty, you've been working at Trenoon two or three times a week for how long? Four months? You like Lucy, you're friendly with Jaz and young Katie, and they've all been involved with Paul Stradling. In case you've forgotten, you took an axe to the Stradlings' boat and did more damage to Paul's cabin than anywhere else on board. The police see you as a possible suspect for his murder.'

This time he didn't wriggle his shoulders. He simply looked at her with the brown eyes that were so like hers, and said, 'Well – they're wrong.'

'*You* know they're wrong, *I* know they're wrong, but that'll make no difference if they find you had another motive for damaging the boat besides getting the sack at the yard. That's why I'm not easy about you staying on at Trenoon – it keeps you connected to the Stradlings through the Pascoes.' She grabbed his arm. 'Marty, *did* you vandalize the boat because Paul was starting to see Lucy?'

'Yes, I did,' he said calmly. 'I told you many a time it wasn't fair that he had so much. Why should he have her, as well?'

'Because they liked each other – maybe they were in love. They were seen together more than once.'

Martin gave a small, chilly smile. 'They won't be seen together again, though, will they?'

She gasped. Was he – what – what was he saying? No, no, of course he wasn't saying *that*! But it had crossed her mind, hadn't it, just for a minute when she first heard about the murder? But then Marty bent his head to her, like he sometimes did, and shook it from side to side in reproof. 'I didn't cut him up and kill him,' he said. 'I'd have liked to, of course, but I didn't. Don't ever mention it again.'

There it was, that tone of voice that made him so different, so old – older than her; but she couldn't do as he ordered – she wouldn't. 'I believe you,' she said, and at that moment she meant it, 'but if I see you doing something that could put you in a bad light with the police, then I *will* mention it, whether you like it or not.'

For a moment there was silence, and she thought he was considering what to say in reply. Then he took his scarf, tied it neatly round his neck and picked up his crash helmet. 'I'd better get off then, or I'll be late,' he said briskly. 'I'll be back at the usual time, soon after one.'

A minute later she heard the roar of his motorbike. So much for doing what his mother tells him, she thought bitterly.

Blue sparked with silver, water lapped lazily against *Daphne*'s hull as the two detectives went up on deck. Some boat, thought Channon as they crossed satin-smooth teak to go back to the dinghy. 'The SOCOs will be here soon,' he told the constable. 'Nobody else allowed on board unless I say so.'

Bowles was eyeing the water with pretended nonchalance, so he spared him any conversation until they were out of their suits and back on dry land. The sergeant concealed his relief and at once mounted his hobby horse. 'How the other half lives, eh, boss?'

'It's a beautiful boat,' Channon agreed. 'The space, the luxury, the style; and if that's how Stradling wants to spend his money – why not?'

'How much, then?' Bowles persisted. 'How much do you reckon it cost?'

Channon sighed. Envy was the blight of Bowles's life. 'I should guess an initial outlay of perhaps three-quarters of a million. Usage and maintenance, I don't know, but hardly peanuts. Forget the money, Bowles, forget the luxury and think of the reason for going on board – we didn't find much, did we?'

There had been no visible signs of murder done, no signs of violence at all; no naughty pictures to be found on the computer – at least, not without forensic examination. But in the sleek fitments of Paul's cabin they did find stacked printouts from a digital camera, and on a lower shelf the camera itself, tossed there as if after hurried use. Channon left the camera alone, but together they looked through the printouts: a variety of pretty young girls displaying their all, some eager and willing, others less so, but none showing signs of force or even coercion.

As Bowles bagged them up for routine removal, he said, 'Not exactly hardcore stuff, boss.'

'No, and none of Lucy Pascoe,' said Channon, adding silently, thank the Lord, and wondered whether the same applied to Amos Heaney's young niece. They'd soon know . . . Then he went on, 'I want all girls from all sources traced and checked.'

'It'll take man-hours,' warned the sergeant.

'I know, but there's no option. Put somebody good on to it. Also, check alibis of close family members of the girls for Friday night.'

'Will do,' agreed Bowles promptly, then as they reached the car, he asked, 'Having seen some of the photos, how do you see Paul himself?'

'On what we've found so far, simply as a highly sexed young man, very attractive to the girls, who liked to take pictures of them for his subsequent private enjoyment. Tresillian was shocked, and his innocence is refreshing, but compared to what I've seen in the past, they're mild. What do you think?'

'The same,' said Bowles soberly, and rather to his own surprise felt relief that the awkward, bossy, red-eyed Stradling wasn't going to be questioned about any sickening hardcore stuff belonging to his son. What was this? he asked himself in alarm. Was he getting like Channon? Was working with the older man making him a softie? Sergeant Bowles was known in the force as a hard copper, so he'd better watch it or his reputation would be down the drain.

They were almost back at the room before he asked himself how Channon came to be so successful, so respected, when he wasn't known as a hard copper at all.

It was a courteous letter, written and apparently delivered by hand, because Helen had found it on the hall carpet before the ordinary mail was due. Her heart twisted with pity as she read Richard Stradling's dignified acknowledgement of her awkward condolences and offer of help.

It seemed he didn't need to either join them for a meal at Trenoon, or accept anything else from the Pascoes; but give the man his due, she thought, he'd taken the trouble to write and say so.

Was he aware that Paul and Lucy had been so close? She had no idea, but at least she could tell her daughter that Paul's dad was composed enough to write a letter. With Jaz and Katie at school, now would have been the ideal time for her and Steve to talk things over with Lucy, whose first difficult tears had given way to that awful howling. Within minutes, in the arms of her mother at last, she had wept with such abandon she'd exhausted herself and they'd persuaded her to go back to bed.

Then, instead of discussing what was happening, Steve had marched off to the studio. That was what they'd agreed, of course; after a couple of hours in there he would continue working in his room, clearing the way for her to use the studio herself, though at that moment nothing was further from her mind.

She needed her husband, she thought desperately, but after shutting him out for so long it seemed wrong to try and lean on him now. She could hardly believe it, but since yesterday her distress about his adultery was fading by the minute. Nothing seemed to matter except their daughter having been involved with the murdered man.

It was no use – busy or not, she would have to disturb him. He was Lucy's dad, he was good with her, with all three of them, come to that; he was part of their life. Expecting to find him at the studio drawing board, she gave a quick knock and went in, to see him slumped at the workbench with his head in his hands.

He turned. The eyes she'd known and loved for more than twenty years were like two black holes in his head. Misery stared at her. It came to her then that he felt just as she did about the horror that engulfed them. Separated or not, they were still as one when it came to their family. The realization of it was like the peal of an organ somewhere inside her. 'Steve, let's talk,' she said.

'Right,' he agreed, 'but first let me say this, Helen. I've got to give the agent an answer today about the barn conversion. I'm taking it. Murder or no murder I can't stay away from you and the family any longer.'

Then words left her lips without thought or preparation. 'I need you here, not across the water,' she said. 'Will you stay until Lucy's all right again? Let's concentrate on doing our best for her and see how things go between you and me.'

'On the same terms as at present?'

'Yes. No more for now. Shall we give it a go?'

'Is a starving man glad of a crust?' he answered, and for the first time in months she saw him smile. He was on his feet now, facing her across the workbench, while next to them the huge window looked out on a panorama where sun was banishing the frost.

'How about you working in here in the mornings and me in the afternoons?' she said.

'That's fine. I'll let them know at the practice. Now, what about Lucy? That howling and weeping! Do we need professional help with her?'

'I don't know. Maybe it's a bit soon for that. She's letting it all out now so that can only be good for her.'

Then he put into words what she'd been thinking and feeling. 'I can hardly believe she was ready to marry a man who'd been sleeping around as much as Paul.'

'I know, but he did tell her about all the others. Perhaps he really loved her, Steve.'

'Maybe he did,' he agreed, 'but it's pretty clear someone didn't love *him*.'

They looked at each other, still without touching. She didn't even think of a time when she might be ready for that again. What mattered right now was that he was back – for all of them.

Channon was greeting DC Les Jolly. Bowles watched, tight-lipped, and decided not to join the welcome party. The high-ups had told *him* – a sergeant with years of experience – that he was low on 'people skills'. If he was low, then Jolly was absolute zero! He couldn't form a question to save his life, his appearance was so at odds with his name it wasn't even a joke; he looked like a moron with stomach ulcers and he had a manner to match – none of which helped in getting info out of a witness or putting the frighteners on a suspect.

Why the DCI wanted him on the team was a mystery, unless it was because Jolly was good at analysing reports and statements. He could list obscure facts that sometimes proved useful, and Channon was obsessed by that sort of thing. He'd said as much – often. 'We're a local force, Bowles,' was his theme, 'so local knowledge of both past and present is pure gold – it's a fact of history.'

Well, history – local or otherwise – couldn't have much to do with this particular case, because the Stradlings weren't local and they'd only been in Pengorra for four or five years. But wait – it *could* be local history if the killer was from where they lived and worked – it could be *London* history. If that were the case the boys from the Met would step in and take all the credit . . .

But then Channon had finished with Jolly and was jerking his head for his sergeant to join him. Typical, thought Bowles grimly; laughing-boy got a smile and a chat but the right-hand man a mere jerk of the head.

'Now,' said Channon, 'sit down and let's see what we've got.'

'We've got enough to bring her in, boss,' protested Bowles.

'I'm aware of it, but I want to clarify things a bit before we dash round there and upset the family without cause.'

Why not wrap the lot of 'em in cotton wool and have done with it? Bowles asked himself. Aloud, he said, 'Cause? Surely a blood match and fibres are cause?'

'Yes, they are,' admitted Channon.

'Well then?'

'We'll look again at Mr Hunter's pathology on the actual death. He believes Paul was knocked senseless elsewhere and then transported to the Menna to be finished off. If Mrs Pascoe did do it, where did she attack him? Did she meet him away from either of their houses, accidentally or by arrangement after leaving her yoga class, knock him senseless and then toss him in the back of the Freelander? Then did she drive him to the Menna after selecting the sharpest knife in her kitchen, or did she carry one as routine in the car? Or keep one in her handbag? *Then* did she lift him two feet up from the road and across a load of brambles to finish him off? And then did she put some bloodstained stuff in the car and finally, neglect to clean it away properly?'

Bowles sighed. 'We might find out if we take her in and grill her, boss.'

Channon ignored him. 'All that cutting – and the only blood to link her to it was a smear or two that she neglected to clean from her car. If you wanted to remove all traces of a killing, would you leave any visible sign for Forensic to find?'

'I might if I was in a hurry, and I might take all my bloodstained clothes off and chuck them in the river. And listen, boss – about the lifting of the body from the road, I was up there with the SOCOs for a while, you know.'

'What of it?'

'There's access to the stone apart from climbing up. Because of the slope of the land you could leave the road at field level if you travel a few yards further on, then double back and approach the stone from the rear. Less brambles that way, too.'

Channon eyed the sergeant. He himself had seen the lie of the land over there, but that aspect hadn't registered. This was yet another thing against Helen Pascoe. He said heavily, 'Well noticed, Bowles. Evidence is mounting, but I just can't see her killing a young man because he's sleeping with her daughter – even a young man with a reputation for the girls. Say she knew of their relationship, and say she was furious, would she have done it in such a way, and at the limit of her physical capabilities? Is it likely she had help from her husband? We know he was down here because he's told us, and it's clear to any observer that he still cares for her. We'll have to get his alibi, if any, for the crucial time.

'Look, get on to the SOCOs, to Fred Jordan in person. He won't like it if he hasn't finished his report, but tell him I want a verbal on the major stuff they got from the ground: footprints, signs of the attacker including footwear, traces of vegetation brought from elsewhere, angle of dragging the body and so forth. I've had nothing from him yet apart from the obvious – that the killer would be bloodied to hell. What did she do with her clothes, Bowles?'

'Like I said, dropped them in the Fal, or she might have been wearing protective stuff, including overshoes, and removed the lot to drive home.'

Channon's mood was sour. 'Certainly she kept her boots clean,' he said. 'Now, I'm going though every detail of what we've got so far. Then, and only then, we'll go to Trenoon.' As he said the words his reluctance to do any such thing was so powerful he felt nausea grab him by the throat. Who'd have the job? he asked himself.

Chapter Eleven

Inspector Addie Savage surveyed the incident room with satisfaction. If there was such a thing as a hive of activity, then this was it. She tried not to be smug, but knew quite well that the smooth running of the enquiry was largely due to her own skills in organization and deployment.

In spite of that, she wasn't sure if she would rather be here, seeing that the place ran like clockwork, or out and about doing the real detection, with Bill Channon and the sergeant. Giving the impatient twitch of the shoulders which was becoming her trademark gesture, she told herself she'd made her decision to stay on the uniformed side years ago, so it was a bit late to start questioning it now.

Her phone rang. 'Ma'am,' said one of the operators, 'I know you said not to disturb him, but there's a call from the City of London division for the DCI. They want to speak to him personally.'

'Put them through to me,' Addie ordered. When Bill had said he mustn't be disturbed except for something vital, he'd had the look that said he meant it. A minute later she put down the phone. Well, well . . . She'd give Bill another quarter of an hour and then she *would* disturb him. What she'd just been told might not be vital, but it was far from trivial, and must be dealt with.

Fifteen minutes later she was outside Channon's room at the same time as Bowles. The model of politeness, he held the door for her and followed her in. It was clear that the DCI was in deep thought, perhaps visualizing the events of Friday night in the light of the reports he'd been reading. He was gazing into space and only reluctantly brought his gaze round to Addie, aware that she wouldn't have come unless it was necessary. She was no shrinking violet, but she knew when to keep her distance. 'What is it, Addie?'

'The City boys wanted you, but I took the call. You arranged with them to go into the Stradlings' personal affairs as well as the business side, and they think you should know that Paul broke up Nigel Nollens's engagement to be married. Apparently Paul went after the woman, she fell for him and finished with her fiancé, though it was less than a month before the wedding. She and Paul had a brief but very public affair, then he dumped her for the next one in line.'

'When was this?'

'About eight or nine weeks ago.'

Channon thought about the timing. The 'next one in line' must have been Lucy Pascoe. He recalled Nollens's bright hazel eyes, guarded and giving no sign that he resented his employer; but then, it was the son and not the father who had stolen his fiancée. 'When did Nollens arrive in Pengorra, Bowles?'

'Yesterday, early afternoon.'

'What, straight from London?'

'That wasn't spelled out, but I assumed so. Stradling had sent for him.'

Channon grunted. If Nollens was still madly in love, he had a motive of sorts for murder, or the humiliation of being dropped so close to the wedding would be motive enough for some people. In his time in the force he had found that motivation for murder varied from the serious and almost understandable to the astoundingly trivial. He well remembered a middle-aged man who insisted that his motive for murdering his wife of twenty years was that he couldn't stand her ideas on decorating the house ... He said, 'Send somebody round to talk to Nollens about how and where he spent the late afternoon and evening on Friday, and to get the usual on who can back his story.'

143

Bowles went out at speed, apparently keen, but thinking that Nollens could have been left to stew until they'd got Mummy Pascoe under the grill. If there was one thing that riled him it was Channon dragging his feet . . .

Addie was still standing there, and asked now, 'Has anything else come up, Bill?'

'Not since Eddie's call about Mrs Pascoe's car. Bowles and I were about to have a final run-through what we've got for Friday night before we go to Trenoon. He's impatient because we have reason to bring her in, but I don't want to do it, Addie.'

'Do you think you're being swayed by the fact that she seems a decent woman and a good mum?'

He answered, 'Yes, to a certain extent, I am, but even if she's the devil incarnate, would she have spent an evening with good friends at the yoga session, sharing supper and chatting, and within half an hour met up with Paul, knocked him out and then killed him in such a way, taking care to leave no clues? I can't see it.'

'Are you saying that the traces in the Freelander were a plant?'

'Yes, I am – a clever plant, arranged so we'd think a hurried clean-up had been done.'

'Was there residue of a cleaning agent?'

'Yes. Faint, but it was there.'

'So if she was telling us the truth about stopping at the Menna because of the plastic bag, whoever did it could have been there out of sight, recognized the car and thought he could implicate her, or at least, throw us off the track. Did he follow her home and then break into the car?'

'I don't think followed her home, because if he hadn't yet killed Paul, he wouldn't have had any blood to plant, would he? Maybe he went round to Trenoon later, in the dead of night.'

Addie pushed up her lips. 'That theory is no easier to swallow than the first one,' she warned.

'I know, but time will tell.'

'You're searching the house?'

He sighed. 'Yes.'

'Good luck,' she said, and left him.

An hour later the two detectives were finishing their work on the reports. Channon bundled them together and tidied his notes. 'Right,' he said, 'to summarize: no source of DNA apart from Paul's, so we'll have no use for the national database; not a smidgen of a fingerprint on his body, on his clothes, the surrounding vegetation or the standing stone itself, but traces of rubber gloves and a fragment of the cuff of one, caught on a bramble. Bog-standard, cotton-lined glove – lightweight; but as the bit we've got hasn't been in contact with the hand itself, no trace of sweat. A minute droplet of Paul's blood, though, even on that tiny scrap.

'No footprints except from rubber boots and we have only two reasonable casts of them because the site was all rough vegetation. No exact sizing, but they were a pair, so it doesn't seem like a joint effort by more than one person. And Fred says the body *was* dragged to the stone by the route you thought of – well done! No traces of the assailant's clothing, so we have to presume that protective gear was worn. This killer was prepared for the act, Bowles. And surprise, surprise, no signs of the knife. Hunter insists Paul was killed some time after the blow to the head, and then –'

Bowles interrupted. 'Why is he so sure, boss?'

'There was a heavy blow to the side of the head, partly on the hair, and subsequent bruising that wouldn't have appeared instantaneously, but over some time – maybe minutes, maybe longer. The skin wasn't broken, but in the hair Forensic found traces of metal grease that's still being analysed. *Then*, on top of the bruise and elsewhere on both the head and any exposed flesh, scratches from the brambles, showing that he was put in place after the bruise was caused. Hunter is pretty reliable on that sort of stuff.

'Also, he's adamant that the killer was fit and strong or was lent impetus by violent rage. That may be the case, but I think that transporting an unconscious man even a short distance would require enough effort to quieten rage.' Channon looked at the sergeant, 'Have I forgotten anything?'

'No, but have you condensed it!' was the reply. 'Boss, even though it seems there was only one attacker, are you going to query exactly how long Papa Pascoe was down here on Friday?'

'As I've already told you, I am,' said Channon wearily. 'Anything else?'

'Yes, you said earlier that one other thing was niggling you.'

'Yes – the earring. The reports haven't said much about it, except that it was pulled off the ear and that it hasn't been found at the crime scene. When the killer took it, would he have slipped it casually into a pocket of his waterproofs? I think not. A diamond worth 100K, however bloodied, is still small in size and easily lost. Most people would handle such a stone with great care, maybe wrapping it up and putting it somewhere safe to be taken away with them.'

Bowles was dubious. 'So what's your point? We've been told the earring was torn off in Paul's final moments of life. Would the killer have paused to wrap it up and put it away when he was about to slit the guy's throat?'

'Perhaps not,' admitted Channon, 'but that diamond is somewhere, and it certainly isn't among what's left of the undergrowth at the Menna. Word went out to all forces on Saturday to watch for it being offered for sale, but the killer will expect that to happen and could be hanging on to it. We might have to wait some time for it to surface. The fact remains – we find the diamond and we find the killer.'

'More likely we'll never see or hear of it again,' said Bowles.

'Possibly.' Channon jumped up. 'You've got the extra men?'

'Ready and waiting.' Bowles would never have admitted it, but after their joint session he was feeling clearer about the mish-mash of facts they were faced with. 'So,' he summed up, 'we're after bloodied clothes, wellingtons, rubber gloves with a bit of the cuff missing, waterproofs or a plastic suit, probably hooded; a slim, strong, very sharp knife, a 100K platinum-set diamond and anything else that could be relevant to the enquiry.'

'Correct. That lot must be listed and read out to the Pascoes, as laid down.'

'Oh.' Bowles could have groaned. Channon always dragged up procedures that pre-dated the Ark.

'The whole shebang is to be strictly by the book, Bowles.'

Bowles sighed. When did Channon do anything that *wasn't* strictly by the book? Then he found himself asking, 'You don't want to do this, do you, boss?'

'I do not,' agreed Channon. 'But if it turns out she's guilty, we don't want errors in procedure, however dated, to prevent us from making a case.'

'So what's the odds on the lads finding any of this lot in the cupboards of Trenoon?'

'You tell me,' retorted Channon grimly. 'Let's go.'

'Hello, Sue, it's only me!' It was Bridget Stumbles' usual cry when she popped into the cottage next door.

Still on edge about her talk with Martin, Sue welcomed her friend. 'Biddy! Come in and have a coffee with me. Why aren't you out on your rounds?'

Biddy stumped into the kitchen and put a damp package on the table. 'I'm not doing Monday mornings any more,' she said heavily. 'Last time my takings barely covered my petrol, so from now on I'm starting my week's work on Monday afternoons.' She patted the parcel she'd brought. 'Jimmy's just been with the fish. A nice bit of plaice, landed this morning. He threw in a couple of fillets for free, so I wondered if you could use them?'

Sue pretended she didn't see through the ruse, telling herself that if you didn't know any different, you'd think Biddy was just a rough, mannish old woman, when in fact her tact and real kindness were legendary. She could come up with more ideas on providing her and Marty with extras to their diet than they could think of ways of refusing. 'Thanks, Biddy,' she said warmly, 'I'll be glad of it. We were only going to have cold beef from yesterday, with maybe a few chips for Marty. He'll come in from his work all hungry, I expect.'

She made instant coffee and was getting out the short-bread when Biddy asked thoughtfully, 'He's gone to Trenoon just as usual, then?'

Sue flopped down opposite her at the table. 'I tried to persuade him not to,' she said uneasily, 'but you know what he's like. The Pascoes have all been involved with Paul, especially Lucy, so I thought he'd be better keeping away for a bit, till the murder's been solved.'

Biddy thought about that, then crossed her legs and jiggled one foot up and down. 'I had a visit yesterday from the detective in charge. He said he might come round sometime to get a bit of local knowledge.'

'He'll be asking the right one, then,' Sue assured her, then added awkwardly, 'Have you heard anything about Marty on your travels, Biddy? You know – are folk saying anything about him having a grudge against Paul?'

'Not a word's been said about him,' declared Biddy stoutly. 'Listen, my love – taking an axe to a boat out of resentment is one thing; taking a knife to do what was done at the Menna is another. I'll get to know the latest when I'm out and about this afternoon – folk treat me like the messenger of the Roads, you know. Going back to the Pascoes – it's getting to be common talk that Lucy was involved with Paul.'

'I'd heard he was one for the girls,' agreed Sue, 'and then the cleaner at the pub saw them together in Truro. Do you know any more?'

'I do cover a bit of ground,' said Biddy, 'in fact, my van's such a familiar sight I reckon folk think it's part of the scenery. I've seen the two of 'em together more than once, and knowing what I know about Paul and his girls, I'd been wondering whether to have a quiet word with Helen to see if she was aware what was going on. I've known her since she was born, don't forget. As a youngster myself, I scattered rose petals at her great-uncle Ben's wedding.'

Sue warned herself to go carefully. Only two or three months ago Biddy's cherished goddaughter had been one of those who fell for Paul Stradling's charms. At first Biddy had been highly pleased that Rosie had attracted a man with money, from London, then on hearing talk from her customers she'd become alarmed about it, and finally shaken to the core that her little girl, as she liked to call her, had joined the ranks of those Paul had tossed aside.

Feeling she should say at least a few words about the girl, just to show she cared, Sue ventured, 'I expect everything's all right with your Rosie now, Biddy?'

The older woman didn't meet her eye. 'She's fine, so I'm told,' she said carelessly. 'I haven't seen her lately, but I did hear she's taken up with the new herdsman at the farm.'

Sue was stunned. Something wasn't right here, she thought. Biddy doted on young Rosie, almost to the extent of being a bore, yet here she was acting as if she didn't know anything about her . . . And then it dawned. It was the murder, affecting Biddy as it was affecting many a one. People were behaving out of character, trying to distance themselves from the Stradlings; anxious to help the police, yet desperate not to become involved. Involved? They'd know the meaning of the word if they had a son who admitted he'd have liked to kill Paul himself, as her Marty had done.

She could hardly credit that she'd been tempted to confide in Biddy about what he'd said. All at once she felt old, very old, and had to remind herself that she hadn't even turned forty. She was tired – tired of her life, it was nothing but hard work and worry about Marty. She looked at the lined, familiar features of the woman across the table and, for the first time ever, wished that Biddy would go back home and leave her in peace.

Helen crept into Lucy's room. If she was awake, she would make the excuse of bringing her a drink, but the real reason she was here was that she needed to be sure they were still in their regained closeness.

She found her awake, propped against a pile of pillows, with sunlight spreading gold across the bed. When her mother came in she sat upright. 'Mum, I can't sleep,' she said tensely, 'but somehow I do feel better after all that crying. It must be true when they say, have a good cry. It *was* good in a way, because my mind's clearer and I've been thinking.'

'So have I, my love.'

'What I want to say is this – I was stunned that someone wanted Paul dead, it was so unreal that everything else seemed unreal as well. I got the idea that everyone had changed and that I was all alone because nobody knew about us being in love. I was aware that you hadn't liked Paul much, and it made you seem like a stranger, or something. I kept forgetting that you're still my mum and dad who love me. I'm sorry for being so horrible.'

Thankfulness flooding through her, Helen sat on the bed and folded her daughter in her arms. 'I think you're allowed to be horrible when the man you love has been murdered,' she said, 'but I'm sorry as well, pet, for thinking I didn't like him. If I'd known you loved him it stands to reason I would have seen all the good things about him, instead of having doubts.'

'That's what I mean. People might see him as just a well-off womanizer, but he felt differently about me than he did about all the others – I know he did.'

In spite of what she'd just said those same doubts were lining up in Helen's mind like soldiers ranking for battle. Ruthlessly she flattened them. History was full of libertines

150

whose lives had been transformed when they found youth and innocence. Perhaps the same thing had happened to Paul? She took a sheet of paper from her pocket. 'His dad has replied to the letter I wrote him,' she said. 'Here, love, I've brought it for you to read.'

Silently Lucy read Richard Stradling's acknowledgement. 'He seems lucid,' she said thankfully. 'In spite of all his money he's a real family man, you know. But now he's lost not only –' She broke off when the doorbell rang.

Helen looked down from the window to see who had called. There were two cars outside the front door, one of them a police car. She could see Martin, garden fork in hand, watching from a border he was working on. 'It's the police again,' she said, taken aback. 'They must have forgotten to ask us something. You stay here, Lucy, unless I give you a call.' Still filled with euphoria about things being right between them, she ran down the stairs and met Steve on his way to answer the door.

'It's the police,' she told him. 'I wonder what they want now?'

'We'll soon know,' he said quietly, and opened the door.

'Mr and Mrs Pascoe,' said DCI Channon. 'Could we have a word?'

What was this? thought Helen. The sergeant here as well! She shot a glance at Steve who was stony-faced at the sight of Bowles. Both detectives were very serious, but Channon was the man in charge, so she concentrated on him. She got the mad idea that he didn't like having to do what he'd come for, and ridiculously, felt the urge to put him at ease. 'Mr Channon,' she said, 'come in and take a seat, and what about your colleagues? Are they coming in?'

'We don't need them at this moment,' he replied cryptically, and the two detectives followed her and Steve into the sitting room, where Channon said briskly, 'You know Sergeant Bowles, I believe? We have a few matters to sort out – with both of you. First: Mr Pascoe – you've already told me that you were in this area on Friday. Perhaps you could tell us the exact times you were here on the Fal, and

151

make a formal statement for our records, which you'll then be asked to sign.'

Steve shrugged with a trace of unease. 'I went to work as usual on Friday morning, then at about nine thirty I took a call from the agent who was acting for me down here. He told me that a property on the Roseland had come up for rent. He described it, it seemed good, and I arranged to see him there at four o'clock. I cleared any urgent stuff at the office and set off at about ten thirty.'

'You allowed yourself five and a half hours. Was that optimistic?'

'Not really. I wasn't leaving London in the Friday afternoon mass exodus, and I told the agent I'd keep in touch by mobile if I was running late. I was at the place ten minutes before he was.'

'You travelled down in your Mercedes?'

Steve blinked. 'No, as a matter of fact, I didn't. It was out of action, having the suspension checked over. They gave me a courtesy car – still a Merc, but a different model, dark blue, soft top.'

'Perhaps you'd give us the details of that car and the name of the garage or dealer who worked on your Mercedes, then, just for the record? And what time did you leave the area of the Fal?'

'I came back across on the King Harry just after five, and set off on the return journey right away. It was a lot of driving, so I stopped for a good meal and a rest at a place just outside Launceston. I got back to Highgate at about eleven.'

Channon was matter-of-fact. 'Perhaps you'll give me a list of names and telephone numbers of people who can verify those timings, including your agent and the place where you stopped for a meal? Also, I need confirmation of the time you got home. Was anyone in the house when you arrived?'

Impatience was simmering in Steve's tones. 'No, there wasn't. What *is* this, inspector? I volunteered the information that I was down here to avoid complications, not to cause them.'

'I'm aware of that, Mr Pascoe, but I must remind you that we're in the early stages of a murder enquiry. I'm merely going through the routine procedure of eliminating you from our enquiries. Perhaps you'd be thinking of those names and addresses while I have a word with your wife?'

Bowles was standing silently in his customary position behind Channon's shoulder, determined not to say a word out of place, but telling himself he couldn't be penalized for thinking. Get a move on, he was urging his superior silently, it's clear as the nose on your face that Daddy-oh has no alibi.

But Channon was already turning to Helen. 'And now, Mrs Pascoe ... did anyone else use your Freelander after you arrived home from yoga on Friday evening?'

She stared at him. What next? 'No, I left it in the court-yard at the back, where we always park our cars.'

'Locked, I imagine?'

'Yes – at least, I think so. Very occasionally I've forgotten. Locking it isn't always on my mind here, as it is when I'm in London.'

'You told me on Saturday, and in your official statement, that it must have been about ten minutes past ten when you stopped at the Menna to try and reach the plastic bag?'

Helen swallowed, suddenly wary. Hadn't she told herself that she wished she'd never mentioned that infernal bag? 'Yes, it was about that,' she agreed.

'So you would have arrived home at, say, between ten fifteen and ten thirty?'

'Yes, I think so.'

'Can anyone substantiate that?'

'What?'

'Can anyone in your household verify the time you arrived home after yoga?'

'My children could, I suppose. Katie was still up, I recall. Jaz was in his room and Lucy – yes – she was watching television.'

'We'll need an extra statement from each of them, then. Jaz and Katie are at school today, I take it? Is Lucy in the house?'

'Yes, upstairs. She's been having a lie-down.'

'We'll see her in a moment. Now, to the main reason for our visit.' Straight-faced, he said, 'Perhaps you'd be more comfortable sitting down, Mrs Pascoe?' then he continued, 'Your Freelander has undergone forensic examination, and I have to tell you that traces of the murder victim's blood have been found inside it, also fibres from the sweater he was wearing when he was attacked.'

Silence descended. Helen could hear her own breathing, quick and heavy as though she was running, rather than sitting down. She knew something awful had been said, but she hadn't taken it in properly. She shook her head. 'I'm sorry, would you repeat that, inspector?'

He did so, with neither more nor less emphasis. Helen was aware that her jaw had dropped because it felt loose and very heavy. 'I don't see how that can be,' she said blankly. 'I told you – I saw nothing suspicious at the Menna.'

Steve, too, seemed to be having trouble comprehending what was going on. 'Did you say the murdered man's blood was found in my wife's car?' he asked in bafflement. 'But it's a mistake – surely you can see that? It must be a mistake.'

'I'm afraid not, Mr Pascoe. There had been some attempt to remove the blood, but traces were left. Our regional forensic experts compared them to copious samples of the dead man's blood, both from his person and the murder scene. They were a match.'

All at once Steve focused. His very dark eyes glittered. 'What's the matter?' he asked in fury. 'Are your superiors pestering you for a result already? You can't find anything to pin on anybody, so you go to the two people who made voluntary admissions – admissions that could be seen as self-incriminating. Can't you see that if either of us had

154

anything to hide, we wouldn't have spoken to you in the first place?'

'Oh, I can see – it's my job to see, Mr Pascoe, and I assure you that I'm not being pestered for a result by anyone. The point you make has already been noted and discussed.' He turned to Helen and said heavily, 'Helen Pascoe, I'm arresting you on suspicion of the murder of Paul Stradling. You do not have to say anything, but it may harm your defence if you do not mention, when questioned, something which you later rely on in court. Anything you do say may be given in evidence.'

'Is that so?' snapped Steve. 'Well, my wife isn't saying anything at all until she has legal representation, and as you seem intent on fitting us both up, I'll have the same.'

'That is your right,' agreed Channon. 'We'll be talking to both of you at the station, but before then I have to inform you, Mrs Pascoe, as the owner of this property, that my men are about to search this house.'

They both gaped at him. Helen felt dread pull at her stomach. *This* was close to home, she thought, it couldn't be closer. This, not those paltry little happenings that had worried her ages ago – no, no, it was only yesterday! She tried to gather her wits. 'What are you looking for?'

He nodded to Bowles, who read out the list they'd worked on earlier. Helen and Steve listened in stunned amazement, each seeming to find a different item remarkable. 'A knife?' she said in disbelief, while Steve, white-lipped, repeated, 'A single diamond?'

Channon was watching them narrowly. 'The law requires us to list what we're searching for,' he said, 'and to offer you the chance to produce the items.'

They continued to stare at him, dumbfounded. He said to Bowles, 'Get the others in.'

Anger was building up beneath Helen's fear. Things were moving too fast for her to keep up. 'What if I refuse? Have you got a warrant?'

'The law decrees that when arresting a suspect, a warrant is not required.'

But this was Trenoon, she thought in confusion, her lovely Trenoon, not some seedy criminal hang-out. This man was going to let his officers tramp around the rooms, searching for things that weren't there. She looked hard into his eyes, and could have sworn she saw pity there, then she turned to Steve, who put his hand over hers. It felt big and lean and comforting, and she relaxed for an instant. This was some horrible mistake. They would sort it out. Everything would be all right – wouldn't it?

Chapter Twelve

The school bus was crowded and very noisy. Jaz and Katie had come on board with their friends, each aiming for the other through the crush. 'Hi, Midget,' he said; 'Hi, Beanpole,' she answered, then by unspoken agreement they found a seat and for the first time in months sat next to each other to travel home.

At once Jaz asked, 'Have you heard the latest? They're questioning someone about the murder. We saw it on the computer news update during IT.'

Katie was aggrieved. 'Well, it must have been after our lesson at two o'clock! We were all chasing the latest bulletin before we started, but when we brought it up there was just a rehash of what was on at breakfast time, with new shots of boats on the Roads and various standing stones. They were still saying that the murder could be linked to prehistoric sacrifices.'

'Yeah, I know, but we saw this update just before the bell went at three thirty. It said a woman was helping the police with their enquiries.'

Katie narrowed her eyes. 'A *woman*? Everyone says that Paul was cut to pieces and then tied to the stone. Would a woman be strong enough to do that?'

'A mature woman,' said Jaz, patting her hand consolingly, 'not an under-age midget.'

She rolled her eyes. 'A midget can do things and get into places where an oversized person wouldn't fit. Listen – do you think Mum will let us go out and around on our own again?'

'Sinbad says he's going to demand it from his parents. We've discussed it and we're both confident that if someone attacked us, we're capable of defending ourselves.'

Katie was nothing if not down-to-earth. 'You're talking about carrying a knife?' Everybody knew it was commonplace for boys to carry knives, even in Cornwall, but she was pretty sure that Jaz didn't. Their mum and dad had made a rule about it years ago.

Jaz shrugged and tried to whisper something, but she couldn't hear him because of the noise. He leaned closer to her ear. 'One of the Year 12 kids has been saying he knows where to get guns. So think about this – if I let you walk with me to and from the bus, would you rather I was armed, or not?'

She hesitated, torn between the excitement of deadly weapons and the thought of her mother's reactions. 'If the police have got someone, then not!' she said. 'Because it wouldn't be necessary, would it? Honestly, Mum would go mental if she thought you were carrying a knife, and she'd die of shock if you so much as mentioned a gun. Sinbad isn't getting one, is he?'

'I don't think so,' he admitted reluctantly.

Katie kept silent for a minute, then asked, 'This woman . . . did they say who she is?'

'No. They hardly ever give the name of someone they've arrested unless it's a celebrity.'

'Everyone in my year thinks the killer's from London, because it's where Paul lived and worked. It could be a wealthy woman who's invested heavily, then lost all her money because Paul gave her bad advice.'

'A woman he's dumped, more like.' Jaz tried to appear worldly-wise, but only managed to sound envious. 'Some of my friends say he had the girls queuing up for him.' Suddenly his voice seemed very loud, because the noise of more than thirty youngsters laughing and chattering had died away to uneasy muttering. Puzzled, they both looked around them, but not even Sinbad or Katie's friend Holly would meet their eyes.

Just then the bus stopped at the first dropping-off point, and several youngsters jostled each other as they got off. Katie's eyes swivelled over those who were left. 'Are they being a bit funny with us?' she asked. 'What's going on?'

Jaz wriggled in his seat. He thought he knew. Earlier in the day some of the kids in his year – ones he'd thought of as mates – had asked smart-alec questions about what was it like to be connected to a murder. They'd thought it was funny, so he'd laughed it off and stretched up a bit to show how tall he was in case it came to a bit of rough stuff.

He shot a glance at Katie. Usually she got on his nerves, but right now he had an overpowering urge to protect her. 'Nah,' he said, seemingly careless, 'they're just talking among themselves. Take no notice.'

There were more drop-offs before Pengorra, and Sinbad was due to alight before them. As the bus neared his stop he made his way between the seats to Jaz and Katie, looking concerned and self-conscious. 'Cheers, Jaz,' he said awkwardly, 'uh – see you tomorrow – you as well, Katie,' then blundered away to the exit.

Jaz stared after his best friend. Something was wrong – he was sure of it. But they'd be in Pengorra in a minute, and after that in the car with their mum or their dad, so why upset Katie by saying he was worried?

In that instant it never even occurred to him to think of his sister as 'Midget'.

Chrissie Boon sat in her car with Lucy at her side, waiting for the school bus to arrive at the village green. They could hear the sound of voices and the ringing of telephones from inside the tent, but out in the fading sunshine it was cold and very quiet, with police cars edging the grass alongside those of parents waiting to meet their children.

It seemed to Chrissie that there was a third occupant of her car, a half-obscured creature leaning over from the back seat, whose name was Unreality, because it wasn't real that Helen had been arrested on suspicion of murdering Paul

Stradling, it wasn't real that Steve was with the police answering questions, with the possibility of being arrested as well. She gave Lucy's arm a squeeze. 'This all seems a bit weird, doesn't it, my love, but I'm sure your mum and dad will be home before you know it.'

Lucy looked at her with her huge green eyes. 'When Mum told me that Channon had cautioned her like they do on TV I simply couldn't believe it, but when he actually arrested her I just cried and cried. I couldn't help it. D'you think Dad will be allowed to stay with her?'

'I don't know, my love,' Chrissie said gently. That was a lie, she told herself. Her limited knowledge of police procedure told her that Helen would be questioned with only a solicitor at her side. Right now she needed to keep Lucy talking so she wouldn't get too worked up about what she was going to tell her brother and sister. 'Did your mum and dad ask for anyone in particular as a legal representative?' she asked.

'They've hardly ever needed one down here. They said that taking over the house six years ago was simple, because it was a straight legacy, but in the past Mum's family dealt with an old-established firm in Falmouth. They've sent a man over to be with them both, but the firm said if it turns out to be more than a single interview they'll recommend somebody who's more accustomed to criminal procedure.'

She sat next to Chrissie and found herself mouthing the words silently to try and get used to them: criminal procedure . . . criminal procedure . . . The idea of her mother being involved in any such thing was beyond her comprehension. She wanted to cry again, but it was becoming clear that she couldn't keep on crying; she would have to be strong, and it was going to be hard, because she knew quite well that she wasn't a strong person.

She looked at the woman next to her. Darling Chrissie, who had been dragged across to Trenoon at a moment's notice . . . She clutched the older woman's arm and said, 'Chrissie, I'm so worried that I won't be able to do what I

160

should do for the family. I'm so tired, you see. I've hardly slept since it happened and I haven't a scrap of energy or initiative. It's as if my brain has stopped working.'

Chrissie was a great believer in squeezes, so she gave her another one. 'My brain can work for both of us,' she said warmly. 'I'll be with you for as long as you need me, and – oh, here's the bus! It's just possible that they've already heard what's happened, you know; but whatever we say to them, I think it will have to be the truth, don't you?'

Lucy dredged resolve from the morass that had replaced her mind. 'I'll tell them,' she said, 'but will you be right next to me, in case I cry?'

Lucy was waiting as they left the bus. Lucy – with Chrissie? Jaz and Katie stopped in their tracks, and without knowing he was doing it, Jaz held his sister close. They both spoke at once. 'Where's Mum and Dad?' asked Katie, but Jaz, forewarned, said quietly, 'What's wrong?'

And Lucy – emotional, bereft and always doubtful of her own capabilities, somehow managed to put her arms round both of them. 'There's been a mix-up,' she said calmly. 'They're both at the station helping the police.'

His mind racing, Jaz looked down at the other three. This was why Sinbad had been weird, why the kids on the bus were muttering to each other. Someone had heard what had happened – maybe they'd ignored the ban on mobiles and had theirs with them. He felt a bit sick and was furious with himself. This was no time to start throwing up.

Katie was staring at her sister. The last time she saw her she'd looked ill, really ill – yet she'd come to meet them, to tell them, and so had Chrissie. She had to ask. 'They said on the news that a woman is helping the police – a *woman*. Is it – is it Mum?'

'Yes,' said Lucy, and didn't shed a tear.

Just then one of the parents called across as she walked away with her child. 'What a to-do, eh? They'll be after me next, I shouldn't wonder!' Another woman with two

161

teenagers came across and gave Katie a kiss. 'Don't you worry, my precious,' she said, 'they have to follow their funny old rules, you know, do the coppers.' There were one or two other reassuring comments, and a rapid, embarrassed hurrying away by another woman, and then the three Pascoes and Chrissie were alone beneath the big oak tree.

'Your mum asked me to come over in case I was needed, with Lucy being so tired, and things a bit mixed up,' explained Chrissie. 'I'll be in charge of your evening meal – so you've been warned!'

But as always, Katie was concerned with facts. 'Why are they *both* with the police when it only mentioned a woman on the news?' she asked, scowling in concentration. 'Chrissie, they haven't arrested her, have they?'

Chrissie opened the doors of her car, and couldn't help sighing. 'Yes, my love, they have.'

Katie ran fingers through her hair and exchanged a look with Jaz. Then she waved a hand at the tent and the caravan. 'So is she here, in Pengorra? Is Dad here, as well?'

Lucy spoke up. 'No, they've both gone to the main police station with Mr Channon.'

'Not the sergeant, then? He's not with them?' That was Jaz, all at once looking so tall and thin it seemed that a puff of wind could blow him over.

'No,' Lucy said firmly, 'just some rather nice men in uniforms.'

So much for sticking to the truth, thought Chrissie. A minute later she drove away from the village and headed for a mist-wreathed Carrick Roads and the warmth of Trenoon.

'How's it going, boss?' Bowles had to ask, even though he was livid at being kept out of the interview room.

Earlier, Channon had been unmoved by his protests. 'You want to know my reasons for not having you in there with me?' he asked quietly. 'Where shall I begin? One, Mrs

Pascoe doesn't trust you to be unbiased – and don't say you're surprised by that. Two, she's so tensed up I'll get more out of her when I've calmed her down, and I'll do that more quickly without you. Three, unlike you, I'm pretty sure it's a fitting-up that's given us grounds to bring her in, and I wouldn't have done it if there'd been any other option. Four, I don't want to feel disapproval oozing out of you when I treat her with basic respect and consideration, and five, her lawyer is one of the old school who probably doesn't know the meaning of grilling a suspect like a pork chop. How's that for starters?' He looked at the sergeant, flipped a dismissive hand, then went into the room and closed the door behind him.

Teeth gritted, Bowles decided to think about all that later. For now, he wasn't going to waste his time on mumbo-jumbo. He would chase the team he'd put on to checking the girls in the diary and photographs, just to make sure they were earning their wages.

Now, fifteen minutes later, Channon had emerged, leaving Helen Pascoe and her elderly adviser still at the table. Swallowing the remnants of his pride, Bowles asked again, 'Boss? Did you get anything?' A likely scenario occurred to him. 'Don't tell me she's weeping?'

'No, she's quite calm, Bowles – in fact, she's unshakeable. She says she didn't know how close Paul and Lucy were until after the killing, but admits she thought he was too sophisticated and worldly-wise for Lucy. She's adamant that she saw nothing untoward at the Menna, and didn't see Paul all evening. She has no idea how the blood and the fibres got into her Freelander.'

'Is she lying?'

'No.' Channon didn't soften the word with an 'I don't think so' or 'Not as far as I can tell'.

The single negative made more impact on Bowles than a detailed analysis would have done. Grimly he told himself that Helen Pascoe was proving an unlikely killer. 'I've had a call from uniforms at the room,' he said. 'They've checked with Jaz-boy and the gremlin. They've both given

163

times for their mum getting in from yoga, and they tally with what Lucy told us – ten twenty, give or take a couple of minutes. None of the three can confirm or deny if she went out again later.'

'Unless we find somebody who saw her elsewhere after ten twenty we're going to have to let her go,' Channon told him. 'You can join me in a final session with her when I've dealt with the husband.'

'Oh, yes, the husband.' Bowles didn't allow even the vestige of a smile to surface. 'Before you start on him, here's a copy of a message from the City division of the Met. Inspector Savage faxed it through while you were with Mummy-oh. You might see it as significant, or you might not.'

Channon read it. 'Of course I see it as significant!' And how, he thought. His contacts in the City police were saying that Stradling and Son had driven a tough deal when putting up capital for a massive extension of both the premises and the practice itself at the firm of architects where Steve Pascoe was a partner. Not only that; quite legally, they'd exacted a penalty clause when the first and largest repayment was late by only a matter of hours. He looked at Bowles. 'Another motive surfacing, would you say?'

Bowles lifted his shoulders. 'Only if it affected Pascoe personally. I should have thought a firm of top architects could have weathered a penalty or two.'

'What if they were coping with a cash-flow problem or a liquidity block – you name it – and they were already in debt to the firm they usually turned to for help?' asked Channon thoughtfully. 'What if the partners had to stand surety, or whatever these people do when they're guaranteeing big money? That would hit Steve Pascoe's pocket, wouldn't it?'

'Yes, I suppose it would.'

'Look, said Channon, 'here's the number of the man who got me this information. Talk to him – tell him I've authorized you to do it. Get his opinion on Pascoe's involvement and report back to me. To save time I'll start on the interview, and – wait for it – you can interrupt and tell me what you've found out.'

Bowles was highly pleased. Better to talk to a big noise in London than sit listening to Channon pussyfooting round the demon king. With a spring in his step he made for the stairs and the privacy of his own tiny office.

When Steve Pascoe was brought in his first words were, 'Where's my wife?'

'Relax,' said Channon. 'She's being looked after and somebody's getting her some tea.' The young constable on duty at the door listened with interest as he started: 'Now, I've gone through your recent statement and we've checked with the place where you say you stopped for a meal on the way back to London. They have no record of a payment by card.'

'Probably because I paid cash. It's not unknown, even today.'

'Quite. So you confirm you paid cash for the meal. Do you happen to have the till receipt? And what did you have to eat, Mr Pascoe?'

'I don't think I kept the receipt. I usually throw them out if I pay cash for food and drink. As for what I ate – standard stuff, but it was good. A steak and salad, fruit juice to drink, then various cheeses followed by coffee.'

At his side the solicitor leaned back in his chair, maybe thinking that his client discussing a meal was less harrowing than the client's wife answering questions about a murdered man's bloodstains.

From across the table Channon watched Steve Pascoe with interest. He seemed to be just an intelligent man who had cheated on his wife and now bitterly regretted it. The instinct that sometimes screamed at him about a witness was at this moment dormant. Irritation was there in the man; frustration, concern for his wife, maybe even fear of being involved in a murder, but either he had acting ability

165

to match his theatrical good looks, or he had nothing to hide about how he spent Friday evening.

'You've said you have no witness to confirm what time you arrived back in Highgate, Mr Pascoe, but tell me, how did you spend your Saturday morning?'

'I slept late. It must have been about ten by the time I finished breakfast. After that I did some work on my current commission. I didn't go out.'

'Did you make or receive any phone calls during the morning?'

'There was a message, but I didn't listen to it until later, when I found it was somebody at work about seeing a client on Monday – today, that is. It's been put on hold because I'm here.'

'I believe your younger daughter rang you and asked you to come down to join the family? What time would that be?'

Steve shifted on his seat. 'This is all a matter of checking up, isn't it? Is it usual for an officer with the rank of Chief Inspector to question a witness about this sort of thing in an official recorded interview?'

Channon's dark eyes observed him carefully. 'Only when we're investigating a brutal murder and the witness's wife is under suspicion, Mr Pascoe; or, as in your case, when there seems to be bad feeling between the witness and the victim.'

'Bad feeling? What do you mean by that? I hardly knew the man.'

'Our colleagues in the City have been checking on the Stradling company's affairs. It seems they drove a hard bargain recently when dealing with your firm.'

'Yes, as a matter of fact, they did, but it was just business. They were pretty tough and my firm had a difference of opinion with them, but –'

There was a knock at the door and Bowles showed his face. 'Boss – a minute?'

Channon went out to him. 'Well?'

'You were right. Your contact says the four partners all had to stump up a considerable sum. He isn't sure how much, but if he finds out he'll let you know.'

'Right. Come in and join us, then.'

Channon switched on the tape again, noting the look of dislike that Pascoe directed at the sergeant. 'Now, Mr Pascoe,' he said firmly, 'we know that you and your partners each had to put a sum of money into your business because of the Stradlings.'

'Then no doubt you also know what the senior partner had for breakfast and the colour of the tea lady's eyes?' asked Pascoe tightly.

'We know a great deal,' agreed Channon, 'and I assure you we'll know even more before long. Did you put money into the business?'

'Yes, but only as a temporary measure. It wasn't a good time for me, as I was a bit pushed for capital.'

Oh, diddums, thought Bowles. You could have sold your Merc to raise a bit, then you could have driven an ancient banger, like I had to do for years . . .

But Channon was forging ahead with his questions. 'So were you upset at the way the Stradlings were dealing with you?'

'I was annoyed. I thought they were high-handed and almost ruthless, even for financiers.' Dark eyes looked into dark eyes. 'I was *annoyed*, inspector, not demented enough to come down here and hack the Stradling son to death.'

Channon eyed him calmly. 'My colleagues in the City will be continuing their investigation. Now, to return to the phone call that brought you down to the Fal on Saturday. How did your daughter contact you? On your landline in Highgate, or on your mobile?'

Pascoe glared at him. 'I hope you haven't been badgering her about it?'

'Strange to relate, we rarely badger twelve-year-olds, and then only on matters of extreme urgency. I'm asking you, not your daughter. If you can't remember we can find out from the phone company.'

Reluctance to answer showed in the thinning of Pascoe's lips; he was well aware of what would be checked. 'It was on my mobile,' he admitted. 'Katie always contacts me on it because I'm out and about so much.'

'So you could have been anywhere when you took her call?'

'Yes, I could. But I wasn't anywhere, I was at my drawing board in Highgate. I think it was about 3 p.m.'

'Thank you. We haven't yet finished our work on eliminating you, but you're free to go for the time being. Your wife can join you when we've had a final word with her, but neither of you must leave the Falmouth area without telling us.'

Pascoe flipped a weary hand. 'We're hardly likely to make a bolt for South America! We won't be going far, inspector.'

'I'm glad to hear it,' said Channon smoothly. 'The constable here will show you to the waiting area and your wife will join you there, then my men will drive you home. Let me say again, Mr Pascoe, our enquiries are proceeding.'

'You've made that abundantly clear,' was the icy reply, and Steve Pascoe allowed himself to be led from the room.

Channon watched him go, and turned to the silent Bowles. 'What do you make of him?'

The sergeant said carefully, 'He's bright, angry, sarky as hell and aware he's on a tightrope. So what's next, boss?'

'What do you suggest?'

Bowles let out an impatient breath. Every now and then Channon put on his mortarboard, as if he was working with an amateur. 'Pretty obvious,' he said coolly. 'Give the courtesy car a going-over.'

Channon almost smiled. 'Just checking! Contact the nearest station to the Mercedes dealer. Tell them I say will they go and get the car and take it straight to the London Forensic. I'll see they deal with it quickly.'

Bowles went off, thinking that this was his lucky day. He'd been spared Channon pussyfooting around the demon

168

king, and now he was to escape the final soft-soaping of Mummy-oh.

As it turned out there was no soft-soaping of Helen Pascoe, no word of apology from the detective, no word of sympathy. He found her draining a mug of tea to the very dregs, and telling herself she could have drunk a gallon of it. Her mouth was dry, her lips were dry, her eyes were dry, because she was beyond weeping. Earlier, she wouldn't let a single tear fall, because she knew that once she started she might not be able to stop. She was very tired; but that was hardly surprising – it wasn't every day she was arrested on suspicion of murder.

'You and your husband are free to go, Mrs Pascoe – he's waiting for you. I've explained to him that we may need to talk to both of you again. Don't leave the area without telling us.'

'That's it, is it? I think you should clarify my position, inspector. Am I still under suspicion of murder?'

'I'm afraid so. I could keep you in the cells here, but I've chosen not to do that.'

Through the fear and tension it came to her again that this man didn't want to do all this. 'Thank you,' she said quietly, and went to join Steve.

Chapter Thirteen

Chrissie watched the three young Pascoes with bemusement. She'd aimed for a simple family meal of pasta with a cheesy sauce, garlic bread and a big salad, but it seemed the young ones had other ideas.

They were so relieved their parents were coming home they were behaving as if planning a celebration. Lucy had done a smoked salmon starter, then she and Katie laid the table with good linen and china and ranks of candles, while Jaz unearthed the best glasses and raided the wine rack for something that looked special. Chrissie went along with it, but couldn't help feeling that a celebration might be premature.

When Helen and Steve arrived there were hugs and kisses from the girls, a squeeze for his mum from Jaz and, animosity forgotten, a vigorous handshake for his dad; then they were ushered to a sofa in front of the fire and given a gin and tonic each. Next to them Lucy wept quietly, presumably from either joy or reaction, Jaz hovered with more cut lemons and tonic water like a wine waiter in a restaurant, and Katie ground her teeth and studied the list of questions she'd prepared.

Helen was exhausted, but couldn't help thinking that it was almost worth being arrested if it brought her children to such a degree of harmony. At her side Steve was trying to appear relaxed and good-humoured, but she could tell he was still on edge after his session with Channon.

Then Katie came to stand in front of them on the

hearthrug. 'Well,' she demanded, 'are we going to have a family discussion?'

'What do you want to know, pet?' asked her father.

'Why did they arrest Mum when she was at yoga all evening and then with us? Why did they question you as well? Are they questioning anyone else?'

Steve exchanged a look with Helen. Each knew that the other was wondering how much to say in front of Lucy. They'd discussed it on the way home in the police car, but it wasn't quite so easy to tell nothing but the truth with her mopping her eyes and trying to be brave.

'You remember the police taking my car away to be examined?' she said carefully. 'Well, they found a – a clue inside it that made them suspect me, and so they had no option but to take me in. I just told them the truth about what I did on Friday evening. They had no further grounds to keep me, so they sent me home.'

'They found a clue?' echoed Katie. 'What?'

'Something to do with Paul,' said Steve flatly. 'Look, pet, we're not going to go into details at this stage. Leave it at that.'

But Katie wasn't prepared to leave it at all. 'Paul's never been in Mum's car,' she said. 'Somebody must have planted evidence.' Even to herself it sounded thrilling, and she tried not to look pleased that she'd thought of it.

'Maybe they did,' agreed Helen wearily. 'Inspector Channon is working on it. Things aren't really sorted out yet, and he may have more questions before we're cleared.'

Jaz didn't like the sound of that. 'But we're all set to celebrate you being free of suspicion,' he protested hoarsely. 'We intended it to be a sort of party.'

Helen swallowed a sigh. The thought of sitting through a celebration meal with the memory of Channon's calm dark eyes assessing her and with Lucy at the table trying to look as if she was enjoying it was more than she could stand, but all she could say was, 'Then we'll celebrate that we're back home. Thanks, Chrissie, for being here when we needed you.'

Chrissie gave her a hug, 'I'm always here when you need me,' she said. 'Haven't I said so, many a time? I'll put the pasta on as soon as you're ready to go to the table.'

But Katie wasn't going to listen to such ordinary talk. First things first, was her motto. 'Why did they question you as well, Dad?'

'Because I was down here on the Fal on Friday. I hadn't told any of you, but I mentioned it to Channon, and he needed to eliminate me from his enquiries, that's all. And before you ask, I came down to look at a place to rent over on the Roseland, but your mum has asked me to live at Trenoon until they catch the murderer, just to keep an eye on things.'

Katie beamed. 'Good. We need you here. That's what I've been saying for ages.'

'I'm starving,' announced Jaz. 'Can we eat?'

Lucy said nothing. She simply draped herself over her mother, gave her a kiss, then led the way to the dining room.

Following the others, Jaz let out a long, relieved sigh. He wasn't sure how he felt about his dad coming back to live with them, but having him here was a lot better than being the only man in the house when there was a murderer on the loose.

Channon was pleased to find that it was DC Yates who had talked to Nigel Nollens. He liked Yates; he was conscientious, unassuming and intuitive – no intellectual, but with a real gift for hearing more in a person's answer than mere words. Now, the young detective was ready to report on what he had learned from the jilted Nollens. 'So what did you think of him?' asked Channon.

'Self-confident, clever, efficient and prepared to be Stradling's secretary as a stepping-stone to better things.'

'Did he say as much?'

'Uh, no, sir, I just sort of picked it up.'

'I see. So how did you tell him that we know he was dropped by his fiancée?'

'I put it to him that our investigations were revealing that Paul was a womanizer, and had he any views on that.'

'Didn't he see it as an obvious opener to get him talking?'

'Of course he did. He was pretty rude about it, and made it clear he thought I was a prying busybody.'

Channon remembered being sent out on similar interviews many years ago, and nodded in sympathy. 'Did you manage to get him talking?'

Yates half-smiled. 'I think he was wanting to talk to somebody, and saw me as a thick copper who was no threat. He was careful not to sound bitter about Paul; in fact, he said he was glad his fiancée had fallen for him before the wedding, rather than after.'

'Do you think he was humiliated?'

'I'm sure of it. He says she was beautiful and that when they got engaged everyone thought they were a perfect couple. I got the impression that Paul simply crooked his finger and she went running. Nollens's actual words were, "He tempted her and she was like a woman bewitched."'

'What did she do when Paul dropped her?'

'Went back to Nollens and said it had been a terrible mistake.'

'And?'

'He told her she'd spared him making an even bigger one by marrying her.'

'So there's no reconciliation?'

'No chance of one, as far as I could tell.'

'Do you think he was so angry with Paul he was driven to murder?'

'It's hard to say. He's a pretty deep type, but he seemed more angry with her than with Paul.'

'Mm. Has he got an alibi for Friday evening?'

'He was a bit stunned when I asked him. I don't think it had occurred to him that we'd do a check on him. He says he was at home in his apartment and didn't go out. No witnesses or phone calls. He's coming here at six to make a statement.'

'How did you see him in relation to Richard Stradling?'

'Nollens is a self-contained type for a secretary, but seems to respect his boss. In his case the term secretary covers a lot – he's a sort of PR man for Stradling – a general factotum and a bit of a fixer.'

Channon was thoughtful. 'Right. Good work. Will you see I get a copy of his statement? And Yates, if anything strikes you as important, or odd, you can come to me direct, you know. I've told you that before, haven't I?'

'Yes, you have, sir. Thank you sir.'

Channon watched him leave the room, and let out an irritated breath. Clearly, Nollens was just one more to add to the growing list of suspects. He went to find Bowles, who was holding forth to a group of uniformed officers. Seeing Channon, he left them and said, 'Boss, we're getting bogged down with Paul's girls.'

'Bogged down or not,' replied Channon, 'they've got to be sorted and eliminated. What's Les Jolly doing?'

Mentally Bowles rolled his eyes, but showed no visible signs of impatience. He was getting a bit tired of Yates and Jolly being spoken of as if they were the cream of the force. Good-boy Yates was too soft and as for Jolly – he was halfway to being a moron. How he'd ever managed to cross over from uniforms was a mystery. 'Les is doing what you told him to do,' he said evenly, 'going through the house-to-house stuff and checking statements with that lad from the station and Honor Bennett.'

'I'll have a word with him later,' said Channon thoughtfully, 'and Bowles, liaise with Inspector Savage and arrange a full briefing for 8 a.m. tomorrow.'

But before Channon had time to seek out Jolly, the mournful detective came to his office with a sheet of paper. 'You did say to mention direct anything I saw as relevant,' he said.

'Yes, yes, so what have you got?'

'A report just in – on a doorstep interview in Flushing. The son of the family says he knows Martin Goodchild – he'd been out with him and a few others on Saturday nights in Falmouth town. The lad – one Ricky Dash – said that a couple of weeks ago their group of friends saw Paul leaving a hotel bar with Lucy Pascoe. They made a joke about her being the latest of many and Martin got very annoyed and defended her. There's no mention of him making any threat against Paul but young Dash said it was clear to them all that Martin was keen on Lucy – he'll know her because he works at Trenoon.' Jolly said no more, but his sad, drooping eyes were watchful, showing his awareness that what he had said was significant.

Channon recalled the oddness of Martin Goodchild, the fact that he had spent Friday evening alone in the house, without witnesses, while his mother was at her work behind the bar. Now he said irritably, 'I gave instructions to all those on the doors that anything of interest was to be rung in right away, not buried in paperwork!'

'I know you did, sir, but this interview only took place at lunchtime – that's why Ricky was at home. The constable who spoke to them probably didn't see it as particularly urgent.'

'But you did.' Channon nodded with satisfaction. 'Thanks, Jolly – carry on, carry on. And another thing, I haven't had time yet to talk to the staff at Pengorra Court, though Bowles was in charge of taking their statements. Will you have a close look at what they said, and if there's anything to query, let me know?'

Jolly went off with his face contorted in the nearest he ever came to a smile. Bowles, sitting nearby munching a pasty, watched him go. 'Laughing-boy getting well in,' he told himself moodily, and took another bite.

Seconds later Channon joined him, waving his copy of the Dash family's interview. 'Read this,' he said, pushing aside the paper napkin holding the pasty and plonking the report in its place, 'then tell me what I'm thinking.'

Bowles studied it and thought that the question was hardly the conundrum of the year. He sighed. 'One – you're annoyed it wasn't rung in direct, as you'd ordered, and two – we've got to go and see Marty-boy again and maybe talk to this kid in Flushing.'

'Correct. Have a word with the constable who dealt with the Dash family, but later – and don't wipe the floor with him – we all have to learn how to sort the wheat from the chaff. Before that, we're off to the Goodchilds again, with luck in time to see the mother before she goes to work – no – she doesn't go in on Mondays.'

'Or any other night,' Bowles reminded him. 'She's laid off.' He crammed the last chunk of pasty into his mouth and swallowed as they headed for the car. 'Are you having Martin in, boss?'

'Don't rush it, Bowles. We'll see what he says and at the same time watch his mother. She's no good at hiding her thoughts.'

Sue was washing up after the evening meal. The low spirits that had descended when Biddy called were still wrapped round her, seeming to take the air she breathed, like mist on a winter's day. She even felt breathless as she was drying the dishes.

She could hardly credit what Marty had told her when he came in from work – and now folk were talking about it in the cottages and round the village green. There was a feeling of outrage that born and bred Cornish folk were being taken from their homes to the police station because a madman had been at work. Marty was shocked, she could tell, but he wouldn't discuss it. After telling her what he'd seen at Trenoon all he would say was, 'As responsible parents Mr and Mrs Pascoe couldn't have been happy to have their daughter seeing so much of Paul – not if they knew his reputation for sleeping around.'

She would never get used to his way of saying things. His remarks were a mix of old-fashioned pronouncements and modern talk that he'd picked up from his mates. She'd asked him what he meant, but he'd folded his lips together, like he sometimes did, and that was the signal he'd say no more, so she didn't know what to think about Mr and Mrs Pascoe.

Were they still at the police station, she wondered; they weren't *suspects*, surely to God? But if they were . . . *No!* She dismissed the thought, because it was wicked. She was a wicked woman. She'd been ready to tell herself that if the police suspected the Pascoes it must mean that they didn't suspect Marty – her Marty, who was calmly waiting for the television news while she was worrying herself to death as she stood at the sink.

When the doorbell rang she called to him to answer it, coming from the kitchen in her pinny to find the chief inspector and the sergeant walking through the door. It was funny, but she really was breathless. She stood at Marty's side as Channon said politely, 'Mrs Goodchild, Martin, we'd like another word, if you please,' and she knew, she just *knew* what it was about.

Bowles weighed her up and told himself he knew fear when he saw it. This woman was well aware of what her son had been up to, but she was trying to conceal it, ushering them to seats and talking fast to cover Martin's silence.

'We have some questions,' Channon began briskly. 'Martin is of age, Mrs Goodchild, so we could talk to him alone, but we have no objections to you being present. Now, Martin, our enquiries have revealed that you were aware of Paul Stradling being close to the Pascoes' daughter, Lucy.'

Sue let out breath. She'd known it, known they'd find out about him being keen on her. Marty, she warned silently, be careful!

Martin wasn't pleased by the question, but he looked Channon in the eye. 'Yes, I was aware of it.'

'For how long, Martin?'

'Several weeks – since they met at the party at Paul's house.'

'Were you there?'

'No, but a friend of mine plays in a band that had been booked for the evening. He told me about the party.'

'And what did he tell you?'

'That Paul started the evening with one girl but spent all his time with another – Lucy.'

'How did you feel about that?'

Martin's eyes rested for a moment on his mother, and she knew that, though he would never say so, he was remembering her warning against him going to Trenoon that morning. 'What do you mean, how did I feel?' he asked edgily.

'Did you feel jealous?'

'Why should I?'

'Because I think you liked Lucy yourself. She's a very lovely girl, isn't she?'

Martin wriggled his shoulders and stretched his neck, which was turning brick-red as blood rose beneath the skin. 'Yes, she's very lovely,' he agreed stiffly, 'but she liked Paul and, from what I was told, he liked her. It was nothing to do with me.'

'Oh, but I think it was,' said Channon. 'You'd got to know Lucy when you went to work on the gardens at Trenoon, hadn't you? She was having a year at home before she started university, so sometimes she must have been there at the same time as you.'

Sue was so on edge she wanted to answer the questions instead of her son, but she had to admit he was doing really well. So far he'd only admitted what Channon already knew. But detectives were clever, weren't they? In a minute he would ask him something that would upset Marty, and then what would he do?

Next, Channon said, 'Paul was a fortunate young man, wasn't he? Did you sometimes wonder why he had so much and you had so little?'

Martin was silent for several seconds. Then, to his mother's amazement, he said, 'That remark is very patronizing, chief inspector. How can you say I have so little? I have the best mother in the world, and I live in this beautiful place.'

Bowles leaned forward. There was more to Marty-boy than met the eye, but whatever he said, it couldn't be true that he wasn't envious of Paul ... Then Channon said, 'I meant materially little, Martin. Paul was wealthy – in his

178

own right, not just because of his father. He drives an Aston Martin – you ride an old motorbike. He works as a financier in the City of London – you have part-time jobs. I'm stating facts, not being patronizing.'

'So what exactly are you asking?' said Martin.

'I'm suggesting, not asking – that you were so envious of Paul having so much, and then sleeping with Lucy, that you decided to put an end to him.'

Bowles was conscious of a strange feeling coming over him: a tightness in his chest that he couldn't even recognize, all mixed up with a sneaking admiration for this weird, uptight lad. Why was he feeling like this? A minute ago he'd been impatient for Channon to bundle him in the car and take him in for a grilling, but now –

'I do know that they slept together,' Martin said doggedly, and all at once veered to his sing-song mode. 'It's a well-known fact that high achievers have a voracious sexual appetite, inspector. Surely you know that? If Lucy chose to love such a man what could I do about it?'

Bowles tried not to goggle, and Channon was momentarily lost for words. He was stunned to find this odd young man coming out best in the confrontation. He saw pride pass over Sue's face as she studied the three of them, and gathered himself for a final shaker. 'Martin, I appreciate what you say, but I warned you on my last visit that you are automatically a suspect because of what you did to the Stradlings' boat. You have no alibi for Friday evening, you have no witnesses that you never left the house. I think it's highly likely that you decided to get rid of Paul once and for all. Give me one good reason why you didn't do it.'

But Martin had taken a firm stance for long enough. He started to twitch and jerk his neck. 'I didn't kill Paul,' he said, swallowing hard. 'I was upset that he and Lucy were lovers, but what could I do about it?' For the first time he turned to Bowles. 'Sergeant,' he said, 'can you understand? I'm not a fool. I'm aware she's out of my reach, so to speak, but I enjoyed dreaming about her. I knew she'd have men after her all the time, and I was sorry that the first one I

179

found out about happened to be Paul, of all people, but I didn't kill him. Do *you* believe me?'

And to Bowles's own astonishment, he heard himself say, 'Yes,' and to his even greater astonishment, he knew he meant it.

Sue slumped in her seat. This was one of the strangest sessions her Marty had ever, ever taken part in. She couldn't believe it. Neither, it seemed, could Channon. He shot an astounded look at Bowles, turned his attention to Martin, and said heavily, 'We may have to ask more questions, Martin. Don't leave the area without letting us know. Goodbye for now, Mrs Goodchild. We'll see ourselves out.' Seconds later they were outside in the lane, with Bowles almost writhing in embarrassment.

'What's happened to your motto of Go for the jugular?' demanded Channon.

The sergeant lifted his hands, palms upwards. He was bewildered. 'Boss, I simply don't know. All I can say is I believed him.'

'So did I,' replied Channon. He stood there in the light of a solitary street lamp, adjusting to the fact of Bowles showing a humanitarian instinct. 'Come on,' he said heavily, 'let's get back to the room.'

Addie Savage was waiting and marched towards them, holding a small plastic bag in the air like a trophy. 'Look what I've got,' she smiled.

Channon took one look. 'Paul's wallet,' he breathed. Carefully sealed inside the bag was a wallet of soft cream leather, apparently empty and somewhat damp. 'Where was it?' he asked.

'About a quarter of a mile away. A farmer – the same one who owns the field behind the Menna – had put his man to clearing the ditch on his side of the hedge fronting the road. The wallet just came up on top of a forkful of dying vegetation that was clogging the ditch. Almost certainly it had been tossed over the hedge from the road.'

'Did the workman touch it?'

'No, our teams have warned all locals to call us if they

find anything. I sent two uniforms to bring it in, and tape the road off at that spot. I've asked the SOCOs to give it the treatment.'

'Good, good.' Channon stared absently into her clear bright gaze. 'This makes it look like an opportunist thing,' he said, 'not a planned in advance job as I'd imagined.'

'Or it was made to look like it?' suggested Addie.

Bowles joined in. 'Paul would have had to be out on foot for it to be unplanned, surely? Do we know if he ever walked the lanes on his own – at night?'

Addie shook her head. 'Nothing has come in about him going anywhere on foot – he was too fond of the Aston M. He had the grounds of the house for exercise, and the gym. Why should he go tramping on a wet and windy evening?'

'Why indeed?' answered Channon. 'Tell Forensic I say the wallet's urgent.'

It was good to be home after a busy day . . . Channon put a match to the fire before he took off his coat. The house was warm, of course, but since early autumn his house-keeper always left the fire laid ready for when he got home. Deep in thought, he made a mug of tea and sat drinking it as the logs started to flame in front of him.

It was very quiet apart from their crackling and the dis-tant thud of the waves, and after the noise of the incident room the silence was wonderful. There had been little time during the day for thought, but now he could open his mind to points that might have eluded him.

He wasn't sure why he was at last feeling closer to the dead man, unless it was the result of going on board *Daphne*, but even that had only served to confirm Paul's obsession with female flesh. His lifestyle wasn't one he himself had ever admired or yearned for, his promiscuity had been extreme, but gradually an understanding of the young fellow with the earring was coming to him.

Apparently he was good at his job. The City boys had uncovered no shady deals or sharp practice in his work at

Stradling and Son, just a keen aptitude for dealing with money – evidently a case of the son following the father. The enquiries had shown Paul as a high-spending womanizer – maybe a compulsive womanizer, travelling light and travelling alone – until he met an eighteen-year-old girl ... or had Lucy Pascoe been just another one he romanced to the skies while intending to drop her?

With the scent of burning apple logs around him, Channon let his mind run free. Had Paul been searching for something? A soulmate? A sex goddess? An uninhibited lover? Or – the sentimental option – had he been simply a restless, over-sexed young fellow looking and maybe longing for love? Had his mother's illness and death affected him? What had they thought of each other? Had they been close? Had he taken after his father and been devoted to the elegant, dark-haired woman who looked out from her portrait with love in her eyes?

His mind turned to Bowles at the Goodchilds' house. That had been a surprise. Well, he'd always said the sergeant should soften up and not be so abrasive, so envious of privilege. Were they to see the beginnings of change in the hard-boiled Bowles? More captivating still, was the sergeant aware that a certain young constable was interested in him?

Channon stared into the burning logs and almost chuckled. Young Honor Bennett, whose family farmed near the Helford River, had seen quite a bit of Bowles when they were all busy with the triple murder on the Lizard. She was a pretty, wholesome little thing; hardworking and slightly naive – an unlikely admirer for the unpopular, divorced sergeant; but only that afternoon she'd looked at him in a way that, to anyone who chose to see it, revealed a definite interest ...

Channon finished his tea and went to see what meal had been left for him to put in the microwave. His real thinking-time – in the bath with a glass of whisky – would come later.

Chapter Fourteen

The people of Pengorra were getting used to the jumble of police properties on their village green. At first they'd been dismayed to lose their cherished peace and tranquillity, but they were soon saying that when staff were at work in the tent all night long, and the whole site was lit up and buzzing before folk in the houses were out of their beds, it was clear that the police were doing their best.

Channon was parking his car at the edge of the green, having left home with no more than a glance at the dark, rain-washed beach below his garden. He'd made a decision during the night – belated, he knew – but still, he'd made it. When this case was over he would check on Sally Baxter; he would discover if she still lived in that round, beautiful house along the coast, how her children were faring, and above all, whether she was still with her husband. If she was, well, that was that. If she wasn't, he would go to see her, he would talk to her and find out if the strange bond that had drawn him to her during her time of trauma was still there. For now, though, another busy day lay ahead of him.

As he left the car a cold, fine rain was blowing in from the sea, but light shone through the canvas of the tent, and inside it was warm and steamy and smelled of hot toast and bacon. Men and women who had left homes over a wide area were lining up for a snack, chattering together before starting work.

Addie Savage lifted a hand in greeting and gave him a pile of printouts. 'Latest reports from the door-to-doors,' she said briskly. 'I haven't had time to go through them yet, but there's sure to be something to follow up.'

Channon took them to his office, glad of a spell of quiet before the eight o'clock briefing, but his phone was already ringing. 'What's this then,' came Eddie Platt's loud baritone, 'the early bird catches the worm? I'm ringing now so I can go home for a spot of shut-eye. My team are complaining that I'm turning night into day on this crossroads stuff. I do have one or two other jobs lined up, you know.'

'I know, Eddie – you're a star,' Channon said diplomatically. 'Have you got something?'

'Nothing untoward on the Bentley or the Aston Martin – some cars, eh? Had the lads' eyes popping. The Bentley in particular was immaculate – very recently given a top-notch cleaning, leaving traces of nothing except whoever cleaned it. Local vegetation in the tyre treads overlying main road traces – what you'd expect from a London to Falmouth run. The Aston M. same tyre tread result, but with rather more of the local vegetation. Traces of the deceased here, there and everywhere, though that's no surprise, and of another occupant, probably the father as they were both known to use it, but we're checking just to be sure.

'No traces of any weapon – oh, and your query about the grease in his hair – my team have narrowed it down, and they're still on with it. So far they've got that it's a common enough, high quality substance used to protect tools – in this case they think a steel implement that may well have been used as a weapon – but to knock him out, not finish him off. And that's about it, for now.'

'Written reports when you're ready,' said Channon, 'and thanks a lot, Eddie. You can get back to less important stuff, now.'

'*Sleep* isn't less important!' Platt retorted. 'That'll come first, and then I'll start on lesser jobs. I'll see you, Bill.'

Channon picked up the printouts from the house-to-house visits. When he'd gone through them he'd pass them to Les Jolly. If someone on the team found pleasure in detail, he might as well keep him happy.

Bowles was feeling on top form. He was getting to be an expert at his breakfast routine. Today he'd had a fruit smoothie, cereal, crispy bacon and scrambled eggs, followed by organic coffee. If anybody had told him a year ago that he'd be planning and cooking decent meals all by himself he'd have laughed his head off, but now it didn't seem even remotely ridiculous.

He'd been thinking about how Marty-boy had turned to him the evening before – an odd moment if ever he'd known one. In his time in the force it had been almost unknown for anyone to appeal to him for support, and now he asked himself if he was losing his edge, because though he didn't particularly like oddball Marty, he had liked being turned to for help. Watch it, Bowles, he warned himself, you'll be getting a soft centre to your tough old shell.

The thing that was niggling him – though it might be stretching it a bit – was that if he could do something so very unlike himself with his meals, could he do the same with the way he tackled his job? Nothing drastic, of course, but suppose he tried to keep the lid on when he felt the urge to be stroppy, and just see how it went?

Then Channon appeared, on time to the minute as usual, and all agog to start the briefing session. Deliberately Bowles subdued his critical tendencies as he watched the older man in action. Until yesterday he'd always been ready to think of the DCI as 'old clever clogs', but now he couldn't get it out of his mind that the term, though pretty apt, held no respect. Did he *have* to respect him? Well, did he? And if so, why?

Because the man was good, that was why. Good at his job, or a good man? Both, Bowles decided. Right now he was questioning the rank and file about the reactions of the public. 'What's the general opinion out there?' he asked.

'What are people saying on their own doorsteps about the murder?'

A young constable spoke up. 'All the ones I've dealt with think that someone from London did it,' he said. 'Everyone round here knows everyone else, and they can't see one of their own doing it.'

'Why not?' asked Channon. 'Because it would be like killing one of the geese that lays the golden eggs?'

There was a murmur of unrest. 'No, sir,' said Soker. 'Old man Stradling might have more money than a local man will see in a lifetime, but he chooses to spend some of it round Carrick Roads, like many a well-heeled sailing type. You could say he does lay the golden eggs, and he's an outsider, but I get the impression he's respected. His son – well – maybe less so.'

'You mean the womanizing?' asked Channon.

'There's resentment about that,' agreed Loverack, a talkative little man from a remote rural area, 'but there's a sneaking admiration from some of the men – if their wives aren't listening.'

Channon nodded. 'Some of you are already checking on the families of Paul's girlfriends, and we've only just started on them, remember. Be tactful, be respectful, but keep your eyes and ears open. People round here may well be the salt of the earth, but an angry family member is still high on our list of possibles.'

Bowles watched silently. He knew other sergeants who could run a briefing without any trouble, but it simply wasn't his scene – it wasn't his style. Style? It dropped into his mind what Channon's response had been when he'd told him that treading softly with the Pascoes wasn't his style. He'd retorted, 'You want promotion – *make* it your style!' And did he want promotion? There was only one answer to that!

But Channon was still in full flow. 'Now, who was it that sent in this message last night about the Pascoe boy having a disagreement with Paul?' he was asking. 'Oh, that's right, it was you, wasn't it, Cloak?'

186

Good intentions forgotten, Bowles couldn't stop himself rolling his eyes. The Cloak without the dagger, he thought wearily. You only had to look at him to see he was thick, but what he'd reported could be of interest.

The stolid Cloak was quite calm and self-possessed. 'It wasn't an interview on the doors as such, sir,' he said, 'but you did say to look out for anyone who'd had a disagreement with Paul. What I heard about was probably only a squabble, I think. I got talking to a gang of teenagers who were hanging about near the ferry in Flushing – decent enough lads, not roughnecks. The only disagreement with Paul that they knew of was when he invited them all to use the games room and the gym at the Court. They had a special evening there, by all accounts.'

'Right. And what happened?'

'It seems Paul arranged a snooker match during the evening and they were all having a go. Paul was a pretty good player, it seems, but young Pascoe accused him of cheating. Paul told him to leave, and then a minute later changed his mind. They shook hands, sort of an old-fashioned making up, but the next day at school Jaz Pascoe insisted he'd been right and said he was never going to Pengorra Court again to be patronized by a man who thought he was God's gift to women. Actually, sir, I think some of the lads felt they were letting Jaz down by even mentioning it.'

Well, well, thought Channon gloomily, the Pascoe clan again. This had never been mentioned to either him or Bowles. 'Well done, Cloak,' he said, 'the sergeant here will get a check done on that. The rest of you remember, all such cases to be reported immediately. I know you're working hard, but I have to say progress is slow. As you're all aware, the arrest and questioning of Mrs Pascoe came to nothing, but along with her husband, she's being watched and assessed, and now it seems we have another member of the family to talk to.'

Within minutes Channon was bringing the briefing to a close with final questions and answers. The men and women trooped off, leaving Bowles and Addie Savage with the DCI. 'What do you think, Addie?' he asked keenly.

'I suppose you'll have to talk to the Pascoe son,' she said, 'but I really can't see it leading to anything.'

'Teenagers are often a bit unstable,' said Channon doubtfully, 'but I've talked to the lad and he seems pretty well grounded. What did you think of him, Bowles?'

By now Bowles had remembered his earlier resolves. 'It sounds like a teenage whinge versus an older, more sophisticated man,' he said judiciously. 'Do you want me to look into it, boss?'

This was make or break time, thought Channon. If Bowles made a hash of it and harassed the lad unfairly, then hard words would be said, and maybe hard actions taken. Keen dark eyes met suspiciously guileless pale ones. 'Go ahead, sergeant,' he said, 'remembering our previous conversations, of course. I think you'll be too late to talk to him before school, though. Send word to the parents to say somebody will call at the house in the late afternoon.'

Steve had finished his spell in the studio, and Helen was telling herself that in spite of the turmoil around them she needed to get back to the design work she'd been doing on Friday – the day that in retrospect seemed a golden, trouble-free time of performing routine tasks, when she'd been merely unhappy, as opposed to worried sick, frightened, guilty and filled with dread.

It seemed so very odd that the painful coolness between her and Steve had taken second place to the ramifications of the murder. They were having a snack lunch at the kitchen table, almost like they used to do before the split-up. It was a time when they used to update each other on whatever was currently on their minds. The difference now was that the subject for discussion was once again the police and their sudden interest in Jaz.

'Clearly we were wrong in advising him not to mention the disagreement,' said Steve, 'but it sounded so trivial, I

188

just thought it might get blown up out of all proportion and put him under suspicion.'

'That was before the worst things happened,' she reminded him, 'before they arrested me and gave you the third degree. I still can't believe it.'

'Neither can I,' he admitted, 'but the fact remains that none of us have done anything wrong, and I think Channon knows it. We'll be there when they talk to Jaz, and if necessary I'll take a tough line. Did they say who would be coming?'

'No, just that someone would call round in the late afternoon. It only occurred to me after they'd rung off that I should have said we didn't want the sergeant.'

'I'd already told Channon we don't want any more dealings with him, but he just said he couldn't promise it. If it *is* Bowles, we'll know what to expect and I'll keep an eye on things. Look, my lo – Helen, for goodness sake eat something. You need nourishment.'

'So does Lucy,' she said grimly. 'I almost had to force a bowl of porridge down her throat at breakfast time. I'm so glad, though, that she and I are getting back to how we used to be. Do you think she'll forget Paul in time?'

'I doubt she'll ever forget that the man she loved was murdered, but I suppose she might adjust and eventually get on with her life. I think you and I would find all this easier to accept if we only knew exactly what she meant to him. *Was* she just another in the queue, or did he see her as special?'

'She thinks he did,' said Helen sadly, 'and we might as well pretend that we think the same. I don't see how it will help her if we say we have doubts about him.'

In silence they finished their meal, then Helen went to find Lucy while Steve went up to his attic room to carry on working.

Channon was busy with neglected paperwork when Addie came to his office. 'You wanted an update from the computer boys,' she said. 'Have you got a minute to listen?'

He leaned back. She was good at this; she could condense a long verbal report into a few choice nuggets of information. 'Fire away,' he said.

'They're examining four computers in all, three from the house and one from the boat. They've all been used mainly for the financial affairs of Stradling and Son – a lot of the stuff is just copies of the firm's official files. So far, other interests that have come up, sites visited, etc: there's sea-going stuff including historical navigation, various yachting competitions and a bit about local affairs in this area. The boys think that both father and son accessed most of this.

'Paul's more personal stuff is on the boat's computer. More girls, of course, but at least some of them are already on our lists. Also – and this is interesting – he'd been trawling around for prehistoric stuff – ancient history, archaeology, burial mounds, standing stones and so forth. Not just in Cornwall but in the rest of the UK and Europe. The boys say they've found nothing deep or occult so far, just general interest in the subject.'

Channon had let out a satisfied grunt at the word 'prehistoric'. He'd half-expected this, but it was good to have a first, confirmed link with the site of the killing. There had to be a reason for propping Paul against the stone. The word Menna was clearly a corruption of menhir – the correct name for a standing stone, though not a single local person had come out and said so. The people of Carrick Roads were well informed on their local history, so perhaps they thought it so obvious it didn't need spelling out?

Addie watched with interest as Channon's eyes took on the remote, unseeing gaze that meant his mind was finding its way through unexplored territory. All at once he came back and focused on her. 'The start of progress, eh, Addie? Tell your two experts not to miss a trick because it could be vital. I want to know if anyone else was involved in the prehistoric stuff. Was Paul talking to anyone over the internet? Was he exchanging information or pictures of prehistoric sites – or anything else for that matter? And will you have a word with your door-to-door team to listen out for any mention of ancient history? Get someone to do a check on local evening classes, Women's Institutes and so forth, to see if it's a subject being covered. You're good at this sort of thing, Addie – go for it.'

She marched off with a pleased flash of her eyes, leaving Channon feeling more motivated than at any time since he was first summoned to the murder scene. He knew, he just *knew* that this was what he'd been waiting for.

The same pretty girl as before greeted Channon at Pengorra Court. His visit was unplanned: one minute he'd been at his desk, reflecting on what had shown up on Paul's computer, the next he was in his car filled with the urge to talk to Stradling, which in itself was odd, because a chat with the bereaved father was something he would avoid if given the choice.

This time he didn't need to insist on seeing him. 'It's DC Channon, isn't it?' the girl said. 'Please take a seat and I'll tell Mr Stradling you're here.'

She turned to hurry away but Nigel Nollens appeared and took over. 'It's all right, Jasmine,' he said briskly, 'I'll deal with this.'

Channon greeted him politely. 'Good morning, Mr Nollens. Thanks for giving your statement last evening. A mere formality, of course, but as my men will have told you, subject to checking.'

Nollens didn't even attempt to be pleasant. 'I came down here at short notice, on Mr Stradling's orders,' he said tightly. 'Why that should cause such a song and dance I simply can't imagine.'

'Can't you, Mr Nollens? I thought DC Yates had explained our interest in your movements. If you see our investigations into a brutal murder as a song and dance, then I think your viewpoint must be somewhat biased.'

Nollens blinked. 'The only bias I have is against being victimized, Mr Channon.'

Channon sighed. He wasn't here to bandy words. 'Come on, Mr Nollens – a request for a statement from a possible suspect is hardly victimization. Now, if you please, I want a word with your employer.'

But the secretary wasn't prepared to leave it at that. He squared his shoulders and persisted: 'I want to know why I should be classed as a possible suspect.'

Channon eyed him thoughtfully. Was he protesting too much? Was he feigning innocence? Was he simply mortified that what had happened between him and his fiancée was common knowledge? Or was he just a self-important man, tired of subservience and relishing the opportunity to be forceful?

Trying to hang on to his customary courtesy, Channon explained: 'The City of London police are working alongside the Devon and Cornwall Constabulary on this case. As a matter of routine, our London colleagues informed us that your fiancée broke off your engagement in order to pursue an affair with Paul Stradling. Any police officer in the land would see that as a possible motive for murder by the jilted party. Surely you can see that?'

Nollens glared at him. 'Of course I see it, but can't *you* see that it doesn't apply to me?'

'Why not? You said yourself that he tempted her.'

'What? Uh – well – yes I did, because it was true.'

'So did you never, ever, feel resentment or the desire for vengeance?'

Now it was Nollens's turn to observe the other man carefully. Surprise was there, as if it was dawning on him that this policeman might be more than a quietly spoken country bumpkin. Patience at an end, Channon made his final point with some force. 'For every suspect who is charged and ends up in court, there are many more who are under suspicion, some of them with less provocation than you to commit a crime. That is fact, Mr Nollens – deal with it!'

Nollens's eyes glittered, but without another word he went off to find Stradling. When the man appeared he looked even worse than on the previous day, but his greeting was firm enough. 'Ah, Channon – I was going to ring you. What about the cars? Surely you've examined them by now?'

'The forensic team have finished with them,' confirmed Channon. 'Someone will be bringing them back here shortly.'

'I'm glad to hear it. I feel the need to get away from this house and grounds sometimes, and for that I prefer to drive my Bentley. I had to resort to going out on foot last evening, because I felt ready to see the crossroads – to get my own slant on Paul's last moments. It's still taped off up there, Channon. Why is that? Haven't you got all you need by now?'

'We've got all the forensic evidence that's there,' Channon assured him, 'but we want to keep it untouched for a few more days, just in case. Mr Stradling, I think you'd be wise not to walk these lanes on your own, especially at night, until we've made the area safe again.'

Stradling waved a dismissive hand. 'I won't have to walk them when I've got my car back, will I? Come and sit down and tell me the latest on the case. It was on regional news this morning, but not on national. They were pursuing an occult line again – pagan stuff, black magic, sacrifices and so forth.'

'I know, and I'm sorry, but we can't tell the TV companies what line to take. We're only too glad to use them for publicity when there's a need. The occult stuff might be sensational, but it hooks the viewers. Actually, one of my reasons for coming this morning is along those lines. Experts analysing your computers have found that your son had been on the internet several times looking for prehistoric stuff, ancient history and so forth. Do you know if he was interested in that particular subject? I needn't tell you that details of such an interest could help us a great deal.'

Stradling looked baffled. 'I don't know of it,' he said, 'but Paul had so many interests. He never mentioned that in particular . . . But wait a minute – history was his best subject at school. You'll probably hear of that through your enquiries.'

'Was it his degree subject?' asked Channon.

Stradling gazed into space, remembering. 'No, not history – he hovered between sport and business for university, but in the end chose business studies with maths. He was pretty bright, you know.'

'I'm sure he was,' said Channon gently. 'There's one other matter I didn't feel I could broach immediately after his death – you no doubt know that a high percentage of all murders are committed either by family, by household members or by close friends? My sergeant has taken statements from all members of your staff here, but as their employer, are you aware of any of them having a grudge against your son? Their alibis cover each other, of course, but I want a personal opinion from someone who knows them.'

An expression that might have been derision passed over Stradling's ravaged features, but his reply was perfectly serious. 'I've considered that, of *course* I have, Channon. The fact that you're considering it as well reveals that you're no further forward. Is that the case?'

'Progress is slow at this stage,' admitted Channon, 'but we're following up every lead and exploring every possibility. What I've just asked you comes into that category – a possibility at this stage, however remote. Could I ask you to think carefully about it and let me know if anything occurs to you. I know it must be terribly hard to think about who could have murdered you son, but –'

'Terribly hard to think about it?' Stradling echoed. 'I think about nothing else, man! You can rest assured I'll let you know of anyone and anything that might possibly help. For instance, the earring. I take it you've alerted other forces to keep a watch in case it's offered for sale?'

'Of course we have,' Channon assured him. 'As I said

before, Mr Stradling, we have an augmented team working extremely hard on this case.' He took out the sealed plastic bag. 'One more thing, could you confirm that this is indeed your son's wallet, and then it can be examined by our Forensic team?'

Features completely immobile, Stradling eyed the wallet. 'Yes, it's one of the items his mother chose for his stocking last Christmas. Where did you find it?'

Channon told him, and Stradling made no comment. There was no way of knowing if he was pleased, upset or impatient. 'Whilst I'm here,' said Channon, 'have you any objections to me taking a stroll through your grounds and down to the river?'

'Of course not. Have your men finished their work on *Daphne*?'

'I believe they'll soon leave you in peace, but I want a word with them. You'll be the first to know when you can go on board again.'

Stradling nodded and kept on nodding, which gave him the look of an old-fashioned clockwork toy. Channon found it unnerving and very, very sad. With relief he left the older man, let himself out by the big front door and headed across the damp lawns and down to the shining silver waters of Carrick Roads.

It was four thirty, and Katie was in the summerhouse, wearing a warm jacket and furry boots. She was thinking hard and trying not to grind her teeth.

It had been really good when her mum met them from the school bus, almost as if nothing horrible had happened the day before, but school itself had been awful. Her own close friends had been tactful about her mum being arrested, but some of the others had made snide remarks or, even worse, blanked her out when they came face to face with her. And then when they got home her mum and dad had said that Jaz was to be questioned about his argument with Paul. It simply wasn't fair. Three of the family were under suspicion, one was heartbroken – and as for her, she was going to take action.

The thing she had to decide was what she was going to do. For a start she would remember for ever who had been a true friend to her at school and who hadn't; next she was going to try and help Lucy and to sympathize with her, but it wouldn't be easy because her sister was always crying. It was sad that Paul was dead, of course it was, but what good would come from crying about it all the time? Far better to think of something – anything – that would help the police find the murderer.

That was what she herself could do – she'd be a secret observer; she would keep a diary – that would be good. She eyed her little boat rocking at the jetty. Since the murder she'd been forbidden to use it, even in her usual restricted area, but when the family was all upset surely nobody would bother to keep watch from the bedrooms to see what was going on down by the water?

It was pretty obvious, she reasoned, that a killer could have come to Pengorra by water. Paul's house was near the water, *Daphne* was moored there, and the Menna was within a hundred metres. A small boat could have tied up somewhere near – maybe even at Trenoon's own little jetty right in front of where she was sitting . . .

She would come down here in her every spare moment to make a note of all the shipping that went past, just in case it turned out to be useful, and then, forbidden or not, she would go for a sail, in and out of the little creeks and inlets. She would keep her binoculars in the locker on board; she would make a note of anything suspicious and tell Mr Channon. It was a pity she had to go to school, but as soon as she arrived home she would say she wanted to watch the shipping in the twilight, which was true anyway, then make her escape and go out on the water to see what she could see . . .

She shivered, but although it was cold she didn't want to go back to the house. It had stopped raining and the water was a dark, greenish black, with the lights from St

Just winking at her and a few early stars glinting between the last of the clouds – and oh, it smelled so *good*!

They were all going to have hot chocolate in front of the fire in a minute, but the main topic of conversation was sure to be what Jaz should say to the police. Honestly! Life was awful, but she was going to do whatever she could to make things better. Then from up at the house she heard the slam of a car door. No hot chocolate just yet, then, because it sounded as if the police had arrived. She'd better go up, just to keep an eye on things.

Chapter Fifteen

Bowles had chosen Honor Bennett to go with him to Trenoon. He saw her as the safest bet: Soker was a no-no because he'd been present on the previous visit, while the rest of them knew him as a tough nut sergeant, and would probably snigger to see him having to go softly because the DCI had given him a warning. He swished the car to a stop at the front of the house and saw Honor's eyes widen as she took in the setting.

'Some pad, eh?' he said, leaping out, and then for seconds stood quite still. It was completely mad, but he had a feeling that the old house saw itself as a safe refuge for its occupants, enfolding them within its granite walls, the windows seeming to look serenely across the water, but in fact keeping watch against any who would come to cause harm. You needn't worry about me, he thought wryly, I've been told to be a good boy.

Was he losing it? This was just ridiculous fancy – he was annoyed with himself for giving it space in his mind. Honor was smiling and nodding in agreement with what he'd just said, and standing submissively at his side. She was young, of course, and idealistic. He remembered a couple of times when they'd been on the Lizard killings and he'd found himself behaving with restraint if she was around – he'd never managed to figure out why.

It wasn't her appearance that had influenced him; he liked women better upholstered than her and more mature – a bit brassy, to be honest, and good for a laugh, whereas young Bennett here was the sweet and gentle type – a

198

farmer's daughter. In fact, she had the look of an old-fashioned milkmaid with her flaxen hair and rosy cheeks; all she needed was a blue striped pinafore and a bowl of clotted cream. She might be pretty, but there was something about her that simply put him off. She was ... that was it – she was wholesome. Well, enough said, how boring could you get?

And then there was the flurry of introductions, with him trying to ignore the coolness of the Pascoes' greeting and being only too aware that the demon king would go running to Channon if his son and heir wasn't handled with kid gloves. They went to the big sitting room, and again he had the sense of the house wrapping itself around the parents and their son.

He was very careful, very correct. 'Just a few questions, sir, madam,' he began. 'I'd be obliged if you'd let your son answer for himself, but please feel free to comment or call a halt if you see the need.' He'd expected to feel a fool, coming out with such a load of claptrap, but if anything it was a relief not to see resentment looking back at him.

Steve relaxed a little. Quite a change from Sunday morning. It was surprising what a complaint to the man in charge could do.

'Now, Jaz,' the sergeant was saying, 'first of all, could you tell me why you and your friends were at Pengorra Court on the occasion of your disagreement?'

Jaz was relieved to hear the detective's reasonable tone, and decided to co-operate. 'Paul and his father sometimes sent word to the school to invite a group of boys to their house for an evening of games and a workout in the gym. I think they saw it as making them appear part of the community.'

'Was it always the same group of boys?'

'No. The Stradlings had an arrangement with the head of PE that sixteen- to eighteen-year-olds could go in groups of about twenty to their house.'

'So it was popular with you and your friends, but not compulsory?'

'That's right, but nearly everyone went. We all thought it was good. It's a pretty swish games room and the gym is really cool – a bit over-the-top for just Paul and his dad, but great for a group. It was somewhere to go, and they laid on good food.'

'And when did this disagreement take place?'

Jaz shifted in his chair. 'About ten days ago. We were all in the games room and Paul was joining in. The snooker was pretty popular and he'd set up a bit of a knock-out match. He was good, we all knew that, so we didn't mind him winning.'

'Did he win all the time?'

'Not all the time, but pretty often.'

'And you thought he was cheating?'

'I didn't think, I knew,' said Jaz flatly. 'I saw him.'

'*Is* it all that easy to cheat at snooker?'

'It is if you move the white.'

'That's what he did, is it, moved the white ball when everyone was watching?'

'They weren't all watching. There were only four of us really near, because a table tennis final was going on at the same time.'

'The snooker was between you and Paul, though?'

'Yes. It was a close game – I'm not all that good, so it was a bit of a fluke for me. Then a big shout went up from the table tennis. We all looked across, but I turned back pretty quickly because my mind was on the snooker, and I saw Paul moving the white.'

'So what happened?'

'I just shouted out, "You cheat – you rotten cheat!"'

'And what did he say?'

Jaz moistened his lips. 'He laughed and said, "Grow up, sonny."'

'And you didn't like it?'

'What do you think? I said again, "You cheated, you moved the white," and he said, "In your dreams."'

'So what next?'

Jaz wriggled his shoulders. 'I lost it a bit. I said something like, "Just because you're loaded doesn't mean you can make your own rules – it's you who needs to grow up. You can't stand being beaten by somebody who's still at school!"'

'And?'

'He went a bit red. Everyone was listening by then, and he said, "You'd better leave – go on – get out!" so I said, "Fine by me." Then he said, "What's your name so I can see you're not invited again." I told him, and all at once he said that perhaps he was being a bit hasty, and he might have inadvertently touched the white, and if so, he apologized, and could we shake hands and forget it.'

'So did you?'

'Yes, we shook hands and I stayed on and had some pretty good food. They have a proper chef, just to cook for them and to lay on a spread when they have parties and stuff.'

'Jaz, did you know when you went to the house that Paul was seeing your sister?'

'I knew they'd had a date, but she hadn't told me it was getting a bit deep between them – she hadn't told any of us.'

'So do you think he changed his mind when he realized you were Lucy's brother?'

Jaz shot a look at his parents and said heavily, 'I think so. I knew him by sight, but he'd never met me. When I found that he and Lucy had talked about getting married it all fell into place.'

'Were you pleased to know they'd been so close?'

'No way! Everyone for miles around knew he saw himself as a stud – uh – sorry, Mum. The kids at school used to make up verses about him – pretty funny, some of them, but, uh, a bit crude.'

'Jaz, did you say anything to your sister about the disagreement?'

'I told her how he'd been going to throw me out and the reason for it, but she just said that everyone was against him because his father was a millionaire and he drove a class car.'

Bowles was getting restive. This was pretty mild stuff, even if it did throw a bit of light on Paul. He *had* to get something of interest, no matter how polite he had to be. 'Jaz,' he said, 'you were clearly in the right, but tell me, did this disagreement leave you feeling annoyed, or embarrassed, or resentful?'

Steve shifted edgily, but Jaz merely shrugged. 'Not really, I just thought he was a bit of a creep, and come on – even if I'd hated his guts I wouldn't have killed him.'

Bowles asked silkily, 'Did you hate his guts, Jaz?'

Steve leaned forward. 'Sergeant,' he said warningly.

'Nearly finished, sir, bear with me,' answered Bowles, determined on getting a response. 'Jaz?'

But the boy was no pushover. 'I didn't like him much, but I didn't hate his guts. I didn't know him well enough to hate him.'

'What did your friends think of him?'

'A few thought he was cool, because of the way he lived, but a lot of them thought the same as me.'

'Did anyone in particular say anything about him?'

'Several of them did, but I couldn't possibly remember who they were.'

Oh – clever boy, huh? Don't push it, Snazzy-Jazzy ... Bowles dredged up a smile. 'That's all pretty clear, I think. We'll print everything out in the form of a statement and someone will come round tomorrow and get you and your parents to read and sign it.' He turned to Steve. 'How's that, Mr Pascoe?'

'Fine, thanks,' said Steve. 'There was really nothing so important that you needed to make a special visit, was there, sergeant?'

'Not on the surface of it, sir,' answered Bowles smoothly, 'but it's for our records, you see. Everything – absolutely everything – is checked in an enquiry such as this.'

Once outside and in the car he completed his good

detective performance by asking Honor, as Channon had so often asked him, 'What do you think of that?'

To his amazement she said, 'You were lovely with him, sarge, so polite and understanding. As I see it he's just a teenager in an awkward situation. The fact that he challenged Paul in front of all his mates and that Paul backed down will have boosted his cred and maybe wiped out his anger. His parents had probably told him earlier not to mention what happened because they were on edge about being involved with Paul themselves. I've got everything on tape – do you want me to draft out the statement for you?'

Bowles grunted in disbelief. He'd never had more than a couple of words out of her before. 'Yes,' he answered, 'thanks, Honor,' but to himself he observed, There's more to the milkmaid than soap and water.

Next morning the familiar two-tone horn of the mobile shop sounded outside the white cottage in its peaceful garden above the water. It was the first of Biddy's twice-weekly visits, and Chrissie went out to the road with her shopping basket and her purse. Biddy knew quite well that most of her customers bought stuff at the supermarkets; that with mutual respect they used her for speed and convenience when they ran out of essentials, and more important, for good local produce that had come straight from its source.

The inside of the van smelled of freshly baked bread and pasties, and would have been gloomy but for the ship's lantern that shone high above the till. 'Hello, my love,' was Biddy's greeting. 'It's been a busy morning up to now, but when I've served you I'm going to have a coffee. Have you got time for one?'

Chrissie thought of her warm, comfortable kitchen and compared it to the cramped space and single chair behind the chill cabinet that served as a counter; but this big, good-natured woman was truly one of the pillars of their community, so did it matter if it was colder here than next to her kitchen range? 'Of course I have the time,' she said, and started to look along the shelves. As usual their talk was a jumble of what she was buying and snippets of local information, and Chrissie enquired, 'Have you got any news about what's been happening, Biddy?'

'That's what everybody wants to know!' retorted the older woman, flattening her cap with the palm of her hand the way she always did when she was a bit put out. 'They all think I know exactly what's going on at any given moment, but I only know what I'm told – or, of course, what I've seen with my own eyes.' Beneath the cap her face tightened for an instant, then she gave a little laugh. 'Mind you, all I've seen in the last couple of weeks has been the inside of this van and my storeroom at home.'

'I just thought you might know something I don't about the murder,' said Chrissie. 'On television this morning they were talking about the possibility of it being a pagan sacrifice.'

'They like that angle,' agreed Biddy grimly. 'Oh, by the way, I've got some of the bacon you like from the farm.' She bent and delved in the fridge, coming up with a tray of freshly sliced bacon. 'Harry down the hill wants some as well, but he said he'll be over in Falmouth this morning. Would you have time to take it to him this afternoon if I leave it with you? He can pay me when he sees me.'

That was the way Biddy ran her shop: supplying fresh meat, fish and vegetables to suit her customer's preferences, and stocking groceries at prices that didn't even attempt to compete with those of the big suppliers. 'If I filled my entire top shelf with bags of sugar,' she would say, 'I'd still have to pay more for it wholesale than you'd pay as a customer at the supermarket, because they can buy in such bulk; but my clotted cream was in the dairy only a couple of hours ago, and there's not many shop-keepers left in the county who still weigh out their own fresh-churned butter, nor sell bread and pasties that were baked in the kitchen of a cottage on the banks of the Fal.'

Now she made two mugs of coffee and insisted that Chrissie sat in the only chair. Then she hitched at the waistband of her trousers and put her hands flat on the counter. 'Before anyone else comes in,' she said, 'how's Helen after all that to-do on Monday? I've been told this chief inspector's clever, but he made a bloomer with Helen and Steve. What was he thinking of?'

Chrissie was careful. Helen had said that Channon warned her against talking about her arrest and the reason for it. 'I got the impression it was a genuine mistake,' she said. 'Apparently these things happen in a big enquiry.'

Biddy was unconvinced. 'They're saying young Jaz was being questioned yesterday, as well, and him no more than sixteen. What's going on?'

'I don't know,' Chrissie admitted. 'Helen wanted to come over this afternoon for a chat, but she has some work to finish off. Lucy's in a state, as well, grieving for Paul. I suppose you know she'd been seeing him?'

'Yes, I'd heard. All I can say is it's a funny thing when a Cornish family whose roots go back for centuries all seem to have been involved with a jumped-up womanizer from London.'

Chrissie swallowed a mouthful of coffee. Not much sympathy for the victim from Biddy, then. But wait, there was a reason for it – how could she have forgotten? 'I haven't asked about your Rosie lately, Biddy,' she said guiltily. 'Is she all right now?'

Biddy was still for only a second, with her coffee mug halfway to her mouth. 'She's well shut of him, Chrissie,' she said quietly, 'and yes, she's all right. That's all I can say.'

Chrissie felt awkward. 'I wasn't trying to pry,' she said gently, 'it's just she's always been such a little love, and I know how you used to think the sun shone out of her.'

Biddy looked at her and in the shadow cast by the lantern her eyes seemed very dark. 'I still think that,' she said, 'but she was getting on with her life again long before that Lothario met his end.'

Their friendly little chat had gone sour, Chrissie thought, Biddy herself had gone sour; what was going on in her mind? She wished she'd never mentioned Rosie. The girl's brief romance and its sudden end had hit Biddy hard, of course, but even so . . . Just then all was bustle as a young mother with a baby in arms and a toddler climbed into the shop. Chrissie picked up her basket, put Harry's packet of bacon on top of her purchases and went back to the house.

It was a rare quiet moment in a busy day, with Channon physically relaxed but mentally alert, his mind selecting and rejecting facets of the case for attention.

Nigel Nollens was bothering him. So far they hadn't come up with anything on him, but something about the man made him uneasy, so much so that he was considering talking to Stradling about him, to try and clarify his views. How, though, to tackle the subject with the tense and demoralized father? He could hardly say, 'Let's talk about your secretary, Mr Stradling, because I can't help wondering whether he killed your son as an act of vengeance.' No, it would have to be the old faithful platitudes of 'eliminating all possible subjects' and 'confirming their whereabouts at the relevant time'. After all, from what he'd seen so far, Stradling now relied on Nollens, using him as a fender-off of the press and a knowledgeable link with his business interests, so he wasn't going to take kindly to his acolyte being under suspicion.

And as for Martin Goodchild: his own instincts had told him that the boy was no killer, but when the ever-suspicious Bowles had admitted he thought the same, that had more or less put Martin in the clear – at least, for the time being. Then the Pascoe boy . . . Bowles had reported that his talk with Jaz had at least shown that Paul had been keen enough on Lucy to back down in the argument rather than antagonize her brother, but otherwise nothing startling had been revealed. They had both agreed that teenage boys were an unknown entity, especially if acting as a group. That was a fact, but there was another fact, an inescapable one. 'Bowles, the guilty party has to be the one who planted the blood in Mrs Pascoe's Freelander. If Jaz, with or without his friends, was the killer, would he deliberately implicate his mother?'

Bowles had rolled his eyes in dismay and smothered a curse. He thought for a minute, then said, 'Wait, boss – do you remember that weird kid on Bodmin – the one with the ultra-strict mother and the father in the wheelchair? The kid was done for a string of thefts from supermarkets – stuff he neither needed nor knew how to use. Where did he plant it? In his mother's larder. Maybe Snazzy-Jazzy's efforts were along the same lines, or maybe he thought we wouldn't be stupid enough to fall for it, but that it would waste our time?'

Channon considered it, but shook his head. 'Say she didn't forget to lock the car – Jaz would have had access to the keys. Even so, I saw no signs of him being on bad terms with his mother, did you?'

'No, but it's possible he'd been having a teenage strop. We both know kids who've run away from home after a mere tiff with their parents, and we've come across suicide attempts after rows at home. Kids get things out of proportion.'

That was true. Channon thought of the lanky Jaz and was reluctant to see him as a killer, even with the help of friends. 'See what you can find out – on the grapevine, without another visit,' he instructed. 'If we go round there again they'll be shouting victimization.' Bowles had shot off to see what he could come up with, and Channon was back in his train of thought.

Another point – he must watch that Paul's reputation with women didn't cloud his judgement on the case. With investigations covering a positive multitude of suspects among the families of discarded lovers, there was the danger of overlooking other, less obvious motives for murder ... Clearly, Paul had been a mixed-up young man; possibly lacking in confidence in spite of all the evidence to the contrary. Certainly he was out to show himself as a success in more aspects of life than his womanizing – such as snooker?

His mind went back to yet another possible source of information – one that hadn't at first occurred to him – he still couldn't credit he'd been so unobservant. Yesterday he had walked down through the autumn-damp grounds of Pengorra Court to the water, to see how Fred Jordan and his SOCOs were getting on with their examination of the boat. It had seemed very odd to find the serene little jetty taped off and the white-overalled figures swarming over *Daphne*'s elegant timbers. Even her own little dinghy had been hauled on board for examination, and replaced with an inflatable police version.

Fred was his usual down-to-earth self, watching everything like a hawk but with time to spare for the man in charge. 'Traces of all and sundry,' he announced, 'the victim and probably his father, the girlfriend, the employee who helps with sailing the boat – I think it's the chef – and Uncle Tom Cobley and all; but your boys in Forensic will have the last word on that lot. All will be revealed in due course.'

Then he had said, 'You never mentioned us checking the boathouse, Bill. Do we include it, ignore it, or what? It does seem to me that if you think the boat needs a going-over, then why not the boathouse as well? Tools, implements, rubber gloves, wellingtons, waterproofs – they're all in there.'

Channon was astounded at himself. He hadn't even thought of such a place, let alone seen it, but there it was, half-obscured by trees at the water's edge – a big, beautiful building, apparently Victorian, with arched white-painted windows and huge doors above a slipway. Like everything else about Pengorra Court, it was well kept and elegant; it even had the foliage of climbing roses framing the arch above the doors. 'I'm losing my grip, Fred,' he said ruefully. 'You'll have to apply for my job.'

Fred had laughed but kept his gaze on his team. 'So do we give it the usual? It'll take time.'

'Of course you do. Every rope, every boathook, every oilskin – you name it.' He had left them all hard at work on the boat, and driven back to the room, wondering how he could have missed such a goldmine of clues. There was only one source of comfort, Bowles had missed it as well, though when he was last at the jetty he'd had the excuse of being petrified by the prospect of crossing a strip of water.

But right now phones were ringing, doors slamming, the smell of food coming from the caravan canteen. Channon got up from his chair and told himself it was time he showed his face among the workforce. Before he could open the door Bowles came in. 'Nothing so far about Jaz and his mother being on bad terms,' he announced, 'and that's from people who know Pengorra.' Always energetic when following up leads, he was bouncing on the balls of his feet. 'Everyone sees the Pascoes as an ordinary family, though with the parents separated, of course – Cornish-born and well-off compared to those they left behind when they went to London. I'll keep checking, though.

'Regarding the slog of checking on Paul's girls . . . I've just been talking to the sergeant who's my opposite number in London. They've put in more man-hours than us and cleared their list, and – uh . . .' Bowles now stood flat-footed and almost shuffled his feet.

'Yes, yes?' prompted Channon impatiently. 'And?'

'It was sergeant-to-sergeant and off the record, boss. He's a pretty tough type, and down-to-earth.'

Channon almost smiled. 'Tougher than you?' Eyes met in one of their rare moments of friendship.

'Yes, I should say he is,' admitted Bowles. 'I know you're in charge and you talk to the DCI in London, but this guy more or less spelled out that his superiors say the ball's in our court now. They have enough to do without going any further on Paul. Their view is: London man killed in Cornwall – let the Devon and Cornwall force sort it out!'

Channon nodded. 'They haven't said as much to me, but I've seen it coming. If the positions were reversed we'd be saying the same thing.'

Bowles tried to look grave rather than highly pleased. He wanted credit for solving the case to go to him and Channon, not to some London whizzos with their massive funding. 'One more point of interest,' he said. 'Two Pengorra individuals who live close to the Menna are related to two different girls in Paul's gallery. One is Amos Heaney from the boatyard – I think you know about him – and the other is Bridget Stumbles, who runs the mobile shop. I haven't put anyone on to talking to them, because I thought you might want to do it yourself.'

Channon didn't even pause for thought. 'Yes, I do. Give me brief details and get someone to tell them both I'll see them first thing in the morning.'

'Will do,' said Bowles promptly. 'You're going alone?'

'With you, sergeant, if that appeals?'

It appealed. The wolfish grin flashed out and Bowles left the room. Things were moving. If it had been possible he would have walked on the air. As it was, his feet stayed on the duckboards and took him in the direction of food.

Chapter Sixteen

By eight o'clock on Thursday morning the room was humming with activity. Channon was busy planning the day's work with Addie Savage, and Bowles had snatched a minute to ask Mary Donald's advice on a recipe that was stretching his limited expertise.

Smiling, she went on her way after explaining why it was a good idea to seal beef before stewing it, leaving him somewhat smug because he'd suspected what her answer would be before he asked the question. Then he saw Jolly hovering to catch Channon's attention. 'Laughing-boy wanting another pat on the back,' he told himself but, mindful of his recent resolves, he made an effort to be civil. 'If you want the DCI, Les, we have to go out in a minute. Can't it wait?'

'I suppose so,' answered Jolly. 'It's just that he asked me to look at the statements made by the staff at the Court and give them the once-over.'

Bowles gritted his teeth. 'Did he now? *I* spoke to the staff, and Soker and I prepared the statements ready for signing. I thought the DCI had already seen them?'

Jolly's shoulders drooped. 'In that case I'll leave it for now, sarge.' He trudged away at his usual leaden pace, but there was an obstinate tightness to his mouth. It could wait – but not for long . . .

Minutes later Channon was leading the way to the car, eager to eliminate Heaney and Bridget Stumbles from involvement. 'The boatyard first,' he said. 'Tresillian told us he starts work at eight and it's only quarter past, so we should catch his boss before he gets busy.'

There was no sign of busyness at the yard – no sign of anyone to *be* busy; just the medley of boats with their ropes and chains, the white-painted sheds and the slow, purposeful flow of the water. 'He's expecting us, so he'll be in the office,' said Channon, recalling his Sunday morning visit to Heaney; but no, the office was unlocked but deserted, the counter top clear, with job-lists clipped together and file boxes neatly stacked.

It was silent in the yard, and Channon spoke very low and intent. 'Let's have a look round, Bowles. If there's nobody here we'll go to his house or to Tresillian's, to see what's going on.' The two men separated, peering inside the other sheds and threading their way between the boats.

'Boss!' Bowles's voice sounded very loud. 'He's here!'

Only the lower part of Amos Heaney's body could be seen. He was face down at the end of the jetty, head and chest in the water, wispy grey hair lifting with the current. His legs were in black cord trousers, his feet in ancient working boots and grey socks. A plank of wood was wedged across his back and under the jetty railings, to keep him submerged.

'It's that devil again!' said Bowles hoarsely. Channon had to agree with him – the devil indeed! He didn't speak, but held up a finger, warning the sergeant not to move, then ran to the car and came back with two pairs of gloves.

Together they hauled Amos from the water, laying him on his back on the jetty, while water ran from his mouth and dripped through the boards. He was dead, very dead and very cold. 'Several hours, boss?' asked Bowles, and Channon nodded. The skin was mottled grey beneath the weathered tan; one eye was closed by a bruise and the other, inflamed by immersion, gazed up at the brightening sky. Channon remembered asking him his reason for sacking Martin Goodchild, and in answer Amos had waved an arm to encompass his yard, the waterway and the same clouded heavens under which he now lay dead. 'This was the reason,' was what he had said. 'All this – all of it!'

Channon stared grimly at the body, preparing himself for a doubling of his workload. This second killing changed things – already it was changing his views on what had happened to Paul. Maybe they were landed with two opportunist robberies by some deranged individual, in which case the killings had nothing to do with Paul's gallery of girls. 'We'll have to check if anything's missing – money, valuables,' he said heavily. 'Get the crime scene people down here. You know who and what to send for.'

He wanted a moment of quiet to take in the scene, the essence of it, but as the sergeant took out his mobile there was the slam of a door. Luther Tresillian left the yard's own van by the entrance and called cheerfully, 'Amos? I've got everything we need!' Then he saw the two detectives standing side by side. 'Does Amos know you're here?' he asked in puzzlement. 'He'll be in his office.'

Channon silenced Bowles with a look. 'You've been out early in the van, Mr Tresillian.'

'Yes, round to Falmouth by road to pick up some spares for a rush job. Amos wanted them here by eight thirty.'

'Did you speak to him before you set off?'

'What? No, I took the van home with me when I finished yesterday, and set off from the house.' He headed for the office. 'I'll just make sure he knows you're waiting.'

Channon breathed out. This was no act. 'Wait!' he said. 'Amos is here.' He and Bowles moved apart and revealed the body. 'Mr Tresillian, I'm deeply sorry. Mr Heaney is dead – we believe murdered, we found him only a minute ago.'

Later, he was to remind himself that nobody could make himself lose colour as Luther Tresillian did then. Chalk-white and unbelieving, he stared down at the body. 'But why?' he asked blankly. 'Why do this to Amos?'

Channon nodded to Bowles to go ahead with his calls and tried to lead the other man to the office, but Tresillian resisted. 'You'll not leave him lying here, inspector?'

'No,' Channon assured him. 'We'll move him with full respect as soon as the police physician has seen him. Right now we need to notify his family.'

'Amos has no family – at least, not here in Pengorra. His wife died years back and there are no children. He lives on his own.' Tresillian nodded at the white cottage set among trees at the side of the yard.

'I thought he had family near Devoran,' persisted Channon. 'He mentioned a great-niece there.'

'Yes, yes – his nephew and family are over there. Inspector, will you be sending one of your officers to break it to them? I wouldn't like them to hear it over the phone.'

'We'll tell them in person,' Channon promised. 'I have to ask one more thing, Mr Tresillian. Can you formally identify the body for us?'

'But you already know him!'

'It's required by law, and we need it done as soon as possible. Could you manage it?'

So Luther Tresillian bent over the body of his employer and friend, and did as he was asked.

Steve was hard at work when Helen went to the studio. It seemed so right, so natural to find him there at the drawing board that she hesitated for long seconds, not wanting to tell him this latest news. It would drag them deeper into the unreal horror that was weighing down their lives; but he was looking at her, waiting, knowing that something was wrong.

She sat down. 'That was Chrissie on the phone. There's been another murder.'

Just as she had done when Chrissie told her, he focused at once on the children. 'I put Jaz and Katie safely on the bus,' he said in relief. 'And Lucy – is she still in bed?'

'She's having a shower. Steve, it's Amos who's been murdered – Amos Heaney. He was found in his yard, just along the riverbank.'

'*Amos*? But he's not connected to Paul, is he? What did Chrissie say, exactly?'

'It's on the grapevine that police cars raced off at half past eight. Those who live round the green saw them go, but didn't know what was happening. Nobody knows for certain but they've put two and two together, because the police have got the entrance to the yard taped off, and a white tent like the one they used at the Menna has been put up by the jetty. The path to Amos's cottage is taped off, as well.'

'And his man Luther?'

'They say he's in a state. He's at home with his wife and he won't say a word until he's sure Amos's nephew and family have been told.'

They stared at each other, and Steve said tightly, 'No doubt Channon and his sidekick will be here before long, checking on us.'

'Well, they can check all they like,' she said, 'because we've all been here together since the sergeant came.'

We've all been here together, she repeated to herself. How good it sounded. She didn't agree with him about the inspector, though. 'You know, Steve, I really can't see Channon trying to pin anything on us. I'm sure he was reluctant to take us in on Monday.'

'It didn't stop him doing it,' he retorted.

Then Lucy walked in, wearing her robe and a towel round her hair. 'I heard you on the phone, Mum. What's going on?'

Her parents exchanged a look. 'Sit down, my pet,' said Helen, 'something else has happened.'

To their amazement, once she'd heard the news Lucy seemed relieved. 'Don't you see?' she said. 'This could mean that Paul wasn't killed because – because he was Paul! I'm sorry about Mr Heaney, it's ghastly, but there might be a weirdo around who's murdered two people because they just happened to be in the wrong place at the wrong time – maybe it was to steal something, like Paul's earring.'

Steve shook his head. 'According to Chrissie, Amos was murdered in his own boatyard. How can that be the wrong place, never mind the wrong time? Listen, love, we don't yet know why Paul was killed, but you must be right in saying the two deaths are connected.'

Another terrible thing had happened, Helen thought, so why did she feel her spirits lifting? There could be only one reason. It was because Lucy was Lucy again – the real Lucy: still heartbroken, still bereft, but she was talking about Paul, she was communicating with her family.

Soon they would learn more about Amos's murder: when it happened, how it happened, maybe in time they would know *why* it had happened. She didn't think for a moment that they would have another visit from Channon. As it turned out, she was wrong about that . . .

By mid-afternoon the new enquiry was well under way. Addie was in her element, deploying extra staff with the skill of a brigadier before armed conflict, while Channon had closed his door on the bustle in order to have five minutes to himself. He knew he was on edge, not only because of Amos's murder, but because this second enquiry could jeopardize the first. He wondered what the abrasive Richard Stradling would make of another death being investigated side by side with that of his son.

Two very different victims: the one young, privileged, with dozens of contacts here and in London and several suspects for his murder. The other a quiet elderly man with a little boatyard, a single employee and no immediate family, but a lifelong member of this close community. Two different men, but their deaths could only be – *must* be – connected.

Now, leaning back in his chair, he deliberately slowed the computer-like sifting of facts in his mind. First things first . . . the estimate for the time of Amos's death was late last evening. A blow to his temple – weapon as yet unknown – had stunned him and then he had been

216

grabbed tightly by the neck, shoved face down into the river and held there. Not so ugly, not so bloody as Paul's murder, but equally brutal. The clumsy wedging of his shoulders in the water could mean that his killer was anxious to leave the scene and had made a hurried attempt to ensure that he was actually drowned . . . or could it have been a final outburst of rage after a struggle?

Hunter and his helpers were still on with the post-mortem, but he and Bowles had left them to the detailed work after being present for the main part. Right now Fred Jordan was still there; but his men, newly dragged away from *Daphne* and the Stradling boathouse, were swarming over Heaney's yard. Channon breathed out heavily. Fred was going to find that his obsession for masses of detail was fully satisfied with this lot.

He didn't know whether to be pleased or annoyed to see Jolly's bloodhound jowls quivering in the doorway. 'I know there's never a good time to interrupt you,' said the sad-eyed DC, 'but you did ask me to look at all angles of the statements from the staff at the Court.'

'Yes, I did. You've found discrepancies?'

'Not as such, but points of interest came up in cross-referencing. We've put them in writing as separate nuggets so you can look at them as and when you're free.'

Channon studied the other man. He was an odd individual, apparently uninfluenced by the strict regimentation of years of police work, yet with the insight to assess what would be most helpful to a senior officer. 'Thanks, Jolly. I well remember your selection of points when we were on the Lizard case. Having information laid out like that suits my way of working.'

Jolly left him with just two A4 sheets. Channon marched out of his office and, unusually for him, picked up a cup of tea. 'Give me a few minutes free of calls,' he said to the girls, then went back and began to read. No sooner had he started than the phone rang. 'Yes,' he snapped.

It was Addie. 'I know, don't tell me,' she said, 'but Lucy Pascoe is asking for a word.'

'All right, put her through.' Remembering the girl howling in her anguish, Channon braced himself and said calmly, 'DCI Channon.'

'It's Lucy Pascoe, Mr Channon. I won't keep you a moment, but I'm feeling more with it now, and starting to think things through a bit.' She was speaking very quickly and clearly, as if she'd been rehearsing what she must say. 'I just wondered whether you know that Paul was keen on prehistoric stuff? I thought it might have something to do with him being put against the stone.'

Channon swallowed a sigh. Here was another one aiming to solve the murder. Still, it had taken effort to ring him. 'As a matter of fact, we're just starting to look into that particular angle,' he said gently. 'My computer men have just found that Paul was searching for information on ancient history. Do you know if it was a new interest of his?'

'Not exactly new. He'd always been interested in it. It was when we were talking about my degree subject that he became keen to know more.'

'And what subject are you taking?'

'If I go to uni – and I might not – it will be classical archaeology and ancient history.'

Channon's mind raced. Did this explain the words next to her name in Paul's diary: *This one's different*? Or had he found her different because she was so very lovely, with the silver-blonde hair and those vast green eyes? Or because she was so refreshingly unspoilt? Or had he, quite simply, fallen in love with her?

'Lucy, this is important. Was anyone else aware of his interest in prehistoric times?'

'I don't know of anybody,' she said rapidly. 'Oh, yes, he did mention that the gardener at the Court knew a bit about Cornish standing stones, but that's all I can recall. You see, Mr Channon, I was thinking that maybe a maniac had killed him,' she was starting to gabble, evidently not as calm as she wanted to appear, 'or at least a weirdo out to steal his earring, and then when it happened to Mr Heaney it seemed as if it might be just someone going round murdering people at random, and if it was random it couldn't have anything to do with the standing stone and then I knew you'd have to sort it out.' She faltered to a stop.

'Lucy,' he said, 'I'll have to sort it out because it's my job to do that. I usually manage to solve my cases, and you'll have to trust me to do my best. If something really vital occurs to you, or if anything frightens you, you can ring me here at the room, or come in to see me. If I'm not here, ask for Inspector Savage – she'll help you.'

'Just checking, boss.' It was Bowles, full of bounce because of all the activity. 'Have you remembered you wanted to talk to the old bird with the shop as well as to Heaney? I did ring her earlier to say we were delayed.'

Channon looked at his paperwork, including Jolly's notes, still unread; on the other hand, shopkeepers could be useful, and this particular shopkeeper might be more useful than most . . . 'We'll give her ten minutes,' he said. 'Tell her we're coming.'

'Mr Chief Inspector,' was Biddy Stumble's greeting. 'I won't complain about waiting in for you and losing trade because I'm that upset about Amos. He was my friend, you know. We were in the same class at school, and I've supplied him with home-baked bread and farm stuff since long before his wife died, God rest her soul.'

Channon replied gravely, 'It's bad, Miss Stumbles, but we're working on it.'

Biddy slapped her cap with the flat of her hand. 'If you'd been any later I'd have been out,' she said. 'As it is I can only give you five minutes because I have to catch my regulars before it goes dark. Do you know folk don't want to walk down their own garden paths to my shop except in broad daylight?'

Oh, spare us, thought Bowles, she's seeing herself as hard done by because she's affected by a crime. She? Was it a she? The trousers, the man's cap kept on indoors – it was a wonder she wasn't wearing braces, as well.

They all moved to the little room that was a duplicate of the Goodchilds' next door, and equally spotless. It seemed to Channon that her eccentricity was confined to what she wore, not how she lived. But time was pressing. He began, 'Our enquiries have shown that a young relative of yours, Rosie Stumbles, was one of Paul Stradling's girlfriends.'

Biddy's lips twisted. 'What of it?'

'We're here to see if we can eliminate you from our lists of people who might have a grudge against him.'

'They'll be very long lists,' she said.

'And we check every person on them,' put in Bowles.

Biddy turned her attention to the sergeant. She'd heard he was hard as nails, though as far as she could see he was just a skinny young fella whose shirt had never seen an iron. But did the pair of them take her for a fool? 'If the detective chief inspector and his sergeant call on each and every one, then it's no wonder you haven't had time to solve the case!' she said.

'I don't visit each and every one,' said the DCI briskly, 'just you and Mr Heaney, because you both live so close to the murder scene. Now – in a nutshell, Miss Stumbles, what were your movements on Friday evening?'

'Well, I wasn't sitting at home watching the box,' she retorted, 'and I've no doubt someone will have reported seeing me and my shop out on the lanes between eight and nine thirty. I deliver my special orders on Friday evenings to those who aren't at home during the day. I've done you a list of those I called on.'

'Oh, so you were expecting to be asked?'

'I expected your men on the doors to ask, come to that, but all they wanted to know was what I'd seen, not where I'd been.'

'When my officers spoke to you we didn't know you had reason to resent Paul Stradling,' Channon said evenly, and wondered if there was more to her aggression than mere bluster. On impulse he asked, '*Did* you see anything unusual on your travels that night, Miss Stumbles?'

Biddy pushed back her cap. 'I saw young Stradling in

his posh car driving fast along the lane from the Court to the Menna.'

They both stared at her. 'We haven't got it on record,' said Channon.

'That's because I didn't tell you,' she said gnawing at her lip.

'Why not?'

'Because I didn't want to do or say anything to help you find the man who cut him up,' she said simply.

'That could be classed as withholding information, Miss Stumbles, and what makes you so sure the murderer was a man? We've been told that a strong woman could have done it.' He let his gaze rest for a moment on her well-built frame and muscular shoulders.

'All right,' she said, 'man or woman – whatever. I'm not proud of this, but just after the murder all I could think was, serve him right.' Tears of outrage filled her eyes and edged down her cheeks. 'My little Rosie was sixteen – *sixteen*. He tempted her, he used her, and within days he tossed her aside.'

Bowles couldn't stand weeping and had tensed up at the sight of tears. He wondered uneasily if this hitherto tough old bird knew that photographs existed of her dear, innocent little Rosie. If she'd seen them she would have gone for Paul with a meat cleaver, if she had one.

'I'm really sorry about young Rosie,' Channon told her, 'but to get back to Paul in his car. Did you see where he went?'

'No. He slowed before reaching the crossroads, then stopped about twenty yards away with his headlamps on full beam. If it had been daylight I'd have thought he'd stopped for a good view of the stone. As it was I drove past him and went on my way.'

'Do you recall what time you saw him?'

'I was on my last few calls, and running a bit later than usual, so it would be about a quarter past nine.'

'You're sure he was alone in the car?'

'Yes, he was alone, so that in itself was a record.'

221

'Quite,' agreed Channon. 'One more point, did you see or hear anything unusual from the Goodchilds' house at any time during the evening?'

'I did not.'

'You didn't see or hear anyone leaving the house?'

'No, except Sue going to her work early on, as she usually does.' Reluctance to discuss her friends was behind every word.

'You'll have to make a statement about all that you've told us, and then sign it,' Channon said. 'We'll be in touch about that.'

They left her standing in the neat little room, wiping her eyes with her fingers. Once at the car Bowles said, 'What an old crab!'

'Not an easy woman,' agreed Channon, 'but she's still upset that somebody she loves was badly treated. Bowles, you do realize that Heaney's murder will broaden the enquiry? It could mean that Paul's death wasn't necessarily connected to any of his girls.'

'I realize, right enough,' confirmed the sergeant grimly. 'It will be a case of DNA and forensics morning, noon and night, I suppose. By the way, boss, at the time we found Heaney the SOCOs had just about finished on the Stradlings' boat and boathouse, so – wait for it – Fred Jordan has sent preliminary notes for you to enjoy while he prepares his final mountain of info. They'll be on your desk.'

'Fred won't have time to prepare anything for a while now he's got another crime scene to deal with,' said Channon grimly. 'Listen, I'm going out for half an hour. I'll be unavailable – and use my mobile at your peril. Liaise with Inspector Savage if anything turns up.' Without another word he marched to his desk, gathered up his papers and left Bowles staring after him.

Sitting in the back of the car with Jaz and her dad in front, Katie was in low spirits. Everyone at school had known about the second murder, and now the thought of it was making her feel a bit sick. She'd liked Mr Heaney – he used to let her watch him and Mr Tresillian at work on the boats, and once he'd called her 'Miss MacArthur'. That had pleased her. She'd told him she intended to be an even better sailor than her heroine, and he hadn't laughed.

The trouble was that now he'd been murdered, her parents might not let her go down to the water's edge as she'd planned, especially as the murder had taken place so near to Trenoon. She ground her teeth hard. Even if she told the lie she'd been practising about wanting to watch the shipping, they would probably insist on her staying indoors . . .

Once at home she and Jaz left their dad checking that the big gate and outbuildings were secure and went inside to find Lucy and their mum having an argument. Jaz grunted and went off to his room, but she wanted to hear what it was about and, giving her mum the usual quick kiss, busied herself getting a drink of ginger cordial.

'I can't believe you didn't tell them when they were here,' her mum was saying. 'You know it's important or you wouldn't have told me now.'

All ears, Katie tried to make herself unnoticeable. 'So what time did you see him?' her mum said next.

'When I was coming home from – you know – after seeing Paul on the boat.'

'Was he on his motorbike?' So it was Martin they were talking about.

'No, he was on foot. He was out of the beam of the headlights, so I only glimpsed him, but I recognized him from his woolly hat and the jacket he wears when he's in the garden. Mum – it was just Martin. You know what he's like – he can't have done anything!'

Helen stared at her sadly. 'All right, he's just Martin, and I honestly don't think he's capable of murder, but the fact remains he was sacked from his job because of Paul's complaint, and the man who sacked him was Amos Heaney, *and* he tried to wreck the boat with an axe! You'll *have* to tell Channon. Here's your dad, we'll see what he thinks.'

Drink in hand, Katie edged quietly out of the kitchen. The three of them were going to be so busy talking she could make her escape without telling any lies at all. She would change her clothes and go right down the garden to do what she'd planned, and when she came back they wouldn't even have missed her.

Channon sat in his car at the edge of a field high above Carrick Roads, yet only minutes from the incident room at Pengorra. The winter sun was sinking to a dull glow far beyond the Lizard, and below him the waterway sparkled as lights came on in riverside houses and passing boats.

He told himself he needed this spell of quiet, so was half an hour too much to ask? Lowering a window he breathed in cold, salt-laden air that cleared his head at once, but it was getting darker, so he switched on the light before starting to read. He could have felt foolish – a senior policeman studying data inside a car parked in a deserted spot – but such a feeling never even impinged on him. The case was what mattered.

He tackled Fred Jordan's stuff first, unsurprised to find that the head SOCO's 'preliminary notes' ran to several pages. The first point of interest was that yet another knife of the right size and strength had been found, spotlessly clean and kept in its place in *Daphne*'s ultra-modern galley. All human traces from the boat were in the hands of Forensic, and Fred suggested that they might prove to be those of Paul, his father, the boatman-chef, Lucy Pascoe and possibly Luther Tresillian. So far then, not a single interesting clue, pending forensic reports.

The big boathouse had been more revealing, but with so many waterproofs, wellingtons, protective gloves and nautical implements that even a regular user of the place would find it hard to say what was missing. One item, however, was absent from the ranks of expensive tools. There was an empty space where a large, well-greased implement had rested. Forensic would assess what it might have been and whether it could have been the pre-death weapon. No fingerprints around, but there were smears and smudges, possibly from rubber gloves. The last item of interest was that the boathouse doors had not been forced. And that was it, except for technical details in moderation and a massive list of what had been handed to the forensic team.

And then there was the letter from the Met in London, confirming their fax saying that the solving of the Stradling case now lay with the Devon and Cornwall force. No surprise there, but stapled to the letter was a note from his opposite number in the City. It said simply, *Sorry we've had to draw a line under this, Bill, but we both know that man-hours are money. Our side of it is all in computer records, but I'm still – unofficially – keeping eyes and ears wide open on it, so if you need any more inside info, give me a ring.*

Did he need more inside info? What detective in his position didn't? Channon thought for all of twenty seconds and rang the man on his direct line. 'Bill Channon in Falmouth,' he said. 'Thanks for your note. Before we say a last goodbye have you got anything new on Nigel Nollens, or anyone else, for that matter?'

'As far as we can see, Nollens is clean, as I told you. I got the impression he'd been useful to the Stradlings. Earlier this year when the wife was gravely ill he and Paul took on a lot of Stradling's routine work, leaving him free to be with her. It seems he seldom left her side – he was some devoted husband. The doctors had to be on their toes when he demanded an update.

'He reported one of them to the GMC for negligence, maybe with grounds, I don't know, and then Nollens came into it, or at least Nollens senior did – he's a legal wheeler-dealer. It seems Stradling threatened violence to a consultant who was treating his wife, and the doctor kicked up a fuss. Nollens senior was brought in – he hushed it up and settled out of court. One odd thing about the Nollenses – the father's a bit of a brain, a high-flyer, so I don't know what he thinks of his son being a mere secretary, even to someone with clout, like Stradling. That's about it, Bill.'

Channon was thanking him before ringing off, when the London man said, 'Oh – one other thing. You asked me about Steve Pascoe having a grudge against Paul, and I told you about the loan to his partnership, didn't I? Well, in addition to that I've heard from a source in finance that there was a junior architect in the practice – the niece of a friend of Pascoe's – doing a year's practical before her finals. She was a pretty little thing, and of course Paul got to her. He did the usual, romanced her and then dropped her flat. She was devastated.

'Pascoe was livid, and tackled Paul in front of witnesses, but meladdo just brushed it aside and went on his sweet way. The girl had some sort of breakdown, I think, but she's back at work now, part-time. And that's your lot. Only unofficial contact from now on, and the best of luck.'

Channon stared into the gathering darkness. More issues, more enquiries, just as many suspects. This case was complicated . . . He picked up the two sheets of Jolly's 'nuggets', laid out in separate blocks for easy assimilation.

He read them through, switched off the light and sat back in his seat. Two early stars were hanging above the distant area where his home beach lay. He visualized the silver sand under the stars, with the moon climbing high. Not for him to see, though, not yet . . . He started the engine and headed the car down to Pengorra's village green.

Chapter Seventeen

Channon faced Bowles across the desk and wasn't prepared to argue. 'Accept it,' he said, tapping the papers in front of him. 'There are points to be queried in the staff's statements and it was DC Jolly who spotted them.'

Bowles seethed. 'All I'm saying is I'd have liked the chance to study these so-called points for myself before we dash off to the Court.'

'You took the statements; you and Soker prepared them for signing – how much more chance do you need? There's one aspect in particular I'd have thought you would pounce on.'

Bowles let out a noisy breath. He was a sergeant, for God's sake, not some goggle-eyed constable, wet behind the ears. 'And what aspect is that?'

'You're masterminding the checking of Paul's gallery – you must have seen the list of names?'

Bowles was wary. 'Yes.'

'The chef-cum-boatman at the Stradlings' is one Simon Bowen, is he not? Bowen is also the surname of a seventeen-year-old girl from Carnon Downs, who had a one-week stint in Paul's gallery. Simon Bowen lives at the Court, but his home address is in Carnon Downs. I think that just might be something to look into, don't you?'

'Yes, if you're taking the line that every single relation of the girls is behaving as if it's the 1800s and defending their honour', said Bowles acidly. 'She'll be on the list for a visit, but they won't have got to her yet. What's more, I'm not the only one who could have spotted it.'

'No, you're not,' conceded Channon, 'but you're one of the very few to have seen the list of girls and also taken statements from those close to Paul.'

'OK, so I missed it! I've been working like a dog.'

'So have we all, sergeant, so have we all. Now – as a matter of courtesy we'll have to talk to Stradling before we question his staff. Let's go!'

At the Court they found Nigel Nollens playing guard to the bereaved father. 'What do you want now?' he asked impatiently. 'Mr Stradling isn't too well. He was distraught to learn there'd been another murder.'

'In that case we won't disturb him, but please inform him that we're about to interview his staff. Then perhaps you'll be good enough to bring them here and we'll speak to them either separately or together as we see fit.'

Give the DCI his due, thought Bowles, when he spoke in that tone nobody argued with him, not even Nollens. Five minutes later Mr and Mrs Bradley, their niece Jasmine the maid, Simon Bowen and Sandie Goolden the gardener were all gathered in the hall. Not one looked other than tense and slightly apprehensive.

'We won't keep you for long,' said Channon. 'You'll all have heard about the second murder, and there'll be routine enquiries about that in the next day or so, but right now all we want is to clear up a few queries about the evening of Paul's death. We have your statements, of course, but we just need another word. I think it might be better if we see you one or two at a time, so Mr and Mrs Bradley – perhaps you'd step inside here for a moment?'

In the office the housekeeper and her husband faced the detectives among all the high-tech trappings of the Stradlings' business. 'First, Mr Bradley, could you confirm that you cleaned the Bentley as usual, within a short time of Mr Stradling arriving?'

Stolid, fiftyish, Bradley faced him. 'Yes, I did. It was in the garage, spotless, before Mr Stradling and Paul sat down to their meal.'

'Thank you. Now, you said in your statement that you had seen nothing out of place or unusual in the grounds and outbuildings on Friday or Saturday. We're not quite clear if that included the boathouse?' Point number one, Bowles told himself grimly.

'No, it didn't. Simon sees to the boathouse and the boat itself. They're his responsibility, along with the cooking, of course. Mr Stradling liked the boat kept immaculate, the same as his car.'

'Was the late Mrs Stradling just as particular?' asked Channon, and Bowles rolled his eyes. Why not ask for a family tree and have done with it?

Mrs Bradley answered. 'Yes, she was one proper lady. She liked things nice, she did, right to her end. She was a lovely woman, inspector.'

'Yes, I've been told she was beautiful.'

'Beautiful, admitted, even when she was nothing but skin and bone, but I mean lovely in her ways, and in her heart.'

'Ah. It must have been a sad time for all of you when she was terminally ill?'

'For all of us, yes, but as she became weaker we only saw her at intervals. Mr Stradling watched over her day in, day out. We were all worried he'd give way under the strain of it, but he kept on going just for her, and when she passed away he kept going for his son.'

There was such grace and simplicity in her answers that Channon felt slightly uncomfortable to be delving into the motivations of the staff. It sounded as though they were all completely loyal to their employers. He said, 'We were told that Mr Stradling and Paul had coffee by the fire after their meal. Did you serve them with it, Mrs Bradley?' Bowles sighed; was this point number two?

'No, Jasmine serves them at table, and with anything else they might want during the evening, but as we told the sergeant, Mr Stradling likes things to be informal down here, they like to do their own thing, sort of. We're rarely needed after we've cleared away.'

'When they arrived did Paul and his father seem any different than usual in their behaviour, or in what they said?'

'None of us noticed anything, inspector. They were deep in talk, as they always were. If it wasn't business, it was local stuff. They were great ones for the Carrick Roads area, you know.'

'Yes, I believe Paul showed an interest in Cornish history – standing stones and so forth, and talked to you about it, Mr Bradley?'

'Well, he mentioned it, and asked me a few things when I told him it was an interest of mine.' Bradley was looking slightly sick. 'When we chatted I little knew what would happen at our own standing stone in Pengorra.'

'You didn't discuss standing stones on Friday?'

'No, we talked a couple of times about them on his last visit a fortnight ago.'

'Have you any idea why the Menna should have been the site for his death?'

Bradley shook his head. 'It's as big a mystery to me as it is to everyone else,' he said.

'One last point. At what time did you and your niece separate after watching the DVD?'

'Like we said before, about eleven.'

'Thank you very much, that's all,' said Channon.

Next came Jasmine; curvaceous, pretty, and like her aunt and uncle, somewhat wary. Channon was at his most disarming. 'Ah, Miss Bradley – may I call you Jasmine? Thank you. I believe it was you who served coffee to father and son on Friday evening. Did you notice anything different about them, or hear what they were talking about?'

She looked puzzled. 'They weren't talking all that much, as I recall.' Point number three, Bowles told himself. 'I thought perhaps Mr Stradling was tired after his journey. He's always on the go, you know, and we try to let him relax when he comes down here. As for Paul, he went off to his room to make his calls while I was clearing their coffee things. He was still there when I went in to turn down his bed and make sure everything was in order for the night. I apologized and said I'd come back later, but he just flipped a hand to tell me to go ahead.'

'He was on the phone while you were in the room?'

'No, as a matter of fact, he wasn't. He was sitting there, staring into space. I remember it because it wasn't like him.'

'He wasn't one for sitting around thinking, then?'

'Not him – he was a mover – all for action. Just at that moment he looked as if he was deciding on something – I thought maybe it was to do with one of his calls.'

Channon shot a look at Bowles. Stradling had mentioned the phone calls days ago, so surely they'd done a check on them? The sergeant merely nodded and managed not to sneer. He might have missed a paltry point or two, but please – give him credit for the basics . . .

Channon asked next, 'Jasmine, could I ask you for your views on Paul? He was one for the girls, I believe?'

She surveyed them both with dark blue eyes that were very like her uncle's. 'He liked girls and they liked him,' she said simply.

'So I gather. Now, don't be offended by my next question, it's just that we have to eliminate everyone who was close to Paul – at any time. Did he ever make a pass at you?'

'Can a duck swim? It was as natural as breathing to Paul. It was ages ago, but it didn't last. I didn't want to be one of such a long line, and in any case, he told me his father didn't want him to be involved with the staff.'

'But you'd been involved? Sexually?'

'Yes, for three weeks or so. We finished by a sort of mutual consent.'

'What did your aunt and uncle make of it?'

'I don't know. I didn't tell them I used to sleep with Paul on the boat, but maybe they guessed.'

'Do you know if Paul was ever involved with the young gardening lady?'

'Sandie?' Jasmine half-smiled. 'You'll have to ask her about that, inspector, her or Simon.'

'I'll do that,' said Channon mildly. 'Thank you, Jasmine.' When she'd left the room he said to Bowles, 'Keep an eye on Simon's reactions when I ask Sandie about Paul, will you, then I can concentrate on her.'

Simon Bowen looked more like a sailor than a chef: tall, lean, weather-beaten, with sun creases at the corners of his eyes. His partner Sandie would have fitted well into Paul's gallery; slim, long-legged, clear-skinned, with her hair in a thick, honey-gold plait down her back. Competence oozed from her, but Channon saw with interest that she and Simon were holding hands.

'Just a quick recap on one or two points from your statements,' he said easily. 'First, Mr Bowen – Simon, everyone is agreed that on Friday night you and your partner went off to your own cottage at about nine thirty, leaving the Bradleys and Jasmine watching a DVD. Could you remind me how you spent the rest of your evening? Were you together?'

Simon nodded. 'We opened a bottle of wine and listened to some of our music, then we had an early night – we were in bed by about ten thirty.'

'You didn't go down to the jetty to check on the boat?'

'No. All was in order down there. I'd checked it was immaculate and left everything locked early in the evening. If Paul chose to sleep on board he had his own keys and so did Mr Stradling.'

'And what about the boathouse? Did you leave that locked?'

'Of course I did. There's equipment in there – expensive tools and sailing gear.'

'Did you check on the boat and boathouse on Saturday morning, Simon?'

'No. Paul had told me he might be on board on Friday evening. When he's down here with Mr Stradling I keep out of their way as much as I can. They like – liked, I mean – to do their own thing, just as if they're here on their own.'

Apart from being looked after by five members of staff, Channon thought wearily, and knew that Bowles was

232

thinking the same. 'I know you haven't been allowed on board or in the boathouse since Saturday morning, but very soon my men will be asking you to check the tool racks and lockers to see if there's anything missing. Tell me, did you ever take Mr Stradling and Paul out in *Daphne*, or did they always sail themselves?'

'Sometimes I went with them if they went on a trip of two or three days and wanted a restful time. I'd take over the running of the boat and often sail through the night to save dropping anchor. At other times they would go out either together or on their own. Mr Stradling was more expert than Paul, I'd say, but they were both pretty good.'

Channon turned his attention to Sandie. 'I believe you're in charge of the grounds and greenhouses, Miss Goolden, but you have help from Mr Bradley?'

'That's right. He's just as good as me, but I hold the title. We work together, and he spends some of his time on odd jobs around the place.'

'Sandie, I have to ask you this. We all know that Paul was one for the girls. Were you ever involved with him – maybe before you and Simon became partners?'

Clear blue eyes looked straight into his. 'No, inspector, I wasn't. I know Paul had lots of girls, but I wasn't one of them.'

Relief outweighed surprise that this lovely girl had never been one of Paul's gallery; while Bowles, watching Simon carefully, decided that the chef had never regarded Paul as a rival.

Then Channon said suddenly, 'Simon, the young girl Flora Bowen from Carnon Downs was one of Paul's many sleeping partners. Is she by any chance a member of your family?'

Simon Bowen was very still. 'As I'm sure you already know, she's my sister,' he said evenly.

'It's part of the enquiry, Simon – we have to check these things. She'll have a visit from my men very soon – just a routine procedure. May I ask how you felt about their relationship?'

233

'Of course you can ask – I can't stop you, can I? If Flora chose to sleep with the biggest lecher in Cornwall, that's her affair. She's over the legal age, inspector, so I wasn't about to challenge Paul to a duel.'

Bowles kept a straight face. What had he pointed out half an hour ago? All this fuss about a few country bumpkins falling into bed just for the glamour and the earring! It was over the top – he'd said so all along!

But Channon was observing the young ones. Sandie was looking at the floor with an air of careless disregard; Simon was holding her hand – tightly by the look of it because she was wiggling the tips of her fingers. It was clear that controlled tension linked the pair of them. On impulse he said, 'Our forensic samples from the boat and boathouse are still being examined, so we might be asking you both for samples of your DNA – just as routine, of course.'

Simon blinked, then resumed his stolid, earnest expression. 'Of course,' he repeated, and waited for the next question. Channon, however, had finished, and with a pleasant nod sent them on their way.

Nollens approached as the two detectives crossed the hall. He blocked their way and said, 'Mr Stradling wants an update.'

Channon looked at him. 'I thought he was too unwell to be disturbed?'

'He is,' agreed Nollens, 'but he needs to know what's happening.'

Channon nodded and followed the secretary. Bowles trailed behind them, reluctant to face the financier, but curious to see his reactions to another murder. They found him sitting in the lamplight of the big sitting room, with an impressive log fire crackling in the hearth.

'Ah, Channon – and your sergeant, eh? I'm sorry to be on my backside instead of on my feet, but I'm not quite myself – a bit weak at the knees to be honest. Mrs Bradley's twittering about getting the doctor, but I think this Heaney thing has just thrown me. I can't seem to take it in, and I'm worried it'll distract you from dealing with Paul's case.'

'We've had extra men drafted in,' Channon assured him, 'and everyone will be working flat out.'

Bowles was trying not to stare at Stradling. Since he saw him four days ago he'd turned into the closest he'd ever seen to a walking corpse – or in his case, a sitting one. He was deep in an armchair of soft, caramel-coloured leather that looked as comfortable as a cloud – probably his favourite chair in this beautiful room. On the wall facing the chair was a vast blow-up of *Daphne* at sea; atmospheric, mesmerizing, almost breathtaking. Then Bowles saw that the red-rimmed eyes behind Stradling's glasses were wet. He looked away hurriedly. Surely the guy wasn't going to weep?

Weeping, it seemed, was unlikely. Stradling bent his head and eyed Channon sideways from under his brows. 'The two deaths are connected,' he said flatly. 'You must agree on that?'

'We believe so, of course, but so far there's no proof of it. I can't discuss our work on Mr Heaney's case, but is there anything we can tell you about your son's enquiry?'

'Yes, there is. What about suspects? You arrested the Pascoe woman, didn't you, and then you let her go.'

'We had grounds to arrest her,' Channon told him, 'but insufficient grounds to keep her. We also questioned her husband and her son, as we've questioned many more people in this area – and as I think I told you, our colleagues in London have been doing the same. I'll keep you informed on our progress, Mr Stradling, and now we must go.'

'Just a minute, just a minute – you've been interviewing my staff! Is that the best you can do – badgering those who care for me and my property?'

'Not the best, no,' said Channon. 'My personal best will be when I can tell you who murdered your son, and why.'

With that they left Stradling, walked past the watchful Nollens, and left the house. 'Boss,' said Bowles as he got behind the wheel, 'you're always telling me to treat people with respect – especially victims' families – but it's bloody difficult when they're like Stradling.'

'It's bloody difficult when your son's been hacked to death,' retorted Channon. 'He's an awkward devil, admitted, but they come in all shapes and sizes, and what's more –' He stopped as his phone shrilled. It was Addie from the room.

'Bill, I thought I'd better let you know that Mrs Pascoe's just been on, asking for you. She says she thinks you should know that Lucy has just told them she saw Martin Goodchild out near the Menna on Friday night, at about ten minutes to ten. Lucy herself was reluctant to tell you about it, and so was her dad.'

Channon sighed in irritation. 'It was wet, it was windy and these are quiet country roads,' he said, 'but on Friday evening they were more like Piccadilly Circus! Is she sure of the time?'

'Yes, give or take five minutes,' said Addie, and rang off.

'Head for the Goodchilds' place,' he said to Bowles. 'Lucy Pascoe says she saw Martin out near the Menna on Friday evening.'

'Well, well, well.' Bowles turned to go up to the cottages. 'It's taken her long enough to remember that. I wonder what he has to say for himself?' Had he been wrong in thinking Marty-boy was white as the driven? He was an oddball, after all . . .

'So who was Paul talking to on the phone?' asked Channon as they went.

'Need you ask? His sleeping partner Lucy Pascoe, of course – he didn't speak to any of the others – just her; and a call booking a table for two for a meal on Saturday night – that would be one empty table, right enough. There was nothing suspicious or startling – give me credit for that, boss.'

Sue Goodchild was doing her sums at the kitchen table – income against outgoings – but no matter how she tried

236

to adjust them, the answers were always the same. When Martin came in and hung up his coat and helmet, she said, 'Marty, is there any way you can get a bit of extra work for a week or two while I'm laid off? When I get paid on Saturday it'll only be half my usual, and things will be tight.'

He gave her his rare but captivating smile. 'Mum, I told you not to worry. I've just got two weeks' part-time at the fish cellars – cash in hand.'

Born and raised in a fishing family, Sue was used to the smell of those who worked on the gutting benches, but it didn't follow that she liked it. This would mean more washing of his clothes, and making sure there was enough hot water for his shower after every shift. Still, money was money – it oiled the wheels of life, and goodness only knew the wheels of *her* life squeaked and grated as if they'd never been oiled in nineteen years.

But when Marty gave her that smile he looked so – so like an ordinary lad she could only thank the good Lord that he was her son. She got up to give him a kiss and saw the lights of the car through the hall window. It was the police again!

She let them in and tried to stay calm. 'What can we do for you, inspector?'

Channon eyed her gravely. He really hoped that this good, hardworking mother wasn't going to be hurt, yet knew quite well that if she was, he would play a part in the hurting. He spoke gently. 'We just want another word with Martin, Mrs Goodchild.'

He turned to the big, silent young man. 'Martin, we have it on good authority that you were on the road not far from the Menna at about nine fifty on Friday evening, yet in your statement you said you hadn't left the house, that you were listening to music, playing computer games and watching TV. Can you explain?'

Martin sighed and nodded. 'All right,' he admitted readily, 'I went out for a bit.'

'Why, Martin? Where?'

For long seconds Martin hesitated. Then he looked at his mother and gave a little shrug. 'I went down to the Stradlings' jetty.'

Sue uttered a sound that was both a squeak and a groan, but nobody paid attention. Bloody hell, thought Bowles, this was one cool oddball, but Channon seemed unperturbed. 'Ah – so you wanted to see what, exactly?'

'Whether Lucy's car was there. Whether she was on the boat with Paul.'

'And was she?'

'Yes. Her car was there and the lights were on in the boat.'

'So what did you do?'

'I stood there, thinking.'

'What – thinking about Paul and Lucy together?'

'Yes.'

'And deciding you couldn't let him have her?'

Martin looked at him as if he was mad. 'No, deciding there was nothing I could do about it – I'm not a fool. When the hatch opened I knew I didn't want to watch them come up on deck together, so I headed back through the grounds and set off home along the lanes.'

Bowles exchanged a look with Channon. This was so weak it just might be true. Marty-boy was an oddball, but even an oddball wouldn't think he stood a chance against the earring, the Aston Martin and a guy like Paul. Was the DCI going to take him in?

Oh, no. Channon spoke very seriously. 'Martin, we've already told you not to leave the area as we may need to question you further. I'm repeating that now, as we wait for forensic information and the results of DNA tests. We may have to ask for samples of your own DNA, of course.'

As his mother sank down on the sofa, Martin led them to the door. 'I won't be going anywhere,' he said calmly, 'except to work, of course.'

Outside the cottage, Bowles said, 'One cool customer.'

'How do you see him now?' asked Channon.

'As I did yesterday,' admitted the sergeant. 'Pretty weird, but not guilty, m'lord.'

'Same here,' said Channon. 'One quick call on Steve Pascoe and then we'll get back to concentrate on Amos.'

'And have a bite to eat?'

'And that,' agreed Channon. 'Let's go!'

Windows glowing against dark granite, Trenoon sat on its peaceful hillside. The two detectives drove round to the front entrance overlooking the water, but as they passed the rear yard it was clear that something was wrong. Raised voices could be heard through the open kitchen door, and then an overwrought scream. Bowles squealed to a stop, but before they could ring the bell the front door opened and Steve Pascoe hurtled out, carrying a torch. 'Katie!' he yelled. 'Katie!' Then he saw the visitors and gasped, 'Oh, thank God! Have you got her?'

It seemed to Channon that cold hands clutched at his ribs. The child was missing! 'What's happened?' he demanded.

Steve Pascoe let out a frustrated cry. 'Oh, no – I thought you'd found her! It's Katie – we don't know where she is. I brought her back from the school bus with Jaz, but after that there was a lot going on – trying to get Lucy to ring you, arguing about it, talking about Amos. We thought she was in her room doing her homework, but when Helen went in just now she wasn't there. She's changed her clothes and taken her life jacket.' He started to hurry away, talking over his shoulder. 'Helen says she might have gone out in her boat although we've told her not to – I'm going to see. You must come as well – come on!'

Torch jerking, he ran away down the garden. The two men followed, stumbling as they went, but more light appeared behind them as Helen, Lucy and Jaz arrived with more torches and a lantern. Lucy was weeping as she ran, Jaz was a jumble of long limbs in his haste.

Channon hadn't recalled that the garden was so long. They seemed to be descending for ever, past shrubs and rockeries and sloping lawns; even a little summerhouse that loomed from the darkness like some sinister hideaway. His mind was moving faster than his feet. They were all panicking, but was it really likely that little Katie was in danger? Two men had been murdered – *men*, not children: one of them for reasons unknown, the other probably because of something he either knew or had seen. In spite of such thoughts, the cold hands were waiting to squeeze his ribs again . . .

They were nearly there, leaping across boulders to a strip of sand that shone silver under their lights Helen let out a wail. 'Her boat's gone! But she knows she's not to use it until everything's safe again!' Steve turned to take her hand and they all ran to the wooden jetty: six people looking wildly at the dark water backed by the distant lights of the opposite bank.

Channon turned to Bowles. 'Ring the room and alert them, then see if Fred and the SOCOs are still at the boat-yard. Get them here – by water!' To the Pascoes he said, 'We're getting men here and we'll search both upstream and down. She's probably fine, but we don't want her to be out alone, either on water or on land.'

Helen clutched her lantern and held on to Steve's hand. She'd thought life was bad when he was involved with that other woman, she'd thought it was terrible when they were all questioned by Channon. But awful though it was, they'd all been safe! Safe . . . safe . . . safe . . . the word clanged in her brain. Her little Katie wasn't safe – she was out somewhere on this black water. She wasn't safe – not yet – but Steve was here, and so was DCI Channon. They would find her in a minute. They must find her, and then she *would* be safe, because she would never, ever, let her out of her sight again.

Chapter Eighteen

Katie was a bit put out. Things were happening – some of them good – but she wasn't actually in charge, and she didn't like it. She would have to find a way to hide her wet clothes from her mum, but once she was back in her room she could manage that.

She didn't want to admit it, but being wet through out on the water on a dark November afternoon wasn't pleasant, and it was awkward rowing the boat when she was wearing her life jacket. She could use the motor, of course, just to get back quickly, and then switch off before she actually arrived . . . yes, that's what she would do.

At Trenoon's jetty the six anxious watchers heard the approach of a boat, and Lucy let out a sob of relief. 'They're here!' she gasped. 'Mr Channon – your men are coming!'

Her father was looking upstream and listening. 'That's not the police,' he said. 'It's only a little engine – it's Katie's!' Channon felt weak with relief. For a moment back there – just a moment – he'd pictured the worst.

Seeing the lights and the group of people waiting, Katie gave a groan of apprehension. She'd expected to be back in her room before anyone missed her, but now they were all here waiting, with DCI Channon and his horrible sergeant. Weighed down with her sodden clothes she edged her dinghy to the jetty and, letting Jaz tie up, squelched ashore. She faced them all and said, 'I'm sorry.'

Relief made Helen scream at her. 'How could you, Katie? How *could* you go out on the water when we've told you not to? We've been out of our minds! You could have been attacked, you could have been killed!'

Katie thought that was a bit over the top, and in any case she didn't see why she should be told off in front of Mr Channon. 'I'm here, Mum,' she pointed out, 'and nothing's happened to me. Don't you see, I was out in my boat, away from everyone. I was safe.'

'Is that why you're wet through?' demanded Jaz, annoyed to find that, just like his mum, he wanted to shout and scream at her.

'That was a slight accident,' Katie said with dignity. 'I was leaning out of the boat to get hold of something and – uh – I overbalanced and fell in – just for a second, that's all.'

She saw her dad watching her. It registered that he was crying, and she began to see that they'd all been really worried. It annoyed her, but at the same time it made her feel so warm she stopped shivering, and ran into the cluster of lights and her dad's outstretched arms. As he held her close his tear-wet eyes met Helen's, then he bent to kiss the sodden spirals of her hair. 'I'm sorry,' she said for the second time.

'Cancel the search parties,' Channon told Bowles heavily. 'Come on, we'll call back later.'

He turned to go, but Katie wrenched herself from her father's arms. 'Wait, Mr Channon,' she cried. 'All of you – just listen! I went out in secret to see if anything suspicious was happening. I put down the mast and used the oars so people wouldn't know I was there, and I stayed close in to the bank. I'm sorry you were all worried, but I intended to be back before you missed me. And then – well – I found these!'

She unzipped her pocket and took out something wrapped in a wet tissue. Carefully she folded it back and revealed a bunch of keys. 'I found these,' she repeated, 'and I haven't touched them with my bare hands. I think they must belong to Mr Heaney.'

Bemused, Channon exchanged a look with Bowles. 'Where, exactly, did you find them, Katie?'

She managed not to smile, and instead gave a casual shrug. 'Under his jetty, on one of the wooden supports.'

Hitherto speechless at the antics of the little gremlin, Bowles said now, 'But our men should be all over Heaney's yard.'

'Oh, they are,' she assured him, 'in their white overalls, with great big lights shining everywhere, but you see, my boat was below the bank so they didn't see me watching them. And then just when I was thinking that all those men would be sure to find any really good clues, I saw something right beside me, glinting in a beam from the lights. It was the keys, balanced on a cross-brace under the jetty, just above the waterline.'

Not wanting to sound critical of those searching the yard, she added kindly, 'I'm sure your men would have found them if I hadn't seen them first. I used a tissue and reached under the boards of the jetty, and then I fell in, but I held on to the keys, and in less than a minute I was rowing back with them!'

Channon recalled the sweatshirt she was wearing when he first met her. 'Ellen MacArthur herself couldn't have done better,' he said gravely. 'We'll need to put it down in writing where you found them, but for now off you go to get warm and dry – we'll look after the keys.'

The Pascoes all hurried away, leaving the detectives with a single torch. 'Drop me back at the room,' Channon said, putting the keys in a plastic bag, 'then slip round to Tresillian and ask him whether he recognizes these. They belong to someone who handles boats – look at the floats on them. Even if they'd dropped in the water they wouldn't have sunk from sight – unlike the protective clothing our man must have worn. That'll be weighted down at the bottom of Carrick Roads or he's a fool – and I don't think he is.'

Bowles was examining the keys by the light of the torch. 'They look a bit flash for old Heaney,' he said dubiously. 'Boss, I think they might be Paul's.'

243

Channon's eyes gleamed. 'Check with Tresillian,' he said, 'and Stradling as well. We'll have a chat when you get back, and I might just remind Fred to keep an eye on the water's edge, next time he's with his SOCOs in a boatyard.'

It was getting late but the room was still busy, and a group of mixed ranks were gathered together at one end, drinking coffee amid the smell of stale food and damp clothes.

Bowles was feeling better after consuming the last available pizza and Addie Savage was wondering why she had ever doubted being happy to be working with Channon again. As the local bobby and a good friend to Amos Heaney, PC Cloak was there as well, eager to be of help.

Channon himself was having a final run-through before they finished for the day: analysing, recapping, asking questions and considering the replies. 'Right,' he was saying, 'the keys.' There was a ripple of amusement at that. Fred Jordan was known as a stickler, maybe even a know-all, and it had caused many a snigger when word got out that a twelve-year-old had spotted an important clue before his team had found it. 'We've got confirmation that they belong to Paul, so that tells us – what?'

'That he was transported first by water, and then carried up the slope to the Menna?' asked Soker.

'Correct. And it does narrow things down a bit. We think he was unconscious at the time, so it follows he was brought from somewhere close at hand, because nobody would want to risk being seen out on the Roads with a body in their boat. He could have been brought from his own home jetty – we have a lead on the weapon used on him. His keys could have fallen from his pocket when he was dragged or lifted from the vessel at Amos's jetty. His wallet and any other stuff could have been taken later – the killer may not even have known the keys had gone missing.'

Yates, as always at the back of the group, said, 'Or he might have known that Paul would have them with him

244

and that they must have been lost, and decided to have a final search for them – last night.'

Channon nodded. 'And Amos could have interrupted his search, or perhaps he knew him and they chatted together. Then our man, knowing he might have incriminated himself by looking for the keys, made sure that Amos wouldn't be telling anyone he'd visited the yard in the dark.'

'That all puts us back to Paul's body being carried up the slope from the yard,' Addie pointed out, 'with the risk of being seen.'

'True,' said Channon, 'but it was dark, don't forget, and the weather wasn't good – not the night for anyone to be out enjoying a leisurely stroll.'

'The killer still took the chance of being seen,' persisted Addie. 'There were people out on the lanes, weren't there?'

'I've said before it was like Piccadilly Circus,' agreed Channon grimly. 'Sergeant, perhaps you'd remind us of those we know of who were out and about?'

Thanks a million, thought Bowles, then seeing Channon's assessing eyes, understood; it was training-time again, but perhaps that was no bad thing. He himself would have to run sessions like this when he got his promotion, whether he liked it or not. He grunted to himself when he spotted Honor Bennett's rapt attention, then with only the odd glance at his notes, led the others along the lanes of Pengorra on the night of Paul's murder.

'Bridget Stumbles was out in her mobile shop, making deliveries from about eight o'clock. Possible motive for murder, she was outraged that Paul had slept with her sixteen-year-old great-niece. Then at about nine fifteen, Paul sped past in his car, stopped short of the standing stone and sat looking at it. Bridget drove on and left him there.

'Next – Lucy Pascoe, Paul's current girlfriend. Drove past the Menna at about ten minutes to ten, on her way home from being on the boat with Paul. No motive for murder – she was besotted with him. But she did see

Martin Goodchild approaching the stone on foot. Martin's possible motives: he could have thought Paul was responsible for him getting the sack from Amos, and maybe more important, he himself was keen on Lucy Pascoe, but knew quite well that she and Paul were an item.

'Then at about ten past ten, Mrs Helen Pascoe says she stopped at the Menna to recover a plastic bag that was a danger to drivers. She saw nothing suspicious and carried on home. Forensic found traces of Paul's blood and fibres from his sweater in her car, which might possibly have been left unlocked. We suspect the traces were a plant by the killer who was probably out of sight at the Menna and maybe knew her, but at any rate followed her home. No traces of him outside or inside her car, or in the yard where it was parked. Motives for Mrs Pascoe – she didn't think Paul was right for her daughter, though at that time she didn't know the full extent of their relationship.'

'Thanks, sergeant,' said Channon, and to them all, 'See what I mean? These little lanes were far from deserted, and that's only the people we know about. So to recap on those who have no real alibis, but who are possible suspects:

'First, Jaz Pascoe, who didn't like Paul and had words with him in the Court's games room several days earlier. Jaz is only sixteen, but he and his friends may have been envious of Paul's lifestyle and his success with the girls.

'Second, Steve Pascoe, Jaz's father. He was down here on the Fal during the day on Friday, and said he was driving back to London from about five thirty. No confirmation of the journey itself, or of him arriving back in London. Possible motives: Stradling and Son pulled a tough deal with his firm of architects, and I heard this afternoon that a young student at the firm, the daughter of friends, was romanced by Paul and dropped flat.

'Then Nigel Nollens, Stradling's secretary, who says he was in London at the time, but has no corroboration. Motive: Paul stole his fiancée a month before the wedding. Nollens continued to work for the Stradlings, but was that to suss out a chance for revenge?

'Next, the chef Simon Bowen and his partner Sandie Goolden. They alibi each other from nine thirty onwards, and we *have* wondered whether the killing would have needed two people. Simon had access to the boat and boathouse – and he's also confirmed that a large wrench, well greased, is missing from the tool racks in the boathouse. This ties in with the traces of machine grease found in Paul's hair, so it looks as if that could be the weapon for the initial attack. Simon's possible motive: the same old story – Paul seduced his seventeen-year-old sister.

'So bear all that in mind and sleep on it. You can come straight to me or Inspector Savage with any relevant input.' He turned to Les Jolly and the bulky PC Cloak. 'Anything new to report on the checking of Paul's gallery?'

'Two officers still doing the visits,' said Jolly mournfully. 'Those closely connected to the girls fall into two camps: those who shrug their shoulders and wish they had Paul's technique, and those who are bitterly resentful of him. Either way, none of them so far without an alibi.'

Channon surveyed them all. 'With so much work being done on Paul and his contacts, I fear we're in danger of neglecting Amos. We have an estimate for his time of death – between ten and eleven o'clock, last night. Fred Jordan and the SOCOs haven't yet finished at the yard, but we're pretty sure that no valuables are missing. We still need sightings of people or vehicles in the vicinity of the yard last night, and I want to see all those on enquiries first thing tomorrow. Each household, each shop, each boat owner, must be asked for their whereabouts.'

PC Cloak put up a hand like a child in class. 'Even Mr Stradling at the Court?' he asked, and Bowles rolled his eyes in sympathy. Old Cloak and Dagger here had already come up against the vengeful father.

'Ah,' said Channon, 'thanks for the reminder. Nobody is to call on Richard Stradling without my say-so. He's not an easy person, though it's not a case of like father, like son because he's a one-woman man – still grieving for his wife, and with Paul gone as well he's cracking up, but won't admit it. I'll deal with him myself – and his staff, if necessary. Now, those of you on late shift know who you are – the rest of you go home for what's left of the evening.'

They tramped out, leaving Channon pacing the floor. Suddenly he picked up his stack of printouts and announced, 'I'm going home early to have a think.'

'On any particular lines?' asked Bowles, stifling a yawn.

'Several,' was the cryptic reply, and the two men went their separate ways.

Channon was crossing the Fal on the King Harry Ferry, having caught the last run of the day with only seconds to spare. Still restless from the pressures of the case, he edged his car into a space and then got out to stand at the rail and savour the transfer from his working life to the peace and quiet of the Roseland.

The crossing not only saved him thirty minutes of driving time, it transported him from one world to another. Water swirled quietly against the low sides of the ferry; the river banks were steep and densely wooded, almost black, but studded with lights from scattered dwellings. He breathed air that blew cold and salty straight from the sea.

They passed under the hull of a vast merchant ship, resting at anchor in the deep channel of King Harry Reach, where such laid-up ships could spend the winter. Trying to clear his mind of the mayhem of murder, he stared upwards and saw the swing of a lantern as one of the maintenance crew walked a deck far above him; and at that moment a voice he remembered spoke his name. 'Mr Channon?'

He swung round and saw her. 'Mrs Baxter!' he said in amazement. They had always been Mr Channon and Mrs Baxter to each other when murder linked them in the village of Curdower. He had promised himself that he would find her as soon as he was free to do it, but she was here right now.

Dark hair blew across her face. 'I – I just thought I'd say hello,' she said awkwardly.

She was wearing a red scarf, he saw, like the woman on the beach. 'It was you,' he said, his voice sinking lower with the realization. 'I wasn't sure. You were on the beach near my house early on Monday morning, but you went away before I could speak to you.'

'Yes, I was out early on Monday,' she agreed. 'I sometimes do that – just to be on my own. We live near there.'

'You're not at the roundhouse any longer?'

'No. We tried, Rob and I, we tried hard, but it didn't work. I couldn't forget the way he'd been with Luke – the way he'd let him down – and Luke himself wasn't happy having him back. In the end we divorced.'

'And Luke? Is he well?'

'He's fine – in his second year at Cambridge. Tess is in her first year of A levels and Ben is coming up to GCSEs. They're both here with me now – in the car. What about you? I've seen you on television about the crossroads murder. It must be keeping you very busy.'

'Yes, yes,' he said impatiently, 'but Mrs Baxter, I've often thought about you. I saw you once last winter, with the young ones in Falmouth, but I couldn't make myself approach you, not after the way I disrupted your family.'

'You were right to disrupt us,' she said simply. 'It was your job.'

As she spoke the ferry slowed and swished on approaching the Roseland side. 'I have no spare time at all right now,' he said quickly, 'but when I'm free can we talk? Can I ring you? Can we meet?'

He saw the flash of her smile in the light from the wheelhouse. She scribbled on a bit of paper and held it out to him. 'Here's my number. Ring me when you've solved the crossroads case.'

Then, in front of the baffled stares of her teenage children and the interested gaze of the ferryman, he took hold of her hand, turned it over, and put his lips to her palm. He astounded himself by doing it, but he didn't care what anyone thought as long as Sally Baxter didn't think he was mad. He ran his fingers through his hair, and waited.

She didn't seem to think he was mad, and if she was surprised that he'd kissed her hand, she didn't show it. She just looked at her palm and closed her fingers over it, sealing the place he had kissed. 'Ring me when you're free,' she said again, and went back to her car and her children. She was first in line to drive off and that was what she did, with a quick, sideways look at him through the car window.

A minute later he drove off the ferry himself. By then there was no sign of her car, but the scrap of paper was safe against his chest. He headed for home, with the bundle of printouts listing facts and check-ups and timings on the seat next to him.

When his facial muscles started to ache, he realized he was still smiling.

It was just after ten o'clock and all was silent at Trenoon. Steve was finishing a piece of work in the studio, Jaz was watching TV and Katie was safe in bed – Helen knew that because she'd checked on her, twice. As for Lucy, she had actually smiled during the evening at something Jaz had said. She still looked lost, she still looked stunned, but if they carried on loving her and being with her, she might adjust in time.

Chrissie had been round for a couple of hours and they'd talked; it always did her good to talk to Chrissie. It could have been any evening spent with a friend in front of a log fire, apart from what they had talked *about*: the subject, of course, had been the murders, the rumours, the suspects; what the police had done or hadn't done, and needless to say, Katie's little adventure.

Now, Helen lay in bed with the events of the day circling and thudding in her head like a too-heavy load in a washing machine. It seemed to her that life itself was a load – a burden of worry and supposition and dread – but she

250

reminded herself that in spite of two unsolved murders close to their house, in spite of her and Steve and even Jaz having been under suspicion, the family was still together.

She was amazed to find that the nightmare of her own arrest was fading from her mind, brushed to one side by the sight of Steve clasping Katie to his heart, tears of relief on his face. The only times she had ever before seen him weep had been with joy at the birth of each child, and with shame about his adultery.

His adultery . . . Where was the despair she'd felt then, where was the black void of betrayal? If she was honest with herself she could only admit that it had been cancelled out by her need of him, by his devotion to her and the children, his support of Lucy; by the fact that he was ready to leave London to be near the family, and finally by his tears when Katie came home from the river.

She didn't know if she'd been unreasonable about the break-up, she didn't even know if she'd been justified in bringing the children to Cornwall, all she did know was that they were together again, and she wanted it to stay that way.

A shaft of moonlight speared the scudding clouds and lay across her bed. Outside it was dark and cold and windy, but when she closed her eyes she could see sunlit waves kissing silver sand, boats dancing on shining waters, as if summer had come to her heart in the midst of a Cornish winter. She would ask Steve to come back for good. What they used to have – what they still had if she was prepared to rescue it – was too good to lose. She let out a long, relieved breath. The decision made, she didn't even get out of bed to go and see him in the studio. Days of tumult exacted their toll and she crashed into a deep, dreamless sleep.

Channon was in the bath, his favourite place for intensive thought. Instinct was screaming at him that the key to the murders lay with Paul himself – his needs, his aims, his motivations. At last he felt he was getting to know the young man with the earring; starting to fathom the facets of his personality.

The most obvious was the womanizing – from any angle that came first; and the fact that he was a man for action, not thought – that facet had come over from witnesses; and that he was a man who enjoyed his wealth and didn't mind spending it. His own income must have been considerable, and in addition to that he had a doting father who was a millionaire . . . but beneath the glamour and the money and the looks, Channon was detecting a man who wasn't at ease with himself – a restless spirit – someone who must constantly prove himself to be the best – in everything.

No problem there when it came to the girls – his sexual magnetism had seen to that; but on the night of his death he hadn't been his usual self – he'd been silent, thoughtful, abstracted. There had been something on his mind. Could it have been to do with a three-thousand-year-old standing stone? He had sat in his Aston Martin and observed the stone in the light of his headlamps before meeting the young woman who might – who just might have been the love of his life . . . but he hadn't mentioned it to her. No, according to Lucy he'd merely been 'a bit tense, as if he had something on his mind'.

But regarding the stone . . . only days before he was found propped against it with his throat cut, he had discussed the prehistoric monuments of Cornwall with the handyman Bradley. He had always enjoyed history as a subject for study; had he found *ancient* history even more compelling?

The warmth of the bath, the glow of his whisky – both were telling on Channon as weariness tugged at him. This was no time to go comatose! Impatiently he left the bath and stood under the jet of a cold shower. The sting of it cleared his head. He towelled himself dry and put on his robe, then still deep in the day's events went to find his meal to put in the microwave.

Paying scant attention to what he was eating, he recalled in detail the people he and Bowles had listed earlier for the benefit of the others. His fork was merely an implement to lift food to his mouth, the food itself was simply fuel to keep his mind and body active. Later he made himself coffee and sat in the lamplight drinking it, oblivious to the thud of the waves breaking on the beach outside, unseeing when the light of the moon through the window fought with the glow of the lamps.

He thought of Bowles: abrasive, charmless, but at last showing distinct signs of mellowing. This time he must include him in his deliberations – the sergeant had earned the right to take part in the solution – if they could find one. Ignoring the fact that it was two o'clock in the morning, he rang him, and it was clear from Bowles's response that he was awake. 'Boss? Good. I've been thinking,' were his words. 'It was a remark of yours that set me on the track.'

'I'm on a track myself at the moment – one that leads me to an inescapable conclusion.'

'Hah!' said Bowles, clearly intrigued. 'Boss, you recall that stunning big blow-up shot of the boat on the wall in Stradling's sitting room?'

Channon leaned back in his chair while Bowles lay propped against his slightly grubby pillows, and they began to talk . . . two very different men with one single aim.

Chapter Nineteen

Next morning it was after nine before the two detectives had checked all their facts and finished a series of phone calls. Bowles, on tiptoe at the prospect of nailing the killer, asked, 'Who's going with us, boss?' expecting it to be Yates or Soker.

'We'll take Les Jolly,' said Channon, and kept a straight face as he added casually, 'and maybe Honor – she's a hard worker and it will be good experience for her; and Cloak, as he was a good friend to Amos.'

Bowles could have groaned at the prospect of being under the gaze of the milkmaid. As for Jolly the moron – the DCI seemed to think the sun shone out of his backside; and old Cloak and Dagger as well – what a trio!

It was a tranquil scene as the two cars left Pengorra, early sunlight brightening dark winter fields with the sparkle of water far below, but those officers left in the room were far from tranquil: Addie Savage and the others knew what was happening and they were joined together by the tension of a case that just might be about to be solved.

The cars pulled up outside the creamy splendour of Pengorra Court. Pre-warned of their visit, Nollens and Jasmine were waiting for them, but at that moment Stradling himself appeared, wearing a towelling robe. 'Five of you?' he said, eyes widening, then flicked an explanatory hand at his robe. 'My morning swim. Look, Channon, I intend being with you when you talk to my staff. Which of them is it to be this time?'

254

'As a matter of fact, it's you we want to talk to, Mr Stradling – in private, if you please. I'd prefer to use your sitting room.'

The other stared at him, red-rimmed eyes all at once heavy as lead, then he shrugged and led the way. 'If you insist on coming five at a time we may as well give ourselves room to breathe, I suppose.' Lamps were still lit in the room and a log fire scented the air, but as he led them in Stradling stopped in his tracks. 'Ah, I see it now! You've brought news!'

'Not exactly,' said Channon. 'We just need to clarify a few more points. I think I've mentioned to you before that close family members are always our first suspects in cases of murder?'

'What? Yes, yes, I seem to remember you saying something of the sort.' Then he looked from one to the other, his mouth slightly open. 'Are you talking about me? *Me*? Good God, man, is that the best you can do?'

Bowles noted the metallic sheen of his superior's eyes, and kept a low but expectant profile. 'You asked me that yesterday, Mr Stradling,' said Channon, 'but apparently you've forgotten my reply. Members of your staff have said that you and your son liked to live informally when you were down here – "to do your own thing", was how they put it.'

'Yes, yes. What about it?'

'Being left alone by your staff on Friday evening means that we have no word but yours about where you were after they finished work at nine o'clock.'

'And that's not enough? Paul and I were in this very room having coffee – I told you he went out about at about ten past nine, and in case you've forgotten I never saw him alive after that.'

'Didn't you?'

'What?'

'I'm thinking you could have walked down to the jetty later, perhaps to continue a conversation, reasoning that as his car was still at the house he must be down at the boat.

But perhaps you found him bidding a fond farewell to his current girlfriend, Lucy Pascoe?'

Stradling gave a backward jerk of the head and turned down his mouth derisively. Seconds passed. 'I'd been talking to him for half the evening, Channon. Why would I want to talk to him at the jetty?'

'Because you couldn't be seen, or overheard?'

'But what would I have wanted to talk *about*?'

Jolly stood immobile, watching; Honor Bennett stared uncomfortably at the floor; Cloak, as always, was impassive. All three of them were squirming mentally, aware that the DCI was low on fact and high on supposition.

'You wanted to talk about whatever was on Paul's mind. Perhaps he had mentioned to you his interest in archaeology and ancient monuments?'

Stradling's eyes flickered, just for a second. He directed a scornful look at the other four, then concentrated on Channon. 'You and your minions can play at detectives all you like,' he said, 'but don't think you can play with me. It's my son who is dead. Are you hinting that I know who killed him?'

'Yes,' said Channon, 'I am.'

Stradling moistened his cracked and bitten lips, then shook his head pityingly. 'You're saying that I killed him? *Me*? What reason could I have? What motive? We were close, man. I told you how I loved that boy.'

'No,' corrected Channon, 'you told me how you loved his mother and you told me how you loved your boat. We know that Paul was his usual self when you both arrived on Friday evening, but by the time you'd had coffee and he was in his room, he was unlike himself – quiet, deep in thought.

'Later, he joined you and you talked some more, but perhaps you aren't aware that he then went out in his car to sit and stare at the Menna standing stone before going on board the boat with Lucy, where she found him "a bit tense, as if there was something on his mind". Paul had known for weeks that she was hoping to study

256

archaeology and ancient history at university, and I suspect that he wanted to join her there and take the same course. You told me yourself he almost took history as a degree subject.'

Stradling's eyes were swivelling rapidly, as if his thoughts were moving at a faster rate than his speech. 'Uh – well – yes – he thought of it when he was eighteen! What *is* this, Channon? Are you seriously saying I killed my son because he wanted to go back to university? He was a wealthy man in his own right. He was twenty-six years old. He could please himself what he did.'

'Yes, and he was your partner in business, wasn't he? You had him lined up to take over Stradling and Son.'

'I hoped he would, of course I did.'

Channon spoke softly. 'I just thought you might have lost your temper with him, that's all – because you have a violent temper, haven't you, Mr Stradling? You were extricated from a charge of threatening behaviour less than a year ago, and I learned only this morning that two years earlier a charge of wounding with intent was conveniently withdrawn.'

All at once Stradling's legs buckled. 'Oh!' he said. 'I told you yesterday I'm a bit weak at the knees, didn't I? Perhaps you and your sergeant could sit down with me and we'll discuss that?'

The two men sat on a sofa, with Stradling in his big chair not far away, and for the first time Bowles spoke up. 'Mr Stradling, when we were here yesterday I was interested to see that you've changed the picture that used to be on the wall here, opposite your chair.'

Stradling looked at him as if amazed that he could speak English, let alone pass comment on anything of significance. 'Your point being, sergeant?'

'Just to query why you no longer want to be facing a beautiful painting of your late wife, your son and yourself?'

'I always prefer to speak to the organ-grinder, not the monkey,' the older man said, 'but since you ask – isn't it obvious? It upset me too much to see the three of us together when there's only me left.' The broad shoulders were stiff as he sat upright in his chair.

'But it didn't upset you to look at it after your wife died?' asked Channon.

For at least half a minute there was silence, with Stradling deep in thought: unpleasant thought by the looks of his clamped teeth, maybe anguished thought. Channon waited, then Stradling said, 'Could your officers leave us, Channon? I'd like a private word.'

'Sergeant Bowles stays,' said Channon flatly. 'My other officers can leave us for a moment.' He nodded to the other three, who went into the hall.

Stradling breathed out heavily. 'All right, it's clear I've underestimated you. You're right – Paul and I had words when he came down from his room. He announced he was leaving the firm to take the same degree as the girl – at the same uni, if he could fix it. I – well – I was incensed. We argued and he went out, as I told you. Later I decided to reason with him and went down to the jetty, where I found him blowing goodbye kisses to her. I kept out of sight for a moment. When she'd gone I confronted him and we talked – more – we argued.'

'What – in the open?'

'No, it was windy, so in the boathouse. We were used to being in there together. And that was all. You aren't all that clever if you truly believe I killed him. Look at me – I'm a wreck.' As if to back his words, the blood had left his face, which was now dead white, blotched with patches of fading suntan.

'Other emotions besides the grief of bereavement can make a wreck of a man,' said Channon. 'Disbelief, anger, a sense of betrayal – I could name a dozen without effort. Whichever applied to you, I think you exaggerated their effect on occasion – very convincingly, I might add. However, I suspect that one particular emotion could explain Amos Heaney's murder.'

Stradling gave an impatient bark of a laugh. 'If you're thinking I had anything to do with that you're losing it!'

Channon pursed his lips thoughtfully. 'I think that in Mr Heaney's case the killing was very quick – triggered by the all-too-common emotion not of anger but of fear. Fear that he would tell us he'd found you scrabbling around in his yard late at night, looking for something. You knew Paul's keys to the boat were missing, because they weren't there when you'd emptied his pockets, and when you had time to search undisturbed they weren't anywhere in the house, either.

'Did it dawn on you that if they'd been dropped in the boatyard we would soon work out that he'd been taken there from somewhere within easy reach by water? That you of all people would be aware he kept his keys on him, and that if you were found searching the yard it could only have been for them? Oh, yes, Amos seeing you there was dangerous – for you! He had to go.'

Channon shook his head. 'The thing that puzzled us at first was why the Menna, why the echo of a pagan sacrifice, just because he wanted to study ancient history? Was that really enough to cause such rage in you – or was there another, deeper reason?'

Stradling was still very pale. 'You have no proof of anything,' he muttered.

'Not at this stage, no, but we're about to search this house for the diamond you took from your son's ear, and for any other relevant evidence. You're an intelligent man, you did a thorough job of concealing your traces, but there'll be something – there always is. And don't bother to protest about a search warrant – the law says a warrant isn't needed on the arrest of a suspect.' Channon paused to give his next words full weight. 'Then at the station, Mr Stradling, we will take samples of your DNA, to compare with that of your son.'

Weak knees forgotten, Stradling leapt to his feet and actually bared his teeth, opening one of the dried-up splits in his upper lip. 'Don't threaten me with your DNA tests and your search warrants!' he roared.

Channon bent his head. So he was right! 'Temper, temper!' he said reprovingly. 'A DNA test would reveal your real reason for killing Paul, wouldn't it? The real reason for the state you're in? It isn't grief because of your son's death that's eating at you, it's knowing he wasn't your son at all! The woman you worshipped let you believe another man's child was yours, didn't she? Betrayal, humiliation, devastation . . . those are the reasons for how you've looked since Paul's death, and it turned out very convenient to use your appearance to convince us of your grief, of your innocence. So did he throw it in your face? Did he taunt you? You killed him for that, didn't you?'

In front of their eyes Stradling began to shrink. The well-preserved body slumped and lost shape, as if the very life-force was being squeezed out of it. When he spoke it was in a gritty whisper. 'Yes, yes, *yes*! I killed him! Satisfied? Things were heated. I'd just watched him blowing kisses to her – to *her*, the one behind his mad idea. I might, I just might have said something derogatory about her . . .' Stradling seemed to have forgotten that Bowles was present, and addressed himself solely to Channon, speaking now in a hoarse, eager gabble. 'I said that as his father I was entitled to state my views that what he was proposing was absurd.

'He stuck his face up to mine, looked me in the eye and said, "Get real! You aren't my father!" He – he laughed, and the ghastly thing was that something inside me knew at once that it was true! It was true of Daphne, my Daphne! It was knives in my heart – it was agony! Can you see that?

'He said she'd told him just before she died, and asked him never to reveal it to me. I said – I *had* to say I didn't believe him, so he told me who the man was. I used to know him – I'd known him for years. He was a rake – a charmer, a compulsive womanizer. He left the country to escape some horrendous scandal or other, and for all I know he's still at the other side of the world.

'Paul said his mother told him that making love with this – this swine was fun! *Fun*! I was too intense, she said, always desperate to father a child, always loving her, adoring, worshipping her. She felt as if I smothered her, but her one night with this man was simply light-hearted fun! Then Paul did the thing that sent me mad with fury: he yelled in my face that in one night his blood father did what I'd failed to do in years – gave Daphne a baby!

'I can't remember much about what happened next because I was like a madman. I do recall I couldn't see properly. My vision blurred. It had happened to me before. I think it's what's meant by blind rage. I must have grabbed that big new wrench from the rack and hit him with it across the side of the head, because later I found I was holding it. He went down without a sound. I thought he was dead. I wondered what I could do to die as well. I didn't want to live – what was the point? My heart was broken – it was like a shattered stone inside my chest.

'But there wasn't a sound to be heard. Nobody knew we were there. Something took over – self-preservation, perhaps – and before I knew it I was working out a cover-up. I'm not used to being cornered, you see – I like to be in charge, and I no longer saw him as my son – he *wasn't* my son. You know, when he was growing up I used to wonder why I didn't feel more than I did for him. Oh, we got along all right – people used to comment on it, but there was something missing – the bond that I'd always imagined a father would have with a son. Because of that I over-compensated, pretended he could do no wrong; gave him what he wanted, pretended I didn't mind about all the girls, but it never made me feel any different.

'I don't know why I've tried to conceal it – I should have admitted it last Saturday when you came round. I suppose it was because I've always prided myself on being able to handle everything. My life is hell, anyway, pure hell. I thought I knew what a broken heart was when Daphne died, but that was nothing – *nothing* to what I feel now. I've had enough of it, and I'll make sure I don't live to go to prison.'

261

Channon looked at Bowles, who said implacably, 'The diamond earring, Mr Stradling?'

'Oh yes, the little trifle his mother and I bought for him – for *our son*, as I thought at the time. It was glinting up at me through the blood, and if you must know my tears were falling on it. I hated myself for what I was doing, what I'd already done. I almost gave up then, with my heart in fragments. I thought I might be losing my mind, but no, common sense told me to remove the earring and let you think that the theft of it was the motive. I'll show you where it is. I'll tell you everything – how I managed to do it all on my own. I took him to the stone because it seemed only fitting after all his clap-trap about prehistory and archaeology. Red-hot rage lent me strength, you see, but part of my mind was as cold as ice.'

'Was it your ice-cold mind that helped you incriminate an innocent woman?' asked Channon bleakly.

'Helen Pascoe? When she appeared in her car I was almost at the top of the slope from the boatyard, with Paul still out of it and over my shoulder, but showing signs of coming round. The woman delayed me with her stupid staring at a plastic bag. I recognized her car, I knew who she was – the mother of the girl Paul was set on marrying – oh yes, he told me that as well. When I'd finished with him I took a few odds and ends away and later on, in the early hours, I did an artistic little job with them in her car – which she'd helpfully left unlocked, I might add. I knew it would waste your time, and probably give her a fright.'

'Oh, it did both,' Channon assured him. 'So after she'd gone, you got Paul to the stone . . .'

Inexplicably, Stradling smiled. It was a gruesome sight when the awful lips stretched and the cracks widened. One of them bled a little. 'Yes,' he said, 'and do you know, it didn't even tire me.' There was an emptiness to the words, a bewilderment, but then he was talking fast again, wanting to explain. 'Then I did what I'd taken him there for – I had a good knife from the galley. He was just starting to come round when I made the first thrust. I needed to see

262

his flesh cut raw and his blood run, because it wasn't *my* flesh and *my* blood. Can you understand that?'

Channon shook his head in disbelief. 'It was hardly Paul's fault that his mother let herself be made pregnant by another man.'

'It was his fault that he shouted it in my face! It was his fault that he mocked me!'

'And what was Amos's fault? That he discovered you in his boatyard, and came to see what you were doing?'

'Heaney didn't deserve to die,' admitted Stradling. 'He was simply in the wrong place at the wrong time.'

Bowles, to his own utter amazement, was feeling something deep inside his chest: unfamiliar, uncomfortable. He wondered for a second if it could be pity, and dismissed the idea as mad. How could he feel pity for this ruthless old creep when he never felt pity for anyone?

Channon showed no signs of softening. 'Bring in the others,' he said briskly, and when they were all together he addressed the shrunken, white-faced man. 'Richard Stradling, I am arresting you for the murders of Paul Stradling and Amos Heaney.' He nodded to Bowles, who took over with the familiar words of the caution: 'You do not have to say anything . . .'

To the three officers, Channon said, 'Mr Stradling will show you where to find the diamond earring belonging to the dead man.'

Trying to stay erect, Stradling led them not to the office and his safe, but upstairs, presumably to his bedroom.

'You were right, boss,' grunted Bowles when they were on their own, 'when you said it's not a case of like father, like son. You were right about everything.'

'So were you,' replied Channon, 'about almost everything.'

'Are we taking him back to the room?'

'No, to the station – to Truro. Cloak can come with us to keep an eye on him and as some sort of recompense for Stradling treating him like dirt since the moment they met. And he was Amos's friend, don't forget.'

'With the diamond and the confession we won't need anything else.'

'No, we'll have quite enough. With those and a mass of forensic we'll be able to wrap this case and tie it with ribbons,' agreed Channon heavily. 'Would you like to deal with the media?'

'What do you think?' said Bowles, already rising on tiptoe.

Channon took out his mobile to put Addie Savage in the picture. A minute later the three officers came downstairs with a fully dressed Stradling and a small, tissue-wrapped package safely bagged as evidence. Jolly held it out to Channon, who brushed it aside. 'You and Honor go and log it in at the room,' he said, 'and tell everyone I'll be in later to thank them all. Cloak, come with us to Truro and keep an eye on our prisoner.'

Then the five policemen, with Stradling in their midst, walked to the cars past a dumbfounded Nigel Nollens, past Jasmine and the Bradleys, Simon and Sandie. All of them looked shaken to the core.

Outside the sun was still shining. Once in Pengorra, Honor and Jolly parked by the green, but the others skirted it and headed for the main road to Truro. Two women turned as they waited with their shopping baskets at the step of Biddy Stumbles' van, and a passing motorbike swirled to a halt, its rider watching the car as it headed away. Martin Goodchild was taking in what was happening.

Channon told himself that the local grapevine would soon be active. Would the people of Carrick Roads be relieved that it wasn't one of their own who had committed two murders? Would they accept that a wealthy, doting father had killed not only his son but a devout old boatman who had lived in Pengorra all his life? Would Lucy Pascoe be able to understand it?

Behind them on the back seat, next to PC Cloak, Richard Stradling stared unseeingly through the car window. He looked very old and very tired; while the men taking him in were also tired, but well satisfied. Channon said, 'When we've finished in Truro, Bowles, I'll call in at the room and have a chat with them all. Then I think I'll go to Trenoon to have a word with the Pascoes, and to tell Katie that her little adventure proved helpful to us. Do you want to join me?'

You're joking, thought Bowles. Give the gremlin a pat on the back? No thanks! But just a minute; didn't the experts on people skills say that encouragement was a good thing? Praise from the men who had cracked a double murder might encourage her to join the police when she grew up, rather than go racing round the oceans of the world like that MacArthur woman. 'I'll go with you, boss,' he said.

Channon smiled. He was promising himself that when they'd been to Trenoon and he was back home on the Roseland, he would make a certain phone call to arrange a long-delayed meeting. He'd been embroiled in two brutal murders and the murderer was slumped in the seat right behind him, but even so, life was pretty good.